Praise for Lindsay McKenna

"An absorbing debut for the Nocturne line."
—*Romantic Times BOOKreviews* on *Unforgiven*

"Gunfire, emotions, suspense, tension, and sexuality
abound in this fast-paced, absorbing novel."
—*Affaire de Coeur* on *Wild Woman*

"Another masterpiece."
—*Affaire de Coeur* on *Enemy Line*

"Emotionally charged...riveting
and deeply touching."
—*Romantic Times BOOKreviews* on *Firstborn*

"Ms. McKenna brings readers along for a fabulous
odyssey in which complex characters experience the
danger, passion and beauty of the mystical jungle."
—*Romantic Times BOOKreviews* on *Man of Passion*

"Talented Lindsay McKenna delivers excitement
and romance in equal measure."
—*Romantic Times BOOKreviews* on
Protecting His Own

"Classic Lindsay McKenna, with jeopardy,
love, sorrow, hope and enough reality
to make readers shiver."
—*Romantic Times BOOKreviews* on
The Heart Beneath

"Lindsay McKenna will have you flying with the
daring and deadly women pilots who risk their lives...
buckle in for the ride of your life."
—*WritersUnlimited* on *Heart of Stone*

LINDSAY McKENNA

HEART OF THE STORM

HQN™

ISBN-13: 978-0-373-77225-4
ISBN-10:   0-373-77225-4

HEART OF THE STORM

www.HQNBooks.com

Printed in U.S.A.

Dear Reader,

Being Eastern Cherokee métis, I was raised in a Native American household. Our world is very different and I wanted to share it with you. There are sacred secrets in each Nation's culture. And each Nation has powerful and healing ceremonies for their people and "all their relations." I've been fortunate to be involved in some of the sacred ceremonies and have seen their healing powers.

I want to acquaint the reader with one aspect of our culture, to engage and invite you into our world of mysticism and possibilities. There are healing and sacred tools such as a rattle, a drum, a feather, a stone, taking part in a sweat lodge, a vision quest or yuwipi ceremony, among others. In the right hands and with a good heart, these tools and ceremonies become an incredible extension of ourselves, through the will of the Great Spirit. And right now we need this kindness, compassion and good-heartedness to turn this dark world of ours around to light and peace.

Many dismiss Nature, but She is our advocate, the only planet we have. My hope is that as you walk in my moccasins through this story, you will feel the heartbeat of Mother Earth. And in doing so, reconnect with her nurturing, generous heart. *Aho*.

Lindsay McKenna

To Mary Buckner, RN, and Linda Metzler, Physician's Assistant, friends. Thank you for your help and support over the years; I couldn't have gotten this far without you. George Abbott, we couldn't ask for a better neighbor. In a day and age where respect, honesty, integrity and courtesy are dimming in our society, you shine with these wonderful human qualities. We're lucky we live in the same canyon with you.

HEART OF THE
STORM

CHAPTER ONE

"THE VICE PRESIDENT of the United States needs to die. *Now!*"

Rogan Yalua Soquili, known as Fast Horse, was insistent as he stood triumphantly outside the circle of twelve Native American women. Their rapt attention fixed on the Cherokee métis medicine man, they sat in their ceremonial garb. Rogan placed his hands on the strong, capable shoulders of Blue Wolf, a Shoshone woman near his own age of forty-five.

"Make it happen," he declared, his voice booming.

The Sierra Nevadas in early June took on a shadowy, menacing aura as midday thunderclouds grew above them. Rogan looked around gleefully. They were nestled within the Eagle's Nest, his compound built high in the mountains, on a cliff. The wooden walls provided them sanctuary as they stood on the hard-packed earth. It was the perfect place to carry out their task. The air around them leaped and throbbed with living energy.

In the center of the women's circle, a light feathery mist began to gather. It moved counterclockwise, never touching any of the participants. Rogan watched, mesmerized, as the wispy cloud became darker and began to resemble a doughnut whose hole was closing. Cauliflower-like towers grew upward from the sluggishly swirling clouds, and when flashes of lightning occurred, Rogan's jaw dropped in awe. Surely, the ceremonial Storm Pipe and these women were connected to the most powerful magic he'd ever seen. Excitement coursed through him.

The women chanted as one, their voices rising and falling as the thundercloud built with the whipping wind. Rogan's hair fell across his face, but he didn't feel it. His eyes were on the cloud invoked by the sacred pipe Blue Wolf held in her hands. With each chant, the intensity increased and the thundercloud turned more malevolent, eventually shooting skyward to thirty thousand feet. It was coming from the pipe; Rogan could see the energy flowing out of its bowl.

As he stood behind her, he dug his fingers into Blue Wolf's sturdy shoulders. The rhythmic chanting ebbed and flowed, ebbed and flowed. The very pulse of the building storm responded to the women's voices, which rose in a powerful crescendo.

Rogan's order echoed throughout the cedar structure on the side of the mountain. Standing in the west, the position of death, he kept his firm contact with Blue Wolf's elk skin-covered shoulders. Like a bolt of lightning, heat and electricity coursed through his hands, leaped up his arms and shimmered throughout his tense body. Keeping his knees slightly bent, Rogan closed his eyes, took a deep breath into his abdomen and then slowly released it.

The thundercloud manifested by the pipe and the women was inspiring to Rogan. He'd never seen anything like this. Oh, he knew ceremonial pipes were powerful, but to create a mighty thunderhead in a matter of minutes…that was awesome. Lightning continued to radiate from the dark, churning mass far above them. Most of the electricity, millions of volts, was held within cloud. Rogan knew that the powers involved with the pipe would not allow any of it to harm the circle of women. It would be contained within the building storm overhead.

Rogan gazed around at the seated figures. Their knees touched one another to maintain physical contact. In doing so, they became the container for the Storm Pipe's power, and helped direct the energy and the building of the thunderhead.

Blue Wolf lifted a very old pipe made of catlinite, its red bowl glowing in her hands. The smooth, polished oak stem was decorated with small seed beads depicting a thunderstorm with a lightning bolt. She began to sing a ceremonial song to invite the lightning that flashed above them. Her hands grew hot and felt as if they were burning; they were merely responding to the power amassing through the powerful ceremonial pipe.

The women gripped one another's hands at the right moment, as the electrical charge within the churning clouds swirled, growing in strength. The two sitting next to the pipe carrier each placed a hand on her waist, for Blue Wolf needed her hands free, to hold the pipe upward in supplication.

Her voice rose and fell, like a howling wind moving within the circle. She felt Rogan grip her shoulders more tightly with anticipation. He couldn't hold the pipe himself, for the ceremonial object belonged only to women. If he touched it, he'd die instantly. He could focus the energy, however, and direct it to whomever he envisioned in his mind.

Today, the vice president would die. Blue Wolf smiled inwardly as she sang from her heart and soul.

Their song became more strident, in accord with the energy unveiling itself before them. The Storm Pipe felt almost too hot to hold any longer, but Blue Wolf focused, as she had been taught. All the women in the circle felt the same heat, she knew. They held the pipe's energy, carrying the power, just as a womb cradled a growing baby.

Rogan smiled inwardly as he maintained his

grip on Blue Wolf's shoulders. She was trembling physically now. The building energy made her sweat freely, as it did him. Her singing changed in pitch, and at that moment, Rogan pictured the vice president's face in his mind. *Focus!* He must focus one hundred percent.

Dizzy from the gathering, spinning energy, Rogan was trembling so badly he collapsed to his knees. As if he were a lightning rod, an electrical current leaped and flowed through his hands, up his arms and through his body. That was Rogan's mission as he understood it: to ground the power of the Thunder Beings that trod restlessly across Father Sky. He began to slip into a deep, altered state as the chanting continued. It was all Rogan could do to stay mentally connected.

Stealing the Storm Pipe had been the key, he thought with satisfaction. His body was vibrating now, so fast he felt as if he were shredding apart, cell by cell. Too powerful an energy could make a person vanish into thin air. It wasn't happening to him due to the great strength and long training of these twelve women, he knew.

Sweat poured down his tense, kneeling form. His deerskin shirt and breeches were soaked through. Then Blue Wolf moved her arms and pointed the pipe eastward, toward Washington.

Now! he screamed to her mentally. Visualizing

the face of the vice president, Rogan issued his final order. *Force the pipe to release its charge now, Blue Wolf! Now!*

He was unprepared for that very thing happening. As the release was triggered, a flash of light occurred, and he was flung six feet backward. Scrambling to his hands and knees, he looked around, stunned. The sky remained turbulent. Angry purple-and-gray clouds still churned above them. But already the thunderstorm, created by the twelve women's intent, with the help of the pipe, was beginning to dissipate. Had the ceremonial pipe done its deed?

FBI AGENT DAVID COLBY WAS standing next to Vice President Robert Hiram when an incredible wave of heat surged like a tsunami through the large office. His boss, Mort Jameson, was in the middle of his daily report when the bulletproof window began to glow like sun-scorched rocks in a desert, followed by an earsplitting boom. Thrown off his feet, Colby slammed into the wall and was knocked semiconscious. The agent heard the vice president scream. Momentarily blinded, Colby slowly crawled to his hands and knees, disoriented. Automatically, he pulled the revolver from his shoulder holster beneath his dark suit jacket.

As Colby staggered to his feet, sweat trickled

off him. He felt as if he was in a steam room! Mort Jameson was groaning and trying to sit up. That's when Colby noticed the vice president lying flat on the carpeted floor, mouth open, eyes staring sightlessly toward the ceiling.

Beyond the massive cherry desk, the window was still intact. There'd been no sound of a bullet being fired, only that deafening boom. What was going on? What the *hell* had just happened? The agent holstered the gun.

"Colby! Call for backup!" Mort yelled as he stumbled to his feet and ran over to the unmoving vice president. Dropping to his knees, he yanked the man's tie loose, then pressed his fingers against his neck. "No pulse! Get help!"

Colby lurched. His ears were ringing, so much he could barely hear the shouted orders. Why wasn't everyone piling into the room? The door was still shut.

Confused, he grabbed the doorknob. Surely someone had heard the awful booming sound? He swore he'd seen a bolt of lightning lance through the only window in the office.

Saliva dripped from the corners of Colby's mouth as he yanked open the door. He had little control over his body. Unable to stand, the FBI agent called for help and medical personnel, then sagged against the jamb.

His eyes were blurred and unfocused now, his

legs quivering uncontrollably. As his muscles gave way, he slowly sank to the floor.

"THE VICE PRESIDENT IS dead," Dr. Scott Friedman announced to the small group of men in business suits. "From what I can tell, it was a heart attack. An autopsy will be performed shortly and we'll know for sure."

"My God," Mort muttered, wiping his face with a linen handkerchief. The knot of men stood in a room adjoining the vice president's hospital suite.

Mort's frown deepened as he glanced at Agent Colby. Thirty-three years old and one of his best agents, the man was pale and shaken. In fact, after examining him, the doctors had told him to stay in the hospital because he was weak and disoriented, but Colby had steadfastly refused.

"This is…such a shock," the President's press secretary, Burt Daily, stammered. "What are we going to tell the media?" He kept his clipboard and pen poised as he scanned the group.

Mort Jameson glanced at the head of the CIA, Bucky Caldwell, and then at the Chief of Staff, Rodney Portman. The Joint Chiefs of Staff chairman, General Myron Klein, a marine, looked grim. "The doctor said it was a heart attack," Mort repeated.

"But…" Daily looked around the group "…the vice president didn't have a history of heart trouble. The man had low cholesterol, for chrissakes! He'd just had his annual physical two weeks ago. At fifty, he was healthy as a horse. Do you think the American public is going to believe this?"

"I don't have the answer you're looking for," Friedman told them. "I'm just as puzzled over his death as you are. The autopsy will reveal more. I gave the vice president a clean bill of health." Shrugging, he added, "His heart just gave out."

"Agent Colby?" Mort zeroed in on the man. Colby had the face of a lean wolf on the prowl. His gray eyes were focused, the irises large and ringed in black.

Colby shifted his attention to him. "Yes, sir?"

"Escort Dr. Friedman from the room, please?"

"Yes, sir." When he gestured toward the door, the doctor took the hint; said goodbye and left. Colby made sure the door was shut, then turned and walked back to the cloistered group.

"Something hit us in that room, sir," Colby stated, giving each man present a serious look. "I felt heat, burning heat, building up seconds before that bolt of lightning, or whatever it was, struck the vice president. At first, I thought it was a summer storm. But we had blue skies and sunshine. From what I can tell, it wasn't weather induced."

Mort grimly nodded. "I need your help, gentlemen. I had the very same experience Agent Colby did. There was tremendous heat in the room. It hurt to breathe in that superheated air. And then—" Mort clapped his hands together "—there was a tremendous booming sound, something you might hear right after a lightning bolt struck close to you. The sound still has my ears ringing. Something came through that window, but the window's still intact. Somehow this bolt killed the vice president, and it knocked the hell out of me and Agent Colby in the process." He rubbed his jowls and studied the other men in the circle. "You got any ideas?"

"No," the CIA director, Caldwell, said, "but I have my agents combing the room with the most sophisticated gear available. We're trying to discover what the hell went down. Was it an act of terrorism or an act of God? I've got agents talking to the weather service gurus to find out if lightning can strike out of a blue sky and leave a window unbroken."

General Klein, built like a short but powerful pit bull, lifted his green eyes to the group. "Gentlemen, I'd be looking for a more concrete explanation. It was an attack."

"Jesus," Daily whispered. "You're standing here telling us this was a terrorist attack?"

"It's possible," Mort snapped, irritated by the press secretary's whining demeanor. "You think we like what happened? Or the implications? If whatever it was can strike the vice president dead on the spot, whoever or whatever could do the same to the president. Which is why he and his staff have been put into hiding until we can figure this out. None of the ramifications are lost on us, believe me."

Caldwell held up his hand. "Look, everyone stand down. We're all shaken—badly shaken—but we're working on this as fast as humanly possible." He glanced at his Rolex. "I expect to have preliminary results in about thirty minutes. You'll all be privy to whatever we find."

Colby said, "I believe we're dealing with something sophisticated."

"Russian?" the press secretary asked, his face pained.

General Klein growled, "Either that or terrorists have suddenly gotten ahold of the most advanced laser equipment known. The Russians have developed them for defensive purposes. Star Wars technology scared the hell out of them, and they put their focus on weaponized development as a way to counter what we're doing. Lasers are capable of this kind of destruction. We know that Russia was preparing to mount these on their satellites out in space."

"Yes," Caldwell said in a strangled tone, "and they've been testing their version of SDI in the Pacific against our military aircraft off and on the last two years. We have five blinded pilots in different military cargo aircraft who were targeted. We can't prove it, of course, but the Russians are the only ones who have this kind of know-how and technology."

"Laser technology is ready to be used," General Klein agreed wearily. "And all fingers point to them."

"Could it be other terrorists, though?" Daily insisted. "We know that the Russian labs in Moscow were looted six months ago. President Kasmarov never said *what* was stolen by the Chechens. Could it have been their laser equipment? Could they have gotten that stuff into our country unseen? Used it against the vice president?" He gave them all a desperate look. "My God, if that's so…"

Holding up his hand, Mort said, "Don't go there yet, Burt. We need *time* to do a thorough investigation. Right now, we're *all* treating this as an attack from an unknown enemy."

Shaking his head, Burt scribbled some notes on his clipboard. "The American public will panic if that's what has really happened. Lasers loose in the country! My God…"

Chief of Staff Rodney Portman stirred and opened his hands, which had been clasped tightly in front of him. "Look, gentlemen, we all have our work cut out for us. I'm going to put in a call to the Russian ambassador about this, discreetly, of course. We have no proof they did anything." He sighed and added, "I'll make some preliminary forays with the ambassador and be back in touch."

Klein snorted. "I'll tell you what. You should, in the strongest terms possible, issue a communiqué to Kasmarov and let him know that he's in our gun sights."

Gray eyebrows raised, Portman gave the man a thin smile. "Diplomacy is a must here, General. You realize that. We're not going in with guns blazing. We don't have proof—yet."

"I don't need any," Klein said. "No one in the world has advanced laser weaponry except those sons of bitches. This is them or the terrorists, and my hunch is it's Kasmarov pushing his weight around. The president has put us at Defcon Three. And we're staying there until this gets sorted out between all of you."

"Dammit." Daily groaned mournfully and shook his head.

"Go lie to the American public," the CIA director ordered the press secretary. "Heart attack. Pure and simple. No big deal."

"Got it," Daily agreed, his voice grim as he scribbled more notes on his clipboard.

"Our job," Mort told the group, "is to protect the president from any future attack. So, if you'll excuse me, gentlemen? We will remain in touch with one another to unscramble this debacle."

Colby followed his boss out of the room. He was still feeling out of sorts, the dizziness assailing him off and on. He made sure he was near a wall whenever possible so he could reach out and stabilize himself. Something was wrong, but what?

Was it really the Russians? Why would they do this at a time when Kasmarov had his hands full with internal problems of his country?

"Director?" Colby called as they walked out the doors of the hospital into the dusk. "I'm going back to the vice president's office. I want to see if our team has come up with any clues."

"Good idea, Agent Colby. You sure you're up to this? You look like hell warmed over."

Grinning tiredly, Colby said, "I'm a lot better off than the vice president, sir. I'll be fine."

"Go for it." Mort smiled and walked down the sidewalk to an awaiting black limo.

Colby avoided the flock of reporters still hovering around the E.R. doors on the other side of the hospital. He reached the parking lot, opened the door of his dark-blue Toyota hybrid Camry and climbed in. Sitting there, he took a couple of deep breaths. Whatever had happened in that office had made him feel spacey, dizzy and out of his body. It was hard to focus, to stay grounded.

Rubbing his eyes tiredly, Colby realized he was lucky to be alive.

CHAPTER TWO

DORIS RED TURTLE, a medicine woman of the Cheyenne nation, scanned the circle of elderly women. They all sat without expression, even though the eight-sided hogan, windows open, was stifling as the Arizona summer sun beat down upon it. They had gathered in the Navajo nation, at a special place among the red sandstone monoliths near Monument Valley.

The medicine woman's brows, thick and white with age, drew downward. "Rogan Fast Horse murdered the vice president of the United States four days ago. That is why I issued a plea for all of you to come here. He's sworn to kill others in the president's cabinet, and then the president himself."

"Why should we care if he kills them?" Sparrow Hawk, an Apache medicine woman, spoke up. Her hair hung in two thick, gunmetal-gray braids. She wore a knee-length, blue calico gown, and cradled a pipe bag made of elk skin in the crook of her left arm.

Doris held the flashing black eyes of the

Apache. "This is no time to thrash over the history of what whites have done to our nations. Rogan is a threat to *all* people, no matter what their skin color or gender." Her gravelly voice dropped lower in warning. "As you know, two years ago, Rogan stole the Storm Pipe from the Hokahto, Blue Heron Society, of which we are all members. He acquired this sacred ceremonial pipe by murdering our sister, Cora Thunder Eagle, who carried it."

Doris grimaced and added, "Rogan killed her daughter's husband, Hal, as well. This is not news, of course.

"We were all worried what he'd do with this pipe. Sell it to a collector? Try to use it himself? But why would a man want a woman's sacred pipe, which can only be handled by one of the sisters? Men can never access that power, no matter how hard they try. We all wondered what would happen. Well, now we know what he was planning to do with it."

The women, who ranged in age from sixty to almost a hundred, all nodded in agreement. There were twelve of them present, representing a dozen Native American nations. Each medicine woman had been chosen, trained and appointed ambassador to this supersecret and sacred pipe society.

Doris looked to her right, her gaze settling on a tall, thin Navajo. "Agnes Spider Woman, who is our oldest member, will speak now. Grandmother?"

Agnes gave a slight smile of acknowledgment, her light-brown eyes watering, the lids sagging heavily at the corners. Her gaze moved slowly in a clockwise direction around the assemblage. Each medicine woman sat cross-legged on Navajo rugs that Agnes had woven by hand during her long life. Beneath the colorful rugs, the red clay was hard-packed, a reminder that Mother Earth lived with them in harmony. The rocks represented her bones, and the soil, her flesh. The only door to the hogan was open and a slight breeze entered, easing the stifling conditions. There were two small windows, one in the west and one in the south, that were open to allow a breeze. "Thank you, my sister Doris Red Turtle."

Like Sparrow Hawk, Agnes cradled a ceremonial pipe in her left arm, for the Navajo nation. Veins stood out dramatically beneath the coppery skin of her hands. She moved her arthritic fingers gently across the beaded deerskin pipe bag that carried it. "Greetings, my sisters. I had asked Red Turtle, who is a powerful voice among our nations, to bring you here." Her voice was reedy but still strong for her age as she exclaimed, "May the Great Mystery bear witness to our plight and give us direction to change it."

Slowly lowering her birdlike arm, she said, "Rogan Fast Horse, a Cherokee métis medicine man from Nevada, plotted to steal a pipe from our

Blue Heron Society. He made his intentions clear many, many years ago, but we gave his threats little attention. Our mistake was in not taking him seriously. We know there are some arrogant, power-hungry medicine men among the nations. Few, but they are there. Usually, they are blowhards, with no action behind their threats or bragging."

Looking down at the pipe bundle in her arm, the beading of which showed a great blue heron standing near water, Agnes shook her head. Then she gazed around the circle. "Our society was created so long ago that we have no way to know how old it really is. Doris and I figure it may have begun three thousand years ago. We are nations with oral history, not a written one. And from all I have been told, the Hokahto Society is very, very old."

Lifting her hand, Agnes gestured around the room. "Each of you carries a sacred ceremonial pipe from a time long ago that has come to you in the present. Each of you was specially chosen to represent your nation here, because you have a good heart and a good way of walking. Each pipe carried in this room represents Mother Earth, Father Sky, our sun and moon, in some way. Each is different. But each functions in harmony with the others to create a connection for all our relations."

Agnes paused to wipe the corner of her thin

mouth with a white cotton handkerchief. She patted her lips with a trembling hand and tucked the handkerchief away once more. "According to tradition, only women can be members of the Blue Heron Society. Each pipe created was to be cared for and used by a woman. Only one of the sisterhood may open up the pipe bag, look upon the medicine object within, hold it and connect it to the stem for use. We are charged with working with the pipe to inspire life and harmony upon our planet for the good of all beings."

The breeze strengthened and the slanting sun brightened the shadowy space where they sat. Agnes welcomed the cooling breeze and silently said thank-you to Father Sky and the wind spirits. "Each of the pipes has tremendous power that has been gathered over time. That is why a pipe carrier is always chosen with the greatest of care. Each pipe is capable of positive deeds, or can be ordered by the carrier to wreak death and destruction."

Pulling out her handkerchief once again, Agnes dabbed at her watering eyes. "The Storm Pipe was given to the Lakota people. Not only has Rogan Fast Horse stolen it, we now know what he's going to do with it—kill others. A month ago, I heard gossip from a young woman from the Crow nation. She said she'd heard that Rogan had vowed to use the pipe to destroy the white man and his government." Shrugging her bony shoulders, Agnes Spider Woman said, "It was gossip, and I don't like tattling about others. The woman who told me was a good person with a good heart, but it was still gossip. Yet looking back, I know I should have listened and not dismissed her claims so lightly. It was the Great Mystery's way of warning me." Agnes's mouth turned downward. "And I did not listen."

Silence hung heavy in the heated hogan. Finally, Sheila One Feather, of the Crow nation, spoke up. Her square face was deeply lined from eighty years in the mountains of Montana. "Rogan is a two-heart, Grandmother Agnes. None of us here likes gossip. We all know the danger of it. You cannot blame yourself for not listening. We'd all have done the same."

There was a faint murmur of agreement from the group.

Kate Little Bird of the Iroquois nation spoke up. Her eyes flashed with fire. "Let's face it—Rogan has stalked power all his miserable life! He's bent on vengeance against anyone—red or white. Is that not so, my sister?"

Sadly, Agnes agreed. "Rogan killed one of us to steal the Storm Pipe. We all felt that, since he was a man, he could not use it. But he has found a way to do so."

Kate scowled. "How could he use the pipe? It will only awaken and respond in the hands of a woman. I do not understand this. Do you?"

"Yes," Agnes said wearily. "This same young Crow woman told me that Rogan had gathered twelve women to aid him. He taught one of the twelve how to awaken the pipe and use it. With these women willingly cooperating, he was able to control the pipe for his own evil ends. I am ashamed of these women, for they are no better than Rogan. They seek power that is not theirs to use. They are all two-hearts."

"Power," Kate Little Bird said, "is an aphrodisiac to those who have none. We all know that."

"Power is earned through walking in balance and harmony," Doris Red Turtle stated. "It cannot be stolen, nor can shortcuts be taken to work with such power."

"Yet," Agnes said, "that is exactly what has happened here. Rogan knew he couldn't touch the Storm Pipe himself, or force it to work for him. So he's spent the last two years seeking and finding twelve women who thirst after power like he does. Rogan assembled a team of medicine women to support his goals and vision. We all thought that the Storm Pipe would eventually resurface and we'd get it back. I didn't dream that Rogan would devise something like this. None of us did."

"Do not blame yourself," Doris advised the older woman gently. "When the pipe was stolen, we all felt it would return to us sooner or later. Ceremonial objects are taken all the time by those who seek power that is not rightfully earned, or theirs by heritage or training."

"Humph," Agnes muttered. "We all thought since it was a woman's pipe, it would be rendered impotent in Fast Horse's hands. We underestimated him."

"No one has ever done this before," Kate said. "How were we to know? Or guess?"

Again, there was a murmur of agreement from the group. All shared in the blame.

Blotting her eyes, Agnes murmured, "Sometimes it is beyond whoever walks the Red Road with a good heart to plumb the depths of a two-heart, to discover what evil they carry or the plans they create. This is one of those times. We do not think like them and are incapable of such diabolical misuse of power. But we are all paying for it, and so is Mother Earth and all our relations. That is why we must act."

CHAPTER THREE

AGNES SPIDER WOMAN RAISED her thin hand and looked around the hogan at her sisters. "The daughter of Cora was to become the next woman to carry the Storm Pipe. This is as it should be. Since she was nine years old, Dana Thunder Eagle was being trained by her mother to step into her shoes as a ceremonial pipe carrier when the time was right. When Cora was murdered, and Dana's husband, Hal, was as well, the young woman went wild with grief."

"That is only natural," Doris said, shaking her head over the violent deed.

"Of course," Agnes agreed. "Dana is like a granddaughter to me, as you all know. She is Lakota and Navajo, a beautiful young woman filled with such love and care for others, a true pipe carrier in every sense of the word. When she was twelve years old, I gave Dana a personal pipe to train with—the Nighthawk Pipe, in preparation for carrying the ceremonial Storm Pipe. Dana accepted the honor and responsibility, as I knew she would." Smiling fondly, Agnes wiped the corners of her mouth once more. False teeth and old age made her mouth water constantly. "We need to contact Dana and ask her to come home and fulfill her destiny."

"How?" Doris demanded, scowling. "How old is she? In her twenties?"

"Yes, twenty-nine." Wiping her lips, then clutching the damp handkerchief in her thin hand, the elder added, "Dana left the Rosebud Reservation after the murders because both sets of her grandparents were dead. She was crazed with grief. I tried to convince her to come and live with me, but she refused, and disappeared. But I sent out the spirit of the pipe I carry to keep in touch with her. She lives in Ohio right now and teaches first graders at a school near Dayton. It is her way of dealing with her loss of the two people she loved most in the world. Children are nothing but love, and that is where Dana has found refuge...until now."

"Of course," Sparrow Hawk muttered, "the murders were a terrible blow to all of us. At first we didn't know who did it. Over time, we were able to track down the culprits—Rogan and his lead woman, Blue Wolf." She tightened her right hand into a fist. "I wish I could pray for their deaths. I'd do it."

Doris gave her Apache friend a gentle smile.

"As a ceremonial pipe carrier, you are charged with walking the Red Road with a good heart. None of us can use the pipes we carry for anything but good for all our relations."

"I know," Sparrow Hawk growled, opening her pudgy, callused hand. "But I will tell you that, in my heart of hearts, I have dreamed of taking their lives for what they took from the Blue Heron Society and from Dana. It is not right."

Nodding, Agnes said, "No, it's not right, and now it is time to right wrongs. But to right them in a way that the Great Mystery would approve of. We cannot lower ourselves to lies, deceit, theft or murder, as others choose to do. As pipe carriers, we are the symbols of all things good about those who walk the sacred Red Road. We are role models."

"I see a gleam in your eyes, Agnes," Doris noted, grinning. "What plan have you hatched under that messy hen's nest of white hair?"

Chuckles echoed throughout the hogan. Indeed, Agnes's white hair did resemble a tangled nest. With arthritis in her joints, she could no longer braid it, much less comb out all the snarls.

Raising her white eyebrows, Agnes gave a toothy smile. "Hens lay eggs. A nest is rich with ideas." She blinked her watery eyes. "Besides, the dozen hens in my coop think I am one of them now. They come up to me, clucking in their language, and I talk back to them."

More chuckles sounded.

Agnes felt the tension in the hogan begin to melt. She didn't mind making a joke about herself to ease it, and shift attention momentarily from the awful reason why they were gathered here. Humor was most needed in the direst of times.

"We must get Dana to come home," she stated. "Then I will ask her to retrieve the Storm Pipe from Rogan and his women. This is something she must do. She was in line to receive it."

Shifting restlessly, Sparrow Hawk said, "But does Dana have the heart to do this, Agnes? Rogan is savage in battle and gives no quarter. If this woman has not been fully trained in the ancient ways, how can she combat him? Instead of facing the deaths of her loved ones, she ran away, and has remained out of touch with you. I don't find that very courageous."

"I hear your words, sister." Agnes looked down at the knotted handkerchief in her hand. "But I helped deliver Dana. She was born on November 17."

Sparrow Hawk grimaced. "So?"

Doris reached over and patted Sparrow Hawk's arm. "In case you did not realize it, Rogan was born the exact same day and month as Dana."

"Oh." Sparrow Hawk gulped. "I did not know. Well, this changes things."

"Oh, yes," Doris said in agreement, "it changes

everything." She directed her attention back to Agnes. "They are twin souls."

"Indeed, they are. Mirrors of one another. One has a good heart, the other is a two-heart—a person of darkness who's chosen an evil path to fulfill his needs." Agnes lifted her head and said proudly, "You should have been at Dana's birth. Her grandparents were there as well. Everyone was so excited. Because I was there to help with the birth and had been adopted into the family, I assisted in the delivery. When Cora went into the final stages of labor, a thunderstorm came rolling out of the west. I watched from the window as the sky grew black with approaching thunder beings, the spirits who create these powerful storms. Each time Cora cried out, lightning would flash across the sky, followed by a clap of thunder that shook the house like a dog shaking off fleas. And when Dana slid into my hands and took her first breath, a bolt of lightning was hurled by a thunder being. It split the huge cottonwood that grew fifty feet away from their door. I stood with my adopted granddaughter in my hands as the blinding light filled the house, bathing all of us with his radiant presence. Dana did not cry. She did not whimper. As I looked out the window, I saw the cottonwood tree cleave in two and fall over."

Rubbing her chin, which was sprinkled with white hairs, Sheila One Feather groused, "Well, there you go, Agnes. Even then, the thunder beings were telling you that as Dana was born, another of equal power was being born. It doesn't matter that the year of birth is different. When two people are born on the same day and month, there is a connection between them. A sacred cottonwood splitting in two means two of something." Her thick, bushy brows fell. "Now we know who the other one is. Rogan Fast Horse."

"Yes, yes," Agnes said, nodding her head. "As I stood there drying Dana off, before handing her to her mother, I didn't realize what the thunder beings were trying to tell me. It didn't dawn on me until recently." She touched her head. "A little slow, this one."

Laughter again permeated the hogan.

"Rogan was born in Kentucky. Dana was born at the Rosebud Reservation in South Dakota," Kate Little Bird mused. "Otherwise, they are twin souls bound together in a spiral death dance." Her full lips puckered and she looked around the circle. "Only one will survive their confrontation with one another. We all know that. I have seen other twin souls born, and every time, one of them dies early. Usually in a violent or tragic event. And it may or may not be due to the twin causing the death but they will meet and the Great Spirit will decide who lives and dies after that."

"It is a battle between the light and darkness," Doris reminded them. "And no one can foretell the outcome. Dana's heart must be pure and powerful in faith in order to overcome Rogan's dark ambitions."

"She is the daughter of the Blue Heron Society," Agnes declared. "It is in her blood, in her heart, to help Mother Earth and all her relations."

"Well," Sparrow Hawk grumped, "Rogan has plenty of power now. What's to stop him from using the Storm Pipe again? A ceremonial object used for centuries accrues tremendous power. In the wrong hands, such a pipe could be directed to send a lethal blow. But even a ceremonial pipe must have time to recharge after such a feat. Most take six weeks, at least, after unleashing all their power."

"True," Agnes agreed. "I know the Storm Pipe. It will be that long before she can be used again by Rogan."

"I hate the fact that one of our precious pipes is being misused like this," Doris muttered. "They are our most powerful ceremonial tools, which is why the choosing of a pipe carrier takes so long. Years of watching a person, gauging their heart and intent, to ensure the pipe is used only for good, never for evil. Once the connection between carrier and pipe is established, the spirit within must obey the new owner. In this case, Rogan must have had Blue Wolf connect with the pipe, for he cannot."

"That's right." Agnes sighed and wiped her mouth once more. "It is up to us to stop him and retrieve that pipe for our society. Dana is charged with doing this, whether she knows it or not."

"And is she trained in the art of war in the other dimensions? Is she physically fit for such a mission?" Kate Little Bird inquired.

"Let me sing you a song that has always been with the Storm Pipe. Perhaps it may answer some of our questions." Agnes cleared her voice and began to sing in a wobbling soprano.

"Come to me, pipe who works with the storms
I am your friend, I am your friend
Come to me, pipe of the storms
I am your friend, I am your friend
Wind mixes with fire, and Mother Earth cries
I am your friend, I am your friend
Pipe of storms, fire of the sky
Come to me, come to me
Thunder walks, the wind screams and blood flows
Come to me, come to me
Blue heron lies dead, iron hand moves, and the nighthawk rises
Thunder and iron hand join battle, fire holds the key
Come to me, come to me...."

The energy in the hogan throbbed as Agnes finished the sacred ceremonial song linked to the Storm Pipe.

"Fire holds the outcome," Sparrow Hawk said.

"That could easily mean nuclear annihilation for all of us!"

Patting the pipe bag she carried, Agnes said, "That is one possible way to interpret this song. I prefer to think that Dana Thunder Eagle will have the ability to work with the thunder beings, who bring fire in the form of lightning, in order to destroy Rogan and bring the Storm Pipe back to us."

Sheila One Feather groaned. "Agnes, you live in a world of dreams. Few who have aspired to work with thunder beings are alive! For their power is as great as a nuclear blast. No human can physically withstand the surge in order to harness it for use."

Shaking her head, Sparrow Hawk insisted, "No, fire means a nuclear war, not lightning, in this song."

"What choice do we have, my sisters? Do we sit here deciding that the sacred song of the Storm Pipe makes us paralyzed with fear?" Agnes voice lowered with scorn. "I say we contact Dana and get her to help. You forget that if the thunder beings choose to work with and through her, they will protect her from their power and fury. She would become an open conduit for them to send their energy to Rogan and his followers, but she herself would remain unharmed."

"Wait, wait!" Sparrow Hawk held up her palm. "What do you make of this 'iron hand' in the song? What does this have to do with the outcome?" She looked around at the group.

Doris cleared her throat and gave Agnes a significant look. When the older woman nodded, Doris told them, "I have the answer, my sisters. Agnes is aware that one of my grandsons, a Cheyenne Lakota, carries the name Iron Hand." She held Agnes's gaze. "I believe that my grandson, Chase Iron Hand, will work with Dana to secure the Storm Pipe from Rogan and his women. And Chase has strong ties with you, Agnes. You, as our leader, are charged with getting him to help us in our dilemma."

"You are right," Agnes said. "Chase is a member of the Blue Turtle Medicine Society, a group of men and women who are powerful psychic warriors and healers. He is not only trained in the art of warfare and protection on the energy level, but he's also just recently left Delta Force and the U.S. Army." She gave them a narrowed look. "Chase is the 'iron hand' referred to in the song. As I speak, he is up on a bluff on my reservation crying for a vision." She lifted her head, her voice becoming strong and clear. "He came, unannounced, to my hogan a week ago. He asked me to prepare him for a vision quest. His time in the army has left him wanting. He came home to hear what the Yei, our gods and goddesses, have decreed that he become from this time onward. Chase Iron Hand is a man of honor, with a military education and training. I can ask him for his help. Who better to pair with Dana in this effort?"

Sheila One Feather snorted. "Indeed? Does Chase know what he'd be getting into?"

"No," Agnes said pertly, "but he will soon enough. And so will Dana."

CHAPTER FOUR

DANA MOANED IN HER SLEEP and tossed the sheet aside. Brow wrinkling, she shifted to her stomach, stretching her arm toward Hal's side of the bed. The dream that gripped her was the same one she'd had two nights in a row. In it, thunderclouds smudged out the dusky light, looming closer and closer, like angry brooding faces. A chill moved down Dana's spine and she rolled onto her back, dragging her eyes open.

Vaguely aware of the sweat trickling between her breasts, she pressed her hand against her cotton gown.

"Hal?" Her voice was thick with sleep. Husky with hope.

No...he's dead. Two years ago, her mind whispered back to her. Tears formed in Dana's eyes and she shut them tightly. How long was this cycle of grief and nightmares going to last?

The bedroom was silent. It was June in Ohio, and she purposely had kept the window near her bed open. The air cooled her overheated skin, and Dana focused on the crickets chirping happily outside the window. Now and then, frogs croaked. The natural sounds soothed her fractured state of confusion, grief and loss.

It was more than missing Hal. She missed her mother, too. Groaning, Dana tried to escape the questions that often haunted her. Had Cora and Hal suffered terribly after being attacked? Had they died slowly? What were their last thoughts? Panicky ones, probably. Rubbing her moist eyes, Dana flopped onto her back and stared up at the darkened ceiling, those questions like knives assailing her heart and gut.

As she rested her arm across her closed eyes, loneliness snaked through her. The only thing that helped assuage this overwhelming pain was the personal pipe she carried. Reaching out, she found the deerskin bag that lay on the pillow next to hers. Hal's pillow. He was gone, but the Nighthawk Pipe had given her solace on nights like this. Pulling the pipe bag to her breast as she rolled to her side, Dana closed her eyes, tears matting her lashes.

"Nighthawk, help me. I hurt so much," she whispered, pain making her voice hoarse. "My heart feels as if it's going to burst with loneliness."

Dana felt a warmth begin to emanate from the long, rectangular bag. From the spirit that lived within the pipe, she knew—the one she had bonded with when she was young. The spirit answered her plea and sent waves of healing warmth into her heart. Holding the pipe bag securely against her, Dana mentally gave thanks for this unconditional love.

Like rivulets, the warmth spread from the center of her chest outward, flowing throughout her body. With the healing energy washing through her, Dana felt an incredible sense of peace and well-being. Nighthawk's love was dissolving her fear and her anguish.

Dana released a tremulous sigh. Sleep would come now, and with it, escape from the awful feelings that had inhabited her since the loss of her mother and Hal.

Cetan, the Lakota word for Nighthawk, had been her friend, teacher and companion since she was twelve years old. Twenty-nine now, Dana never took for granted the energy the pipe had, the power from the Great Spirit that flowed through it to her. It was always a miracle, and she felt humble and grateful to have such a comfort in times of great suffering. Her mother had taught her that the ancient ways would always sustain those who walked the Red Road of the heart. Now, Dana's faith in those beliefs was healing her bit by bit from the terrible trauma that had occurred two years ago.

Cetan was her best friend, a spirit companion on the unseen levels, and had supported her through this tumultuous time. Dana gently squeezed the pipe bag where the head of the pipe rested in a white rabbit-fur pouch to protect it from being broken. *I love you so much, Cetan. Thank you and the Great Spirit for sending me this healing energy. I don't know what I'd have done without your help and love.*

No less than I love you, Cetan replied telepathically.

Dana smiled tenderly as she snuggled into her goose down pillow. When the pipe spoke to her, it brought feelings of love and nurturance, plus a rich texture of other emotions. Over the years, Dana had come to realize that mental telepathy was more than a concept. When a pipe was given to a human being, an energetic umbilical cord of trust and love was forged between that individual and the spirit within the red, carved stone.

Cetan possessed marvelous powers of healing. It was a pipe of purpose; anything Dana had requested of it over the years had been granted. Sometimes, Dana had allowed an ailing person to hold the pipe bag, and miraculously, Cetan would send the healing energy of the Great Spirit to the patient. Dana had witnessed many beautiful moments of healing and cure with Cetan's help.

A pipe carrier was there to serve her village. Since the White Man had come to Turtle Island—

North America—the bands had been disbursed. But those who knew Dana was a personal pipe carrier sought her out and asked for help.

Dana understood the privilege and responsibility of being a pipe carrier, and she always smoked the pipe for each person who requested that she do so. Connecting through ceremony and prayer to the other worlds, she could help direct special energy to that person, place, animal or thing. Her clients were always grateful and would contact her afterward to tell her of the wondrous changes in their condition. All Dana asked of them in return was to share food, blankets or clothes with those who had less than they, as payment for the pipe's services. Pipe carriers never took money for what they did; they were emissaries of the Great Spirit, and all requests were met with compassion and love. Dana needed no personal reward, for just being a pipe carrier was a reward in itself. She took that responsibility seriously.

Another sigh slipped from her lips as she spiraled down into oblivion. The wings of Cetan beckoned her…. Dana knew what would happen as she nestled in the soft, warm, downy feathers: sleep, blessed sleep without dreams or nightmares, would come. Just to sleep deeply, undisturbed, was a great gift.

This time, though, was different. As Dana slept, she did dream. But this was no ordinary dream. In it, she watched the purple color of dawn approach. Soon, Father Sun would rise—a sacred moment she always absorbed with joy. Dawn was one of the most powerful times of the day.

Out of the red-violet dawn, a dark shape came, flying directly toward her. The wings of the bird were curved and long. Dana watched in fascination as the winged one drew closer. Her heart beat in anticipation, not fear.

As the great blue heron materialized from the shadows, a strange sense of elation soared through Dana. The red-and-gold colors of sunrise were filling the sky when the blue-gray water bird called to her.

Come, Daughter! Ride upon me! I will take you west. Come, mount me and we will fly together!

The heron cocked its head, its black eyes sparkling with life. In the dream, Dana moved forward to mount its broad back. Without fear, she settled astride the bird and gripped the soft feathers of its long, thin neck. The great wings flapped, and Dana felt the power of the heron thrumming through her as it turned and began its journey toward the southwest. Where were they going? A sense of adventure and happiness filled Dana.

The landscape changed remarkably beneath them. Dana gasped as she recognized the red desert of the Four Corners area. It was the Navajo Reservation, where her adopted grandmother lived! How many times had she come here to visit

Agnes Spider Woman? So many, especially when she was a child growing up. Every year, her family had driven from South Dakota to Arizona to visit her Grandmother Agnes. How Dana had looked forward to those warm, happy visits.

As she saw the red desert dotted with juniper, cypress and piñon trees, an ache started in her heart. An ache of loneliness for her grandmother, who loved her fiercely. Since the murders of her mother and Hal, Dana had run away, and hadn't once gone to visit Agnes. No, like a coward, she'd run east and immersed herself in teaching children, trying to forget her pain, to forget her past....

The heron flew over an eight-sided hogan, built of long timbers with mud in between. It was surrounded by tall, mighty cottonwoods to give it shade from the brutal summer heat. Dana instantly recognized the box canyon with its red-and-white sandstone and limestone walls. This hogan was where Grandma Agnes lived. And standing outside, in a long, dark-blue cotton skirt and long-sleeved red velvet blouse, and a heavy necklace of turquoise and silver, was her adopted grandmother. She was waiting for Dana.

The heron landed gently. Dana slid off the bird's back and she thanked it. Turning, she saw her grandmother smiling warmly, her arms opening.

"Grandma!" Dana cried, and she ran up the red clay slope to where Agnes stood.

In the dream, Dana felt her grandmother's thin, strong arms wrap around her. As soon as they embraced, Dana began to cry—deep, wrenching sobs welling up from within her. Agnes murmured her name and, with one trembling hand, gently caressed her hair. She understood Dana's grief.

For the first time since Cora and Hal's death, Dana felt totally loved and protected. She had had to be so strong after their deaths. All the paperwork to fill out, all the meetings with the county sheriff, the detectives… It had been an endless nightmare of ongoing pain for her. No one knew who had killed them. They still didn't know. That bothered her all the time.

"Grandmother…" Dana pulled back from her embrace to gaze at her. "It's so good to see you again. I'm so sorry I didn't come home after… well, after."

"Grandchild, do not worry," Agnes whispered, smiling into Dana's eyes. "I understand. What is important is that when I asked you to come, you did. That is all that matters." She touched Dana's wet cheeks, her fingers shaky. "Tears are good. They are cleansing and healing. You keep crying. Better out than in." She gave Dana a luminous smile.

Stepping back, Dana held her grandmother's thin, worn hand. "Are you all right?"

"Of course. I have come to you in your dream to ask you to visit me. When you awake, you must pack and drive out here immediately. I need your help, and will tell you why once you arrive." Agnes held Dana's startled look. "You will come, won't you, Granddaughter?"

"Of course, Grandma. I promise."

"Good. Come to my hogan. Be here by the full moon."

"I'll be here, Grandma. I will come home."

As soon as Dana whispered those words, she felt herself spiraling downward. The scene with her grandmother dissolved. Accustomed to the sensation, Dana knew her astral body was coming home to her physical form….

Sunlight slanted through the open window, filling Dana's bedroom with brilliance. She rolled onto her back, her arm still wrapped around the pipe bag. Gently, Dana placed it on the pillow again. The dream was alive and vibrant within her. Sitting up and sliding her feet from beneath the covers, she wriggled her toes on the thick, dark-green carpet.

Outside, a robin was singing melodiously. The sky was light-blue and cloudless, the breeze fragrant with the scent of flower blossoms. The world looked different to Dana as she stared wonderingly out the window. It was 8:00 a.m. on a Saturday morning…and the vivid dream became a wake-up call.

Running her palm across her purple duvet cover, Dana closed her eyes and allowed the full beauty of the dream and of her grandma's love to shimmer through her. Her heart opened like a flower, and she drew in a tremulous breath. Home. She was going home. Agnes had asked her to come visit.

As she opened her eyes, Dana felt relief from the guilt she'd carried since the murders. Her grandmother had asked her to come and stay with her. Instead, Dana had run like a coward and hidden in the white man's world.

The familiar odor of burning sage came to her. Oh! How she loved the smell of ceremonial smudge, being wafted to cleanse her of any negative thoughts and feelings. Dana could sense her adopted grandmother in astral form nearby. Even though she couldn't see her with her eyes, Dana felt her loving and powerful presence. She had been taught astral travel at an early age. It was an easy way to visit a friend or loved one anywhere, in the blink of an eye. The sage was her grandmother's calling card. A welcome one.

Lifting her head, Dana looked around her small bedroom. "I'm coming, Grandma. I'm coming home to you…." she said aloud.

Dana could swear she heard her grandmother's cackling chuckle, felt her hand rest gently on her shoulder. The sensation was comforting. Strengthening. For too long, Dana had been off the reservation, disconnected from Mother Earth and all her relations. She'd run to the empty world of the white man instead.

Not happy about her choices, but knowing she couldn't change the past, Dana slowly got to her feet. The warmth of the sun embraced her as she walked to the curtained window. Seeing the robin singing in the Jonathan apple tree made Dana smile.

Her grandmother was near. She could feel her standing at her side, her arm wrapped lovingly across her shoulders. A sharp longing to be back on Native American land plunged through Dana.

There was such a difference in energy, living on a reservation versus in the mechanized world of whites. Indians still had an invisible connection, like an umbilical cord, between themselves and the land. Mother Earth pumped energy and love into the "children" who were still attached to her. As a result, Native Americans cared for and honored the earth. They gave daily prayers of gratitude for being alive, for being nourished and fed. They were reverent toward their true mother, for without her, no one would be alive.

"Yes…" Dana whispered, her throat suddenly closing with tears. "I'll leave today, Grandma. I'll call the school and get someone to fulfill my contract." As a teacher, she would miss her children. Dana felt badly about that. Right now, she needed healing and help. "I'm coming home, back to where I belong." Even though she was born and raised in South Dakota, the southwest was her favorite place to live. Many times in the past, she'd spent wonderful moments with Agnes in Arizona and had come to call it her real home over time.

As she turned from the window, she noticed something on the carpet. Frowning, Dana padded to the end of the bed and picked it up. It was a blue-gray feather—a feather from a great blue heron.

How she had missed the daily magic and synchronicity in her life. Gazing at the feather as she straightened, Dana understood that the dream had been more than just a pleasant experience. The great blue heron was her grandmother's spirit guide. And Agnes had sent her here to call Dana home.

Caressing the feather with her fingers, Dana understood the gravity of the invitation. Finally, after a two-year-long dark night of the soul, she was going home….

CHAPTER FIVE

"I'VE BEEN EXPECTING YOU, Chase Iron Hand.
Enter." Agnes waved into her hogan. Although not
related to him, he had visited and lived with her as
a young boy. Chase saw Agnes as his adopted
grandmother and she loved being that for him. He
had just come off the bluff after a four-day vision
quest, and taken the sweat lodge that must precede
his speaking about his vision with her. Sunlight
lanced in the doorway where he stood, awaiting
her invitation.

He was dressed now in a white cotton shirt, the
long sleeves rolled up to just below his elbows. The
jeans he wore hugged his strong, powerful body.
Agnes was pleased to see that Chase wore the
black buffalo horn choker around his thick neck,
an abalone disk attached to it. She had given it to
him as a departing gift when he was a young man
about to go to West Point Military Academy.

Chase's military short black hair, still damp
from the sweat, gleamed with blue highlights. He

had obvious Indian features, a square face and high cheekbones, and a restless gaze constantly moving around to check out his territory. Golden cougar eyes. Agnes was pleased with Chase's alertness. It was what had kept him alive during his years in Delta Force.

Turning to prop the door open to welcome in the morning air, Chase smelled the wonderful fragrance of sage. He knew that each morning, as the sun rose, Grandmother lit the sage in a rainbow-colored abalone shell, stood in her doorway and sang the sun up. The white smoke was healing and uplifting in a spiritual sense. It got one clean and in harmony for the coming day.

"Come sit." Agnes gestured for her tall, well-built young man to sit on a red-black-and-white wool rug she had woven fifty years earlier. She watched as Chase moved with the boneless grace of a cougar to settle opposite her, legs crossed. She accepted the dried, wrapped bundle of sage that he handed her. That was a sacred calling card, regardless of nation—a gift of sacred sage from one party to another. It was a sign of respect.

Searching Chase's eyes, Agnes saw that the four days of the vision quest had exhausted him. But that was the point of a quest: to wear down the physical body and mind enough so that the Great Spirit could talk to the supplicant's heart in dream language.

When Agnes handed him a cup of steaming sage tea in a chipped blue pottery mug, he took it with a slight nod of his head. Chase had not eaten nor drunk anything in four days. Agnes watched as pleasure wreathed his coppery face, his eyes closing slightly as he sipped the fragrant, life-infusing tea. Sage cleansed a person physically, mentally, emotionally and spiritually. It was one of the most powerful members of the plant kingdom.

"This hits the spot, Grandmother," Chase growled. "Thank you." He savored the medicinal taste as the tea trickled down his gullet into his shrunken stomach and brought him back to life.

Pleased, Agnes lifted a beat-up copper teakettle and placed it nearby so that Chase could drink all he wanted. A person coming off a vision quest was dehydrated, no question. And sage tea was the perfect way to replace lost fluids. "I'm glad."

Without hesitation, Chase drank two more cups of the tepid tea. After pouring a fourth cup, he looked over at the aged woman, whose shoulders were drawn back with unconscious pride. "I've missed sage tea," he admitted, his voice raspy. "I've missed a lot, I think."

Even in her nineties, Agnes Spider Woman was beautiful. Elegant. Chase wondered if he'd ever find a woman who had these inner qualities that shone through like sunlight, as they did in Agnes.

At thirty years of age, he had given up hope of finding such a woman, convinced he had only bad luck with the opposite sex.

"You needed to leave the reservation to find yourself, Chase. There is nothing wrong with that." Agnes spoke gently, seeing pain cloud his golden eyes momentarily. "We each have a journey we must take. And there are many tributaries to the Red Road, paths that we are called to take from time to time. Joining the army to feel your way through the white man's world was one you had to take. I understand this." Agnes watched Chase nod, his mouth twisting in a grimace. His face was deeply weathered by time he'd spent in harsh outdoor elements. Agnes knew that Delta Force was a very specialized unit whose members trained hard physically. That showed in Chase's forearms, where the muscles jumped each time he lifted the cup of sage tea in his large, callused hands.

"Tell me of your vision," Agnes entreated, folding her hands on the dark-blue velvet skirt she wore, her legs crossed beneath the fabric.

Chase wrapped his hands around the warm mug as it sat on his left knee. Closing his eyes, he allowed the vision to congeal before him once more. "I saw a great blue heron come flying out of this thunderstorm that was stalking me, Grandmother. And at her side flew a nighthawk. Lightning danced around the three of us, and I was sure

I was going to be struck by it. The heron landed in front of me, a lightning bolt in her beak. The nighthawk landed next to the heron. Before my eyes, the nighthawk turned into a beautiful young woman." Chase opened his eyes and grinned boyishly at his composed teacher. "She was a looker, Grandmother. Black hair and the most startling cinnamon-colored eyes I'd ever seen. They were the color of fresh, reddish-brown earth plowed up after a hard winter."

Agnes nodded. "And did this young woman speak to you?"

"Yes," Chase murmured, sipping the tea. "She asked for my help. I said how can I help you? She told me to go to the red rock country where you live, and meet me here on the next full moon." Chase frowned. "And then the woman turned into you, Grandmother." Shrugging, he said, "That was the end of my vision."

"A good vision," Agnes said, pleased.

Chase waited. It would do him no good to press her for an explanation of his vision. Patience was one of his strengths, so he waited. Outside, he could hear the merry chirp of a robin, and farther away, the trilling of a cardinal. He had hearing like a cougar, which was his spirit guide.

"I must tell you a story." Agnes filled Chase in on the Storm Pipe being stolen from the Blue Heron Society two years earlier. When she mentioned Rogan Fast Horse, she saw Chase's eyes instantly narrow with rage. His mouth thinned, as if he were struggling to hold back a barrage of toxic comments. Oh, she could feel Chase's reaction, and because she was clairvoyant, she saw the angry red colors swirling in his aura, confirming his reaction.

Flexing his scarred fist, Chase waited until Agnes finished telling him the full story. Then silence fell in the hogan.

Taking in a deep, ragged breath at last, Chase expelled it. Agnes tilted her head to one side, like a bird listening for a worm.

"Just before I went to West Point, I met Rogan at a powwow," Chase told her. "He cheated in the bow and arrow competition to win. I saw him do it. And so did the elders who were the judges. When they announced him as winner and not me, I challenged Fast Horse, because I wasn't going to let him get away with it. The elders were wary of his sorcerer's powers. Afraid that he would harm them or their families if they didn't let him win."

"But you weren't afraid."

"I was, Grandmother, but I also knew what was right. In that instant, I felt as if the Great Spirit had chosen to work through me because the elders were too afraid to confront Rogan about his cheating." Looking down at his hands, his blunt nails and the thick calluses that covered his palms,

Chase said softly, "There was a knife fight." He touched his brow with his index finger. "I cut Rogan across his forehead. He bears the scar to this day. I won the knife match and he swore to curse me, to be my mortal enemy until the day I died."

"Powerful words to invoke."

Shrugging, Chase looked around the shadowy confines of the hogan. The woodstove was in the center, the metal pipe leading up through the top of the mud-and-timber roof. "Rogan doesn't know humility. I taught it to him that day. I won the match and the rewards. I knew he was a sorcerer, but I also had faith that the Great Spirit would protect me from Rogan's rage."

"Did he?"

"Yes," Chase said, a note of sarcasm in his deep voice, "after four years at West Point, I volunteered and was allowed into Delta Force for eight years." He looked at his right arm, which bore many small, puckered scars. "Other than getting caught down in South America by rebels, held prisoner and tortured for six months before I managed to escape, I don't think Rogan got to me."

"He did not," Agnes confirmed with knowledge and conviction. "And I am sorry you had to suffer so much in the army, Chase." She gestured to his arm.

"It wasn't fun," he agreed grimly. Meeting her watery eyes, he asked, "So Dana Thunder Eagle must go after Rogan herself? I've fought him, Grandmother, and there isn't a woman alive who could do what you're asking of her."

"We of the society realize this. That is why the Great Spirit sent you that vision. *You* are the other key to us reclaiming the Storm Pipe."

Chase allowed her words to filter through him. Closing his eyes, he replayed the vision again in his head. Yes, she was accurately interpreting the dream. Sighing, he looked at her once more. Agnes sat there resplendent in her agelessness, the sun touching the silver strands of her flyaway hair. The lines in her face were a road map of her life. Chase knew she was a tough old buzzard, and her lean, thin body proclaimed her power regardless of her age. Admiring Agnes for her strength and great, warm heart, he offered, "Grandmother, I'm tired. I just left the army. I've been fighting the bad guys for so many years. Well, I'm just…tired." Chase didn't like admitting it, but he was. Six months of daily torture had reduced him to a level he never wanted to admit to anyone. And he needed time to reclaim his tortured spirit, heal from the awful, daily beatings, and try to become whole again.

"I understand," Agnes murmured. Reaching out, she placed her thin fingers on Chase's arm and squeezed it. "That is why you came home. Home to find your true calling. Dana must be toughened up not only physically, but to tap into her warrior side emotionally, mentally and spiritually." Agnes lifted her hand and poked her index finger in Chase's direction. "I need you to turn her into a warrioress, capable of reclaiming the Storm Pipe."

"You want me to teach her the art of war? That's all? And I won't have to do anything else other than be her teacher?" That appealed to Chase under the circumstances. Right now, he was at a low ebb. The fact he'd allowed himself to be captured by the rebels was humiliating enough. But to be tortured and finally break, giving away secrets he'd sworn never to divulge, was a blow that had broken his spirit.

When he'd finally made his escape and got home, he'd left the army, defeated and wounded on every level. He'd put good men's lives on the line because he'd squealed like a pig going to slaughter. Chase wasn't proud of himself. And right now, he felt mortally wounded spiritually, which was why he'd come back home to Agnes in the first place.

And now, both she and the vision he quested for were asking him to reconnect with violence and war. Feeling as if he could teach this woman was enough of a demand on him. Chase didn't even want to attempt to take on Rogan right now. It just wasn't in his spirit to do so. "I can train her," he stated. "But I won't go with her to retrieve the pipe."

Nodding, Agnes said, "Then that is enough."

"I'm not a soft man, Grandmother. I'm hard. The training I've had is brutal. I don't know how to be gentle or cajoling. Dana sounds soft. Unprepared. If I become her teacher she may quit. Do you realize that she could walk away, because she doesn't have the heart or passion for this mission you want her to undertake?"

"Choices are always before us."

"The kind of training needed to ensure her survival against Rogan will be harsh," Chase warned grimly. "I won't coddle her, Grandmother. I can't. You're saying we have five weeks to prepare Dana for this mission before the Storm Pipe has recharged enough to kill again under Rogan's direction. Five weeks. That's just not enough time."

"It has to be," Agnes declared. "You saw Dana in your vision. I know she is a beautiful woman and I think you are swayed by that. Beauty can be strong. A pretty face is not always weak, as you assume." Touching her blouse above her heart, Agnes added, "In here, I know she has the stamina and courage to answer the challenge you throw at her."

"So, weaver of people's lives, when do I meet my student?" Chase knew that Agnes had spider medicine. She had the power to combine people and situations together when she felt it best. Trusting her, he acknowledged that spider medicine was like any other kind: good or bad, depending upon how the energy expressed itself through the individual. And Agnes was one of the purest-hearted people Chase had ever known. He trusted her more than anyone else in his world. His father had been a reservation policeman until he was killed trying to stop a bank robbery. His mother had died six months later of a broken heart, leaving Chase to be passed around from one relative to another until he was old enough to go to West Point. His time with his adopted grandmother Agnes had left the deepest impression.

"Tomorrow, Dana arrives. She will come and you will introduce yourself to her.".

Though he had his doubts, Chase said nothing, just nodded.

"The two of you will work as a team here in the box canyon. There is a small hogan farther up where you'll stay. The winter sheep hogan has everything you'll require. Dana will need your brawn and your cleverness as a warrior, Chase. You will pass your experience on to her so that she can confront Rogan and take the pipe back."

Even though Chase had never met Dana, his protective nature was already at work within him. Oh, he knew that women could be warriors; he'd seen his share on the res, growing up, as well as while he was serving in the U.S. Army. Still, that didn't erase the age-old conviction that was alive and well within him: that women and children were to be cherished, loved, protected and defended. Chase knew he'd have to readjust this mindset to work Dana into a tough, well-trained warrior. In five weeks. That seemed an impossible time frame.

But when Chase saw the hope burning in Grandmother's eyes, he kept his worries to himself.

He did not want to disappoint his extended family, especially this most sacred of women elders. He'd already disappointed the U.S. Army, and humiliation still ran hot through him. Clearly, the Great Spirit was setting him up for another test. Perhaps by training this unknown woman, he might salvage his pride, his manhood, and learn to live with what he'd done while imprisoned in South America.

When Agnes passed some homemade fry bread to Chase, and a bowl of fragrant lamb stew, he thanked her. Fasting for four days had left him feeling like a hungry cougar. Dipping the dark, whole-grain bread into the bowl filled with thick chunks of lamb, onions, brown gravy and potatoes, he said a prayer thanking all those who had given their lives so that he might eat.

The moment he took a bite, Chase savored the flavors. Yes, he was home. *Finally.* It had been a circuitous route, he thought, as he swiftly ate to stop the gnawing in his stomach. Restless, he'd left the res because he was curious about the white man's world. And he'd tasted it—at West Point and for eight years after graduating. Now, because he'd failed as a warrior, because he'd broken under torture and interrogation, he'd crawled to Agnes, his pride stopping him from going back to Grandmother Doris on his home reservation. Instead, he'd come here to Agnes on the Navajo reservation to reclaim his shattered spirit. He hoped he would lead a productive, honorable life once more.

As he ate the succulent lamb stew, Chase savored the flavors of rosemary and marjoram. Each bite was more than just a physical gift to his body, it was nourishment for his wounded soul. Already, Chase could feel his battered spirits beginning to lift.

A ray of hope threaded through him. He stopped eating for a moment and felt the tenuous emotion touch his war-ravaged spirit. Healing was taking place. Humbled as never before, Chase finished his stew. Agnes was a powerful medicine woman, and he knew she'd said healing prayers over the food. And he was on the receiving end of her loving hands and heart.

"This meal is wonderful, Grandmother. Thank you…."

Smiling, Agnes murmured, "I'll get you another bowl from the kettle. You're hungry and too thin. You need to regain the weight you lost, Chase."

Watching the elderly woman slowly rise, with the elegance of a great blue heron lifting her wings, Chase admired her lean, graceful form. Agnes Spider Woman was a bright beacon of hope in his life right now, and he was grateful to have such a positive role model. He didn't know how he felt about Dana, and that would be a challenge to him. Women weren't his strong suit and never had been. Tomorrow, he'd have to start dealing with one.

Ordinarily, Chase would have said he couldn't do it, but with the support and help of a powerful elder who believed in him, he would try.

CHAPTER SIX

CHASE SQUATTED on the smooth red sandstone ledge above the winter hogan. A nearby juniper hid his presence. The sun was hot, beating down on his bare shoulders, and he soaked it in like a man starving for life. He'd been six months in a green hell where there was no direct sunlight. Only rain, cold, and high humidity, all conspiring to break his spirit.

His gaze swept down the escarpment toward the hogan near the wall of the canyon. Restlessly, he sifted the fine red sand through his scarred fingers. The grit felt good. He liked having physical contact with Mother Earth. It was comforting to him. A breeze stirred, moving along the thousand-foot-high rock wall behind him, rustling the cypress and piñon trees.

What was Dana Thunder Eagle like? He'd seen her face in the vision, but he knew dream and reality could be very different. He frowned pensively. He hadn't told Agnes how powerfully drawn he'd been to the woman in his vision. Hadn't been able to tell her. It would be his secret. He watched the red grains of sand catch the sunlight, sparkle and then drift to the smooth rock ledge he was sitting on. Of course, Agnes could read minds, so he figured the elder already knew. Maybe it wasn't important. But it was to him. Women had been a thorn in his side, not a pleasure. Oh, he'd had plenty of one-night stands, had found sexual gratification with a number of partners. But he'd never met a woman who made his world stand still.

Snorting softly, Chase decided that his parents must have had something very special that he would never experience himself. They'd been so much in love. As a child, he'd thought all husbands and wives had devoted relationships like that.

He'd been wrong to think true love was the norm. Going to West Point at age eighteen, Chase very rapidly got ensnared in the dating scene. Everyone wanted to stake a claim on the handsome red man who had broken through the white-males-only barrier. Women danced around him like butterflies, there for the taking if he wanted them. He'd been like a beggar in a candy store, grabbing every beauty who wanted to bed him. And for a while, he'd thought he was in a sexual heaven of sorts. But by his sophomore year, the one-night stands were becoming the same; the faces were a blur and the act meaningless beyond selfish gratification and release. Chase broke off the relationships because they were emotionally empty meetings of body only. He wanted more. *Much* more and never had found it yet.

The wind gusted sharply, making Chase lift his head. The sky was a blue vault with white horse's mane clouds stretching across it.

She was here. He sensed it. Dana Thunder Eagle had arrived.

Grandmother Agnes lived at the mouth of this deep, rectangular canyon. The winter hogan was invisible from her summer home. Chase knew that Dana would spend at least an hour talking with her adopted grandmother, to receive her marching orders on how to rescue the Storm Pipe. The elder would then send Dana up here, around the bend of the canyon, to stay for the next five weeks. With him.

The winter hogan was a lot smaller than the summer one, making it much easier to heat during the biting cold and heavy snows. The small potbellied stove was also used for cooking. Navajos were practical about the extreme change of seasons on their large reservation. Still, even though Chase and Dana would sleep on opposite sides of the eight-sided structure, it was a very scant space.

A red-tailed hawk shrieked as it circled the tabletop mesa above the canyon. Chase followed the bird's lazy spiral and enjoyed seeing its rust-colored tail. Only an adult redtail, five years old or more, had that eye-catching hue on its tail feathers.

Chase's mind—and focus—went back to Dana. What was she like? Did she have the right stuff to undertake this deadly mission? Already, he was worried. Five weeks was an impossibly short time to get Dana ready for such a serious undertaking.

Immersed in his thoughts, Chase felt time disappear. He understood that the magic of focus created this out-of-time sense of being. It felt good to Chase, and familiar. And before he knew it, he saw a tall, lithe woman in blue jeans and a white blouse, her hair in long, thick braids, walking up the canyon toward the winter hogan. She carried a red canvas bag in each hand. On her back was a dark-green knapsack. Even burdened as she was, she walked with pride.

Instantly alert, Chase studied her minutely. Knowing he was hidden, he felt the euphoria of a stalker and hunter as he watched the woman draw closer. His heart began to beat more strongly in his chest. Reddish highlights danced in her hair as the sunlight caught and reflected it. There was a deerskin pouch tied on the left side of her black-and-silver concha belt. Chase knew it would contain a mixture of sacred herbs that she would gift to the spirits of this place. One always bade the neighbors hello, like a person inviting another over for a congenial cup of coffee.

As much as Chase wanted to stay distant from this woman who was supposed to save the Storm

Pipe, he couldn't. As she lifted her head to scan the area, behind the hogan and up on the sandstone skirt, where he hid in the shadows, Chase saw a fearless quality in her wide, cinnamon-colored eyes. There was a stubborn angle to her chin, even though her face was smooth and oval. Her Indian heritage showed in her high cheekbones. Her nose was straight, with fine, thin nostrils, reminding him of a well-bred horse.

The horse image suited her, Chase decided, watching her approach the hogan and set her luggage down. Dana was perhaps five foot nine or ten inches in height, with a slender figure. As she pushed open the wooden door, which faced east, Chase noted that every one of her movements was graceful, like those of a mustang.

Taking in a ragged breath, he remained still and watched Dana disappear with her luggage inside the hogan. When she returned minutes later, she stood outside the door and took some of the sacred herbs from the pouch she carried. Facing east, she raised her hand above her head and slowly turned, stopping at each of the major directions until she'd completed her clockwise circle. Chase saw her throw the herbs into the air, the breeze catching and scattering them.

Good. At least she knew protocol. But then, if she was a personal pipe carrier being trained to carry an old and powerful ceremonial pipe, Dana would automatically contact the local spirits of a place. One never came to a strange area without offering a gift and requesting permission to stay. Omitting this critical step was considered rude and wrong.

Chase knew Agnes had directed Dana to climb to meet him, her trainer and teacher. As his eyes narrowed upon her uplifted face, he felt her energy. Indeed, Dana was beautiful. Just as lovely as she'd been in his vision. A part of him groaned in protest, because he was drawn to beauty like a honeybee to a flower in full bloom.

He watched patiently as Dana made her way up onto a ledge of sandstone, and then to another. The walls of the box canyon rose upward like a multilayered cake. Squatting on the third level, Chase saw that Dana had rolled up her sleeves, and her well-worn jeans couldn't hide her femininity. Her long legs seemed to go on forever. A slow grin tugged at the corners of his mouth. Any man would be proud to have her as his woman.

Just as quickly as the thought seeped into his mind, Chase brutally pushed it out. This was business. All business. Besides, Dana was a recent widow. There was no room in her life for an emotional relationship. Maybe he could remold her grief into a driving strength, and a motivation for success in this mission. Perhaps...but that would mean wounding her all over again, and Chase had no desire to do that.

The afternoon air was filled with the scents of

the desert—the medicinal tang of the sagebrush, the sharp wine scent of juniper in bloom and the warm, woody fragrance of the nearby cedar. The blouse Dana wore stuck to her form, outlining her full breasts and long torso. Her braids swung rhythmically as she moved. Sweat made her skin glisten. Her full mouth was set with determination.

Chase watched her come ever closer. Calling on his cougar ally from the other dimension, he ordered him to guide her to within a few feet of the juniper he crouched behind.

Like a lamb being led to slaughter, Dana intuitively picked up on his spirit guardian's cajoling request. Trained medicine people, via clairvoyance or clairsentience, could usually detect a spirit guide, their own or another's. That was how they communicated with the invisible realms. And sure enough, Dana turned and headed straight toward Chase without knowing he was hiding there. She had a lot to learn, he realized.

Dana blew out a breath of air, realizing how quickly she was tiring from the climb up the rear wall of the box canyon. Clairvoyantly, she'd seen a yellow cougar come out and meet her. He'd greeted her warmly and asked her to follow him. Sensing no negativity around the guardian, Dana complied. It wasn't an unusual request; all places had spirit guardians, so she thought little about its greeting or request.

Having lived not far above sea level for the last two years, she felt the six-thousand-foot elevation of the desert plateau taking a toll on her. Her breath rasped as she climbed ever closer to a stand of juniper on the next tier of the sandstone formation.

Somewhere in the back of her mind, Dana recalled dreaming of this place. As a child, she'd come often to visit Grandma Agnes, and had played hour after hour upon these smooth red rock skirts. She'd been like a wild mustang filly, and the elevation hadn't bothered her at all. Now it did.

But the warmth of the sun, the fragrance of the trees and brush, all conspired to relax her after the three-day drive from Ohio. Oh! How Dana had missed all of this—the wildness, the freedom, the silence of Mother Earth surrounding her. What had made her think she could ever be happy in the Midwest? Dana frowned as she recalled again how she'd run away like a coward after the deaths of the two people she loved most in the world. Her adopted grandmother was right: she needed to come home. To be here. To live here once again.

This canyon had always been a place of joy and healing for Dana. She used to play hide-and-seek with her friends up here where the trees grew. Fond memories flowed back, sweet as honey. The wide blue sky, the thin wisps of cirrus that reminded her of threads on a weaving loom, and the faraway song of a cardinal all conspired to dazzle her with the intense beauty of the moment. She should never have left. It seemed like such a stupid, knee-jerk reaction now.

Dana halted near the first juniper and slowly turned east, toward the winter hogan. Gasping for breath, she pressed her hand against her pounding heart. Perspiration on her temples dampened strands of her hair. *Home.* She was finally home. Back where she belonged. As she stood there, embraced by a cooling breeze, and hearing the cry of a red-tailed hawk, Dana felt much old grief sinking out of her, flowing from her body and into Mother Earth.

Yes, the grief that had encased her was finally shedding, like an old, worn snake skin. Closing her eyes, she took a deep, cleansing breath into her lungs, and felt so much of what she'd carried since their deaths miraculously dissolve. Perhaps the biggest mistake she'd made was not staying with Agnes. Her grandmother had pleaded with her to come home, to live with her after the tragedy. Dana regretted not having listened to the wise elder who loved her so fiercely.

As she opened her eyes, Dana inhaled a new scent, one unfamiliar to her. What was it? She lifted her chin, her nostrils flaring as the wind brought a whiff to her once again. It wasn't un-pleasant, and something about it stirred Dana's womanly senses, long dormant.

Chase rose in one smooth, unbroken motion.

Like the cougar at his side, he took three steps toward the woman, who had her back to him. As he threw his arm around Dana's shoulders, his other hand gripping her left arm, he laughed to himself. She was such easy prey!

The instant the steel arm clamped around Dana, she gave a cry of surprise. That same musky scent filled her nostrils. Her eyes bulged as she was jerked back against the hard, unyielding plane of a man's body, his powerful fingers digging into her left arm.

Without thinking, Dana jabbed her right elbow into his midsection. It felt as if her elbow had smashed into an unforgiving metal wall.

Letting out a cry of surprise, Chase nearly lost his hold on the woman. He'd expected her to be a rabbit, to stand helplessly, squeal and surrender without a fight. Instead, she'd fought back! Anger flared in him. It wasn't anger aimed at Dana, but rather himself. A grudging respect was born in Chase as he expertly kicked her legs out from under her. Not wanting to hurt Dana, he monitored the force with which she fell to the smooth sandstone ledge, landing on her belly.

Bringing her left arm up between her shoulder blades, Chase carefully pressed a knee into the small of her back while he held her head down with his other hand. He tempered the amount of pressure he brought to bear on her, and was surprised once more by her fighting spirit. Dana struggled to escape. She didn't scream, but tried to twist free, lashing out with both her feet.

Sweat trickled down Chase's temples as he leaned over, his breath coming in gasps. "You made three mistakes, woman."

Dana froze. The man's husky voice was so close to her left ear it shocked her. The rock bit into her right cheek as he held her head down on the sandstone. His voice was dark, deeply masculine, and sent new alarms racing through her. Dana was receiving mixed signals from her intuition now. Confused, she finally stilled and stopped fighting. Who was this man? Was he going to kill her? The thought momentarily paralyzed her.

Chase felt the tickle of her dark hair against his mouth as he whispered into her ear, "The first mistake was that you didn't pay enough attention to your surroundings." Hard, sharp gasps exploded from her lips. "Secondly, you allowed me to draw you to where I was hiding, by sending out my cougar spirit." He saw her face drain of color, her eye narrowing with rage. Good, she wasn't a rabbit, after all. "Lastly, a warrioress always has her ally guarding her, but you didn't send your own guide out to look for danger."

With a grunt, Chase released Dana. He stepped back, hands on his hips, and watched her with veiled interest.

Dana scrambled to her knees, breathing raggedly. Leaping upward, she whirled around, wildly aware that her captor stood only a few feet from her. When she met his narrowed golden eyes, she checked the urge to run. She saw hints of amusement in those large, intelligent eyes of his. He was laughing at her! Fear turned to fury.

"Who are you?" Dana demanded, her voice low and off-key.

Chase gestured for her to sit down.

Dana refused, glaring at him.

He forced himself to ignore her primal beauty, the way she was crouched and ready to fight him all over again, if necessary. "Sit. Your knees are shaking so bad you're going to fall down if you don't."

Grudgingly, Dana glanced down. He was right. She was feeling terribly shaky from the adrenaline rush flaring through her bloodstream. "How do I know you won't attack me again?" she retorted angrily.

She took a few steps away from this giant of a man. He wore a pair of faded blue jeans, but no shirt, and his chest was broad, massive and without hair. He was Native American, no doubt about it. And powerful. Again, she saw laughter in his eyes. He hadn't made a move toward her. Yet. Nervously, she wiped her damp palms against the thighs of her jeans.

"I don't make a habit of attacking or raping helpless women. Sit down."

Dana felt that same confusion overwhelm her

once more. This man had attacked her. Then he'd released her. Was he her enemy? If so, why had he let her go? Her knees buckled abruptly, and she threw out her hands, cushioning her fall. Landing with a thump on the red sandstone, she felt weak and vulnerable before this warrior.

Searching his tanned, square face, Dana felt a sizzling sensation build within her and momentarily wipe out her fear and uncertainty. Her first impression, of a cougar, had been right. He had topaz-colored eyes that lightened or darkened with his mood changes. His face was hard, weathered by the elements. She couldn't tell if he was a full-blooded Indian; his nose was hawklike, his nostrils now flared to catch even the faintest of scents.

The only hint that perhaps he wasn't a killer appeared in his mouth—the corners curved naturally upward. Her darting gaze took in the powerful breadth of his shoulders. His chest was massive, his arms tight and thick with muscles. But he was far from musclebound; no, this man's body was taut, in shape and honed to perfection. The sunlight made his copper skin glow with an almost unearthly radiance.

Dana blinked, unable to assimilate all that she saw and felt around this man, who stood like a nearly naked god. The jeans he had on were thin and faded from use. And he was wearing leather Apache boots, with their distinctive curled tip—

designed for picking up snakes and hurling them off to one side. That way, the wearer was not bitten, and the snake lived to go about its business.

This man was indeed a cougar, coiled and waiting to leap upon her at any moment.

A sour grin edged Chase's mouth as he studied her.

"Who are you?" Dana said resentfully.

"Chase Iron Hand. Your teacher."

Shock bolted through her. Grandma Agnes had said he would meet her at the winter hogan, but she hadn't found him there. "You can't be…" she choked out, all her bravado dissolving. This man was powerful, physically as well as energetically. There was nothing soft or vulnerable about Chase Iron Hand. Dana could understand why he'd been given such a name. Indeed, he was like a piece of forged metal, far stronger than she would ever be.

Chase watched the fleeting emotions cross her stunned face. Her skin had a golden sheen wherever the sunlight caressed it. She sat with hands flat on the sandstone, her legs crossed. "Grandmother told you to meet me," Chase informed her.

"At the hogan," Dana snarled, anger once again replacing her fear. She felt the terror begin to leak out of her and into Mother Earth. "I thought—" She gulped, her voice tightening. "When you attacked me, I thought you were the same man who murdered my husband and my mother."

Pain slammed into Chase's heart. Damn! He hadn't meant to do that to her. He could see anguish in Dana's wide cinnamon eyes, which were now filling with tears. He opened his mouth to apologize and then snapped it shut. Right now she didn't need his pity. She needed to learn how to work through emotional pain and keep her focus on the job ahead. "And if I had been, you'd be dead, woman. You're supposed to be trained to take back the Storm Pipe," he sneered. "And what did you do when confronted? You didn't think about how to escape."

His words stung her. Gulping back her tears, Dana saw the lack of respect he had for her. Chase was right: she had failed to look for escape. Not exactly what a real warrior would do.

"But then," Chase added, "you have a habit of running away when things get tough, don't you?"

Pain over that truth gutted Dana. She hung her head and placed her hands over her face. It hurt too much to speak.

Chase watched how Dana took his powerful words. She could hide nothing from him. Part of him was delighted with the discovery, but another part disdainful. Warriors showed no feelings, no matter if they were in the worst pain or on a natural high. He didn't look too closely at himself, however. After six months of daily torture, he'd finally surrendered to the pain and given his enemies the information they'd wanted. Was he any different from Dana? Unwilling to go there, Chase hardened his heart against her and his own hidden shame.

"So, you're a coward and you ran," he drawled.

Dana's head snapped up. Rage tunneled through her as she held his merciless stare. "Don't give me that male superiority garbage!"

"Call me Chase." He held out his hand to her. "Come on, let's go down to the hogan, Dana. You've had enough for one day."

Staring at his outstretched hand, Dana saw so many little pink scars on it that she recoiled. There was nothing warm, comforting or nurturing about this man. Her teacher. Oh, Great Spirit, *he* was her teacher? Dana had felt a lack of confidence sitting before Grandma Agnes, as she'd asked her to bring back the Storm Pipe. Now, in the shadow of this mighty warrior, all the rest of her confidence fled.

Scrambling to her feet, Dana lashed out and knocked his hand away. He laughed. It was like listening to the far-off rumbling of her beloved thunder beings.

Chase Iron Hand was beautiful in a rugged way. But in that moment, Dana detested him, because she had none of his confidence or strength within herself. Without a word, she scrambled down the sandstone wall and headed toward the hogan. To hell with him! She wasn't about to walk at his side and chitchat, pretending nothing had happened.

He'd scared her to death! He'd made her think she was going to die, as Hal and her mother had. Hatred toward him rose within Dana as she hurried down the escarpment.

Chase grinned and watched Dana storm down the canyon. Her shoulders were now thrown back with pride, her chin jutting out at a very defiant angle. He eyed her appreciatively as he followed, noting her hips swaying like a willow tree in a summer breeze. Mesmerized by that liquid motion, Chase felt a new trap—longing for a woman. Again he squelched that need. It had no place here, for sure.

There was a barbed wire fence on the last tier of sandstone, a wooden corral nearby for sheep and goats brought up to forage. As Dana bent to slip between the strands, the barbed wire caught on the back of her blouse between her shoulders. She was trapped. She tried to free herself without tearing a hole in the material, and by the time Chase arrived, he saw frustration in her features.

"Go on," she snapped at him.

"I can help."

"That's the last thing I want from you! Get out of here. I'll see you at the hogan."

Chase smiled briefly. Well, Dana was showing some pluck now. "Let me help."

She jerked her head, and Chase saw loathing in her furious eyes. Good, he'd use that to train her with, too. He didn't take her anger toward him personally. No, the Indian way of thinking was that the feelings a person had were his or her own—not someone else's. Why should he take responsibility for how she felt?

Lifting her blouse, he delicately eased the barbed wire from the fabric. "A warrioress knows when to ask for help, too."

What the hell was he talking about? This was the second time he'd made a reference to her being a warrioress. Chase was crazy!

The brush of his fingertips on her back sent a tingling feeling across Dana's flesh. As soon as she was freed, she slipped through the wire fence and hurried away without even a thank-you. Gulping for air, feeling hurt winding through her, Dana walked with resolve toward the winter hogan. Right now, all she wanted to do was run—again. Away from this coldhearted bastard. Away from her mission.

CHAPTER SEVEN

AS DANA WALKED TOWARD THE hogan, she asked herself, *What did I get into?* Grandma Agnes was so loving. So nourishing to her starved and aching soul. This dude, well, he was an irritating, stinging salt in her wounds! Maybe this was a mistake.

Dana plowed on through the rabbitbrush, the yellow flowers scenting the air. Mouth set, she felt fear. Only fear. Chase had scared her to death.

Dana had thought she was being attacked, yet when she stopped being such a drama queen long enough to look at the experience, she had to admit Chase hadn't hurt her at all—at least not physically. Oh, he'd made damn sure she got the message: that she was blind, deaf and dumb out here in the wilderness.

Dana dodged several smooth, red boulders on the steep slope to the hogan below. The wind was warm. The sun felt wonderful on her body. Mulling about Chase Iron Hand, Dana recalled a story her mother had told her as a child. There had been a race of fierce male and female warriors from the stars who had come to Earth to intermarry with the red people. The race was very tall, muscular, powerful and confident. Just like Chase. The star warriors had lived with their people and shown them how to weave, make weapons and defend themselves against invaders. Was he one of them?

Chase was too rough and unpolished, more animal than man, she decided. More wild than civilized. That scared the hell out of Dana. No man had ever sharpened her awareness of herself as a woman like he had in just one, potent meeting.

Pushing open the wooden door to the hogan, Dana stepped inside. She'd placed her luggage on the south side of the structure. The smell of sacred sage and juniper encircled her, calming and grounding. Some had been burned earlier in an abalone shell sitting atop the woodstove. Chase must have smudged the place, Dana guessed.

Rubbing her perspiring brow, she felt her heart opening. And with it came so much hurt and grief that she was momentarily overwhelmed. Chase had been brutal. But Dana was sure he would disdain her feelings and the hot tears that swam in her eyes. Valiantly, she choked down all her boiling emotions.

Tea…she needed some sage tea. Yes, that would help soothe her raw, nervous state. She knew Chase would come down soon enough. Dana didn't want to be standing here like an idiot when he arrived. Nervously, she went through the motions of taking the teakettle off the stove. There was kindling in a cardboard box, and she quickly rolled up some pieces of newspaper. After putting them into the stove, Dona located a box of matches. The fire lit quickly, the dry kindling snapping to life. Dana added several larger sticks and then shut the door.

As she looked around the quiet hogan, the peace of the place infiltrated her tense state. Everything was simple. The floor was hard-packed red dirt, swept clean and then covered by several colorful, handwoven rugs. On the southern walls were pine board shelves holding mason jars filled with various herbs. On another shelf were weaving items— a spindle, herbs for dying purposes and some gathered wool wrapped around spindles, waiting to be used this coming winter. On the western walls were several shelves containing what Dana recognized as medicine tools Agnes used in her healing ceremonies. There was a yellow gourd rattle with a redtail feather tied by a leather thong to the end of the highly polished wooden handle. A fan made of golden eagle tail feathers lay next to it. Dana didn't go over to look at them. Medicine objects were never to be touched except by the owner.

Turning, she set the beat-up old copper kettle back on the stove, after making sure there was enough water in it. The fire spat and crackled. Dana found a mason jar filled with dried white sage leaves. She took a small handful and dropped it into the kettle before replacing the dented lid. It felt good to be doing something rather than waiting for Chase to enter that open door.

Dana could feel him approaching. It was like sensing the invisible pressure of a storm front moving through the area. Steeling herself, she listened carefully, but couldn't hear him. The man was more cougar than human. No one ever heard the approach of a mountain lion, either. Until it was too late.

She took a deep, ragged breath and waited. When he finally entered, like a silent shadow, her heart twinged with fear. Chase was so tall that he had to duck his head at the doorway. Dana guessed the lintel was six feet high, and he was a good three or four inches taller. She tried to ignore the beautiful play of glistening muscles as he straightened and focused those golden eyes on her.

Though her pulse accelerated, Dana compressed her lips and glared at him. She wasn't going to let him scare her again. Or catch her off guard. Yet, as Chase moved on into the hogan, Dana couldn't help gazing at his male body, naked from the waist up. The scars on his chest told her he'd participated in several sun dances up on a Lakota reservation. For that ceremony, wooden pins were pushed through vertical slits in the skin of a man's chest or shoulder. Leather thongs were attached to the pins, and the sun dancer dragged buffalo skulls behind him as he danced for days on end around the sacred cottonwood pole in the center. The sun dance wasn't for sissies, and Dana's admiration for Chase rose whether she wanted it to or not. Any man who had completed a sun dance bore deep scars on his chest or shoulder blades. They were a reminder that he had the strength of spirit and the physical endurance to show his faith to the Great Spirit.

Her own scars, Dana thought, might be invisible, but they were just as deep and as hard earned. All people were wounded, she knew. But some scars couldn't be seen. Staring at Chase's broad, scarred chest, she wondered what other wounds he had endured.

Chase sat down on a rug, legs crossed, his powerful hands resting on his knees. "Sage tea?" he asked.

"Of course." Dana tried not to sound tense and threatened. She couldn't read this man as she could others; it was as if he had a wall up between them. When her back was turned, she could feel his eyes like two hot poker points. Hands trembling, Dana took a wooden spoon, pulled off the lid of the kettle and stirred the bubbling tea. The pungent fragrance of sage drifted upward and she inhaled, absorbing its healing and calming nature.

Dana tried to ignore Chase, but that was impossible. She went to the small sink near the door and found two chipped white mugs. After setting them on the drain board, she retrieved the kettle and poured tea into them. There was sagebrush honey on a shelf above the sink and she reached for it. Desert honey was delicious, and her mouth watered in anticipation as she spooned a thick dollop into each cup. Once she finished stirring them, Dana picked up the mugs and turned around.

Chase took his steaming tea. The moment their hands met, he felt her pull away. If he hadn't wrapped his fingers around the mug, she would have dropped it in his lap. He saw her nervously lick her full lower lip.

"Sit here," he told her, pointing to a place opposite him on the earth-toned rug.

Stung by his curt voice and blunt order, Dana hesitated, staring at the spot. It was much too close to him. She chose another spot a good six feet away and slowly eased into a cross-legged position.

After a few sips, Chase asked, "Did you bring the Nighthawk Pipe?"

"Of course. As a pipe carrier, I go nowhere without it."

"Did your mother leave behind any ceremonial tools for you?"

The mention of her mother sent a sharp ache through Dana. She gripped the warm mug more tightly and gazed at him.

Lowering his eyes, Chase stared down at the red earth floor between the rugs. Ceremonial objects were powerful instruments of their healing trade. He moved his gaze to Dana once more.

"She surely had certain feathers, rattles and sacred stones she worked with," he pressed. Dana looked fetching in her simple clothes, her hair mussed from the breeze, the black braids eloquent testimony to the blood that ran richly through her veins.

Frustrated with his abrupt statements and questions, she snapped, "Of course she did."

Meeting her blazing eyes, Chase stated, "For someone who has such old and powerful tools, you don't use them very well or very often." Pointing toward the canyon wall they'd just descended, he added, "You didn't even have an ally protecting you from my attack. You're giving away power, woman."

Stung, Dana growled, "Just who in the hell do you think you are? First, you attack me up there." She gestured toward her puffy cheek, which had been held against the sandstone. "You're the one who should be apologizing for hurting me! For scaring me to death! And you can wipe that disgusted look off your face while you're at it. I'm not into judgmental people, so back off."

"A warrioress never complains. She does not show her pain, no matter how much she suffers. And she should know the value of silence, of listening. You know none of these things."

"What are you talking about?" Dana began to hate the man. He sat there nearly naked, dangerous to her female senses, and yet supposedly her teacher. A terrible combination. "Who are *you* to question how I walk the Red Road or utilize the sacred objects passed on to me by my mother?" Hot indignation welled up in Dana, something she hadn't felt in two years. She wanted to run from the hogan, down the canyon to Grandma Agnes and tell her that she refused to work with this Neanderthal who called her "woman" of all things. The stormy look in his eyes scared Dana and at the same time fascinated her. His mouth was a thin line and the hard planes of his copper face gave no inkling of what he was really feeling. Disgust at her, most likely.

Sipping his tea, Chase allowed her husky words to reverberate through the hogan. When Dana got her feathers ruffled, she struck back. There was backbone beneath that golden, dusky skin of hers. That pleased him.

The tea and honey were a good combination on his tongue. Lowering the mug, Chase noted how she glared at him. Her hands were wrapped around her own mug, tightly enough to crush it.

"You are the only hope for the Blue Heron Society. Your grandmother already told you that. You are young, strong and possess the genes of your mother, who carried the Storm Pipe." Chase lowered his voice. "I will work with you to prepare you on all levels for the tasks set before you by Grandmother Agnes. That is, if you are brave enough to take on this mission."

Shaken, Dana dragged in a deep breath. The silence between them became oppressive. She stared down at the mug she gripped, her tea barely touched. Her hands were soft and without calluses, unlike his.

"I'll do my best," she finally rasped. Looking up, she met his narrowed golden eyes. For a moment, Dana allowed herself to drown in their darkening depths. Mesmerized by Chase's blunt, powerful energy, she felt an invisible shift within her.

Blinking, she disengaged from his stare.

"Rogan lives up in a fortress in the Sierras," Chase began. "He has a compound near Carson City, Nevada. The twelve women who work with him are true warriors. They are fanatical about keeping that ceremonial pipe for themselves. These women have placed their lives on the line to protect it and Rogan."

"I'm not a killer."

"No, but Rogan is. And his women will kill *you* if you don't know how to be stealthy and protect yourself. This is no game, woman."

"Dammit, stop calling me 'woman'! My name is Dana Thunder Eagle."

She felt stung by Chase's humorless smile. Now, he was laughing at her, as a coyote would a hapless rabbit.

"Better to be called 'woman' than 'child.'"

Drawing herself erect, spine taut, shoulders back, she said, "My name is Dana."

Shrugging, Chase murmured, "So be it."

Something was wrong with her eyes. Or so she thought at first. As Dana stared at Chase, she kept seeing another face superimposed on his own. The visage of an old Native American warrior seemed to overshadow Chase's scowling features. A chill snaked through her as she realized her clairvoyance had come into play.

Having such a teacher or guide from the invisible dimensions was rare, Dana acknowledged. Chase had to be very special for the spirit of such a warrior to work with him.

Though uncomfortable with her staring, Chase remained still. He could feel Dana's energy, like tendrils of light, touching the hard wall of defense he always kept in place. It was tentative. Gentle. Inwardly, he thirsted for the nourishing contact.

He drew his brows together. "What Grandmother Agnes has asked of you is not easy. Your life is going to be in very real danger, Dana. Not only physically, but spiritually as well. Rogan is a well-known sorcerer."

That sent a chill down Dana's spine. She knew about the Other Side, where various dimensions intersected and overlapped the physical reality of the here and now. There were invisible realms that, to someone blessed with clairvoyance, became highly visible. Dana had the ability to perceive these other realities when she wanted to, but also could shut them out when she didn't wish to be aware of them. "I'm no stranger to sorcery."

"Rogan isn't your everyday sorcerer," Chase told her dryly, finishing his tea. He set the mug aside and planted his elbows on his thighs, his gaze on her. A strong woman had no problem maintaining eye contact with him—or anyone. Dana didn't feel like such a woman, yet.

"I'm going to be your trainer on this mission, Dana. Grandmother has asked me to toughen you up, teach you how to defend yourself with and without weapons. I have five weeks to get you ready for that climb up the cliff to Rogan's fortress. You must be stealthy, quiet, and energetically invisible, so no one there knows you are in their midst. Your job is to get that pipe back."

"I'll get it done." Dana winced inwardly. She didn't sound terribly confident, did she?

She saw Chase's scowl deepen. There was such censure and disappointment in his face. Now, he was allowing her to see what he thought of her. And it felt damned uncomfortable.

"I won't coddle you during training," Chase warned. He wanted to goad Dana, to see if she would handle his scalding warning or run. She had to consider seriously her vow to rescue the Storm Pipe. "Once you make the decision to train with me, you belong to me—body, mind and spirit."

Clenching her teeth, she sneered at him. "No man owns me. And you sure as hell aren't going to, either."

For once her voice had some fangs in it. That was good. Chase knew, however, that anger would get Dana only so far. "I'm training you just like I was trained. Nothing more or less. Twenty-four hours a day, Ms. Thunder Eagle. For five relentless weeks. There will be no rest. No days off. Nothing is going to be easy. You're soft and you come from the city. You're completely deaf to your surroundings. Your eyes might be open, but you don't see. And as for being trained, I wonder just how good you really are. You should have sensed me and you didn't." With a shake of his head, Chase added, "You're a runner, I know. When things get tough, you stop trying to cope, and you run."

"I've stopped running," Dana said, her voice uneven. "And I won't run from this. I gave Grandmother my word."

"And will you give me your word?" He raised his brows and held her defiant gaze. "In our world, your word is your bond. You fulfill it or die trying. You know the story."

Yes, she did. Rubbing her chin, Dana said, "I give my word to you, as well. You are my trainer. I accept that. I'll do my best. And I'm not doing this for you. I'm doing it for Grandmother."

Smarting beneath the dark, questioning look in his eyes, Dana found Chase distasteful, threatening and overwhelming. What did she expect in a trainer? She sat there numbly, unable to answer the question. However, it wasn't someone like this—so hard that he felt like a sledgehammer pounding against her bleeding, wounded heart.

Her thoughts were interrupted when Chase rose in one smooth, fluid motion, to tower over her. She grudgingly stared up at him, sensing his utter masculinity, and trying not to be affected by his hardened body. She took a gulp of her cooling sage tea.

"Get up," he ordered.

Dana found she didn't take orders well. Still, she remembered her vow to her grandmother—and to him. All this was part of retrieving the Storm Pipe for her people. Setting the mug aside, Dana unwound her legs and stood up, making damn sure she left plenty of space between them. Chase had an aura that throbbed with such vitality and energy she almost felt buffeted by it. Rubbing her hands on her thighs, she said, "What now?"

"Strip off all your clothes."

CHAPTER EIGHT

DANA'S MOUTH DROPPED OPEN. "What?" The word came out in a strangled tone of disbelief. Tensing, she knotted her hands.

"I said strip."

Panic arced through Dana. "Dude, you're certifiable. There's no way I'm stripping for you or any other man," she said, nailing him with a look of outrage.

Chase seemed impervious to her reaction. His legs were spread apart, as if he were a boxer getting ready to fight—or perhaps ward off a coming attack. Yeah, she wanted to strike out at his implacable features and those slitted golden eyes.

"Did you forget your vow so easily?" he taunted.

"Standing naked in front of you wasn't part of the bargain!" Dana snapped. She took two steps back, glancing around to make sure the door was open. She badly wanted to slip past this giant of a man and make a run for it.

"Think again, Dana Thunder Eagle. A student has no rights. Only her teacher does."

Fingers folding into fists, Dana hissed, "No man owns me, mister. You sure as hell don't, even if I am your student!" Her breathing chaotic, Dana felt the alarming threat course through her already tense body. She crouched a bit, as if waiting instinctively for this man to attack her. Would he rip her clothes off her? The look on his face told Dana that he could, and that frightened her. He'd unexpectedly attacked her out on the escarpment, and she felt equally afraid now.

"I think feminism is dead, sister." Despite his goading taunt, Chase admired her guts. Dana was right—no man owned a woman. In the old days before the white man's arrival, women had been equal partners to men, and most tribes were matriarchal by tradition.

Lifting her chin, Dana held his flat, assessing stare. "I'm a person and I'll be respected as one. I have to learn certain things from you, but that doesn't give you the right to humiliate me." Gulping, Dana tried to force her breathing into a steadier rhythm.

It was impossible. She felt Chase, sensed his aura and his intent. He wasn't going to let her get away with this. He was going to strip her, of all things!

If Dana hadn't been so shocked by his demand, she might have been able to intuitively pick up some of his hidden intentions toward her. Right now, she just felt a stream of power aimed at her. Chase was going to have his way or else.

Backing away, she moved toward the door. Tears flooded her eyes. Modesty was a part of Dana's life. She was a private person, not one to give up anything about herself. No way would she bare her body before this animal!

"Going to cry?" Chase asked. "Going to run like you always do?"

Fury and terror sizzled through Dana. She halted midway to the open door, where the blazing desert light flooded into the hogan. Turning toward him, she snarled, "I'm not going to cry and I'm not running."

The first was the truth, the second a lie. Chase surely realized that, too, and hopelessness flooded her. She stood uncertainly, flexing her hands. Her feet, meanwhile, itched to dash out the door and down the canyon to her grandmother's hogan, for protection from this monster who wanted her soul.

"Running has been a way of life for you," Chase growled. Seeing the fear in her face, the way her body was tensed and ready for flight, he said, "And you stopped yourself from going out that door." He pointed in that direction. "That's good. You might be afraid, but you're not running now."

Blinking, Dana felt herself becoming emotionally unstrung. One moment, Chase was hard as a steel blade cutting through her. The next, there was praise, even warmth, emanating toward her. She felt them now, like an invisible blanket wrapping around her. Instantly, her fear dissolved. The desire to run abated.

Amazed, she straightened and forced her shoulders back. Could she believe Chase had a soul and heart, after all? Searching his hooded, assessing eyes, she decided that he was sincere. Confused, she rasped, "I don't know why you're asking this, your reasons for doing so. And I'm not buying it."

"A warrioress doesn't question her orders."

Anger sparked through Dana. "Then just what the hell would a warrioress do in this situation?"

"Strip. She is a woman who is proud of her body, proud that she is female. There is nothing she wants to hide, because she knows how strong and confident she is. Her body is the vehicle that carries her spirit in this lifetime. She treats it and herself with respect and honor."

Chase's voice was dark and coaxing. Like a reverberation of thunder in the distance, his words seemed to flow from far away until they touched her heart. Carefully studying the look in his eyes, Dana felt his truthfulness. She could find nothing sexual about his statement, nor did she feel it. If she had, she'd have been out that door in a heartbeat.

Chase was her teacher, but what was he trying to teach her? Confusion warred with Dana's natural modesty. She had never stood naked in front of a stranger. It went against her grain in a violent way.

Her thoughts churning, she realized she knew little about this man. Was he playing mind games with her? To bend her to his will?

She thought again of Grandma Agnes. Her grandmother would never leave her in the hands of someone who would harm her. That realization suddenly broke the paralyzing fear that bound Dana. Finding her voice, she said, "I...never thought of myself in those terms."

"White women are trained to be ashamed of their body. You aren't white. You're Indian. Be proud of your lineage. Praise your body by bathing in the warming rays of Father Sun during the day and in the cooling, healing light of the moon at night."

Chase saw Dana waver, unsure. "Why do I have to undress before you?" she asked.

"I want to look at you."

Heat stung Dana's cheeks, and her gaze shifted. But then she gathered up her dissolving courage. "Why?"

"Students don't ask questions. They do as they're instructed. If I decide you should know, then I'll tell you—afterward. Trust me."

Trust. A lump settled in her throat. Chase was so pulverizingly male as he stood there, his copper skin and the firm muscles beneath outlined in the dim light of the hogan. Trust him? She eyed him for a long moment, mulling over his words and gauging the look in his eyes.

Dana realized obliquely that, as a grade school teacher, one of the first things she strived to establish with children in her class was trust in her.

Only, she didn't ask them to strip. No, her methods were far more subtle.

Chase wanted the ultimate sign of trust. This was an awful way to test her. If she was to beg him to take back the order, he'd laugh at that sign of her weakness. A warrioress never showed weakness, Dana supposed, even if she felt it.

A slight breeze entered the hogan and sluggishly stirred the heated air. Finally, she made a decision.

"All right, if I have to strip, so do you. It's all or nothing," she challenged.

A tight grin stretched across his mouth, as if he liked her unexpected boldness. "Fair enough," he rumbled.

Fear arced through Dana. She hadn't expected him to acquiesce so easily—or at all. She watched as his scarred hand moved to the metal button at the waistband of his Levi's. Gulping against her constricted throat, Dana realized her bluff hadn't worked.

Her fingers shook as she placed them around the first mother of pearl button on her blouse. Furrowing her brows, she tried to concentrate on why she was doing this. It was for her grandmother. For her people. And the Blue Heron Society. Dana told herself there was no finer calling than to help her people—and the world—survive something as evil as Rogan Fast Horse.

Button by button, her blouse opened, until

finally, her white silk camisole was exposed. It hurt to breathe. It hurt to feel Chase's imperious gaze burning into her flesh. Dana refused to look up at him. Leaning down, she untied her boots and pulled them off. The wiry wool of the handwoven rug where she stood tickled her feet.

Chase watched as Dana undressed, keeping her gaze fixed on the floor. She slowly pulled her blouse off her shoulders and dropped it. Then she tugged at the waistband of her jeans and reluctantly eased them downward. The material fell away, revealing her long, curved thighs. She was, indeed, all leg. Well-developed legs that held the promise of great endurance.

"You ride a horse?"

Dana's head snapped upward at his quiet question. She nearly fell over, one foot barely out of her jeans. Steadying herself, she got rid of them. "Yes." Right now, she wore only silk boxer panties and the camisole. Crossing her arms defensively across her breasts, she tried to steady her breathing. Never had Dana felt more painfully vulnerable.

Chase had gotten rid of his Levi's. Gulping, she tried to keep her gaze away from his naked body. But it was impossible. He wore nothing beneath his jeans.

Oh, Great Spirit! The black hair around his maleness accentuated his potency as a man. Dana's eyes scanned down his hard thighs to his knotted calves and wide, broad feet. A strangled breath churned in her tight throat as she forced her gaze back up to his unreadable face.

She didn't find laughter in his eyes. That was good. Right now, in her nearly naked state, she couldn't stand to be made fun of by this man. And he seemed completely oblivious to his own nakedness.

"How often do you ride?" Chase demanded.

"Three times a week. More," Dana said, "if I get the chance."

"Your thighs show it. That's good. Keep stripping."

Chagrined, she tensed as he rasped out the order. Why was Chase doing this to her? To humiliate or humble her? To make her admit he was master and she was truly his slave? All the possible answers grated against her feminist mentality.

Clenching her teeth, Dana jerked off the camisole and flung it aside. Off came the silk boxers. Glaring, she lifted her chin, hating Chase. The breath was sucked out of her. His eyes weren't hard or merciless any longer as he studied her in the thick, tense silence. Then he nodded briskly, his gaze like fire scorching her naked flesh.

Dana tried to inspect him just as he was her. The rugged planes of Chase's body gleamed like polished copper. Each set of well-developed muscles flowed smoothly into the next. Her gaze flitted across his barrel chest, devoid of hair, to the corrugated ridges of his abdomen. Trying to avoid eyeing his obvious maleness hanging between his hard thighs, she gulped convulsively. His masculinity was daunting. Threatening. And calling to her.

Challenged by the fact that she could feel her nipples hardening beneath his merciless gaze, Dana closed her eyes. When would this humiliation be over? Every second seemed to drag on like a slug crossing a dry rock.

She heard him move. Or had she? Lashes flying open, she felt her breath hitch.

Chase had stepped to within a few feet of her. Had she heard him, or just sensed the energy change because his powerful aura had touched and integrated with hers? With her heart pounding like that of a snared rabbit, Dana forced her arms to remain at her sides and not cover her breasts. Distrust warred with terror as Chase approached her, his gaze critical and assessing.

As she focused on his body, Dana felt dizzied by his presence so close to her. She could actually feel the heat coming off Chase's naked form. He seemed a wild animal, barely touched by civilization. The scars on his body were many and some made Dana's stomach knot. These weren't all sun dance scars. What had caused them, then? She noticed how some were pink and shiny, and so relatively new compared to the puckered sun dance scars.

Chase cocked his head, perusing Dana as if he were looking at a horse, and checking for conformation as well as possible faults. He spotted a scar on her right shoulder.

"What happened here?" he demanded, pointing to it.

Dana stiffened as his callused fingertip lightly brushed the area. She saw disgust leap into his eyes. Gulping, she whispered, "When I was twenty, I fell off my horse. I smashed against a barbed wire fence with my shoulder before I hit the ground."

Scowling, Chase kneaded the area with his hands, feeling her muscles and assessing any potential problems.

"Stand still and relax," he ordered when she tensed even more.

Chase was so close. So male. Dana could smell the musky odor of his body sweat, as well as the scents of juniper and desert sand. Each time his fingers ran along the sheath of her shoulder muscles, wild tingles radiated outward. To her dismay, her nipples grew taut and erect. What must he think? Dana felt heat spreading rapidly up her neck and consuming her face.

"Muscle damage from it?" Chase demanded.

"W-what?"

Chase saw her nipples grow hard, ripe crowns in the broad crescents of her breasts. He savagely destroyed the sensual response that flowed unexpectedly through his body. She was too skinny for his tastes, he told himself. All skin and bone. He liked women with more flesh and roundness.

She looked dumbstruck, so he repeated his question. "Did you receive muscle damage when you hit that barbed wire fence? What did the doctor say? Do you have full range of motion with this arm?"

The moment he lifted his hands from the scar, Dana whispered unsteadily, "I—never went to a doctor the first six months."

Staring at the curved, ragged scar, he kept his investigation impersonal for her sake—and his. "It doesn't look like anyone sewed you up, that's for sure. The corners are still showing the tears. Why didn't you see a doctor about this?"

How badly Dana wanted to step away from Chase's overwhelming masculine presence. It was impossible. "I—uh—I didn't have money at the time. I was going to college. I couldn't afford a doctor. I went home and put iodine on it and just let it heal up on its own for six months."

"A warrioress, regardless of the situation she finds herself in, can think clearly. What would you do if I was Rogan Fast Horse? He'd strip and rape you, Dana. And then he'd kill you. Would you behave like this? Stuttering and stammering? Or would you be thinking on your feet? Looking for the first opportunity to escape his hold on you?"

Chase's harsh voice snapped Dana out of her confusion and fear. He had done nothing so far to indicate he was going to make sexual advances. Blinking, she stared up at him. "I'd want to be thinking…not be like this, of course."

His mouth twitched. "You show weakness around Rogan and it will get you nowhere but deep into trouble. Now, tell me more about this shoulder."

Dana couldn't believe she was standing two feet away from Chase discussing her old injury. They were naked, and strangers to one another. Yet Chase acted as if being here was the most natural thing in the world.

Lifting her hand, she touched her aching brow and tried to focus. "There was a lot of damage. I remember the doctor looking at it later. The surgeon said the muscles were shortened because I didn't go to the emergency room right away and get the operation I needed. He said it was too late to correct it with surgery."

Grunting, Chase ran his fingers across the area once more. This time, Dana didn't flinch. Good, she was beginning to trust him. If only a little. "The muscle *is* shorter than it should be," he confirmed, then moved his hand to her other shoulder. "Yeah, much shorter than this one." *Damn.*

"It doesn't bother me." Dana was relieved to be discussing such an impersonal topic. A huge part of her was in shock because he wasn't leering at her, as many men might do.

"It may bother you as you get into the hard, physical demands of this mission," Chase growled. Looking down, he saw a scar on the right side of her smooth, golden torso. Dana's belly was softly rounded, a good sign that she could easily carry a baby. It was one of the most sensual parts of a woman's body, as far as he was concerned. Chase stopped himself from going too far with that observation.

"Tell me about this scar."

Dana looked where he was pointing, and some of her initial fear abated. Chase *was* treating her like a horse, checking her out from top to bottom, assessing her potential. "Appendicitis attack when I was fourteen. It was removed."

"Problems afterward?"

Dana shook her head. Her heart began to settle down just a little. But it was impossible to ignore Chase on a sensual level. She'd met few men who had the confidence he displayed. "No, no problems. Not then, not now."

Grunting, Chase stepped back and critically examined the rest of her. He crouched down, placing both palms on her knees.

Dana tried not to react, though the roughened

feel of his hands made her mouth go dry. As warm as she was, Dana could swear she felt embers of heat emanating from his touch.

Chase poked and prodded her knees, front and back. "You've got damage to your right knee."

Amazed he could know that, she looked down at him. "Yes."

"Long ago?"

"A year."

"Another horse accident?"

"Yes."

Chase ran his thumb from her knee down her lower leg, testing one particular ligament. He used enough pressure to make Dana flinch.

"Ow!"

Jerking a look up at her, Chase said, "Is that all you can do? Cry over each little hurt?"

Dana tried to pull her leg free of his grasp, but his fingers tightened just enough to hold her in place. When she stopped trying to get away, they eased their grip.

"That's better," he murmured. At least she had the intelligence to know that if she continued to fight him, he'd outlast her. Carrying on with his inspection, Chase slid both hands down the smooth expanse of her calves. He fought the sensual feeling and kept his body from reacting. This was business, not pleasure.

Dana's breathing came in gulps. The rough slide

of his fingers moving down her calves sent delicious waves of heat up her body. Dana struggled to remain focused on her anger, not the moistness suddenly collecting between her thighs. How could his exploring touch evoke such an intimate response? Closing her eyes, she prayed this appraisal would end very soon.

"Lift your right foot." Chase was pleased when she obeyed quickly. After examining her long, slender foot, he released it and unwound from his crouched position. He walked around to her back. "At least you have good legs."

"I suppose that's a compliment?" Dana retorted, hating that he was looking at her from the rear. Without warning, she felt his fingers slide around her left ankle.

"Lift this foot."

Gritting her teeth, Dana did so. What the hell had he found now?

Chase studied her left foot and saw a pink scar running the length of her sole, from the heel to her big toe. Frowning, he gently ran his fingers along it. "How old is this?"

Pain flooded her and she jerked her foot away from him. Chase seemed caught off guard as she whirled around and faced him. Sudden tears jammed into her throat, and for a moment, Dana couldn't speak.

Chase slowly eased to his feet, his gaze digging

demandingly into hers. Dana opened her mouth to reply, but nothing came out. Her embarrassment over her nakedness receded as a widening pool of anguish filled her.

"The scar," Chase demanded, watching tears form in Dana's eyes.

"I—" She gulped. Forcing back the tears, she said, "Hal and my mother had just been murdered. It was two days after their funeral. I was at my mother's home on the res when it happened. I was exhausted. I hadn't slept in four days. I laid down on my mother's bed and I dropped off, finally. Something in the middle of the night made a noise. I was disoriented, confused. I remember getting up, and I bumped the bedstand. A water glass fell and shattered. I cut my foot open."

Chase stood there, protecting himself against her anguish. "It's done and in the past." His voice hardened. "So this scar is two years old?"

"Y-yes." No tears. Dana swallowed them even as grief from the murders threatened to overtake her.

"Any problems with it?"

"None that I know of. I did go to the hospital on the res and the doctor sewed it up for me. He said I'd been lucky." Taking a ragged breath, Dana whispered, "I didn't feel lucky."

Chase grunted in understanding. "Any other injuries that I haven't found?"

Shaking her head, Dana said in a low tone, "No."

He went to shrug on his jeans. "Get dressed. We've got work to do."

CHAPTER NINE

GLAD THAT THEY WERE both clothed again, Dana watched warily as Chase went to the south wall of the hogan. His hands were beautiful, she realized, even if badly scarred and deeply callused. Those hands had touched her. Trying to ignore her reaction to the evocative experience, she watched as he hefted a black canvas bag and brought it back to where she was standing.

"First things first—good footwear," he informed her gruffly. "Grab that wooden chair and sit down."

As Dana did so, Chase pulled out a pair of socks, and then some leather boots.

"Try these on. Grandmother Agnes gave me your shoe size. These are handmade by a friend of mine on the res, out of buffalo leather. They're supple and they flex easily. That's what you want, because you're going to be scaling a three-thousand-foot basalt cliff to reach Rogan's compound."

Dana first took the thick socks from Chase. Their fingers met briefly, and she jerked back. He scowled at her reaction. *Too bad.* Dana wanted no further connection with him, because it made her feel confused, uncomfortable and yet strangely aroused. As she pulled the socks on, she tried to ignore Chase's overwhelming presence. Hands on his narrow hips, he stood there, waiting. Feeling his impatience, she tightened her mouth as she tried on the boots.

"They fit perfectly," she said, a little awed. They felt like warm butter poured over her feet. Running her fingers across the ankle-high boots, she felt the softness of the leather, the sturdiness of the nylon soles. She almost recoiled in surprise when Chase crouched in front of her and felt each foot, checking how snugly the boots fit.

Though she wanted to jerk her leg away, Dana resisted. She could see the set of his jaw, the intensity of his golden eyes as he ran his hands knowingly along the leather. Trying not to react, she sucked in a breath and held it momentarily. Why did he have to be so damn tactile? She wanted no part of this kind of intimacy with him. For two years, she'd been without a man, and now Chase had crashed into her life, like an eighteen-wheeler Mack truck. It wasn't a pleasant feeling.

"No pinching?" Chase demanded.

"No...none."

"Well, we'll find out tomorrow morning," he

growled, checking her left boot just as closely. "Charley Crow Wing is a pretty damn good shoemaker. He usually nails it the first time around, but in your case, we can't take his word for it. You'll be climbing tomorrow, so we'll find out pretty quickly if they are a perfect fit or not." Rising, Chase said, "Get up."

Though she obeyed, Dana didn't like his terse orders. Biting back a response, she watched Chase pick up another black canvas bag, heft it to his shoulder and head for the door.

"Let's go. We've got work to do."

Grabbing the straw hat that her grandmother had given her, Dana settled it on her head. She shoved on a pair of sunglasses, picked up her knapsack and slung it over her shoulder. Then she hurried to catch up with Chase, whose stride was twice as long as hers. They were heading up into the box canyon again. The sun was hot, the breeze still, as if the world were holding its breath.

As she jogged after Chase, Dana felt slightly winded. She reminded herself that she'd lived near sea level for two years, and her body needed time to adjust to the higher altitude.

She glanced up at Chase as he climbed the slope ahead of her. No question, he was a mountain of a man. Yet as he wound around the rabbitbrush and prickly pear cactus dotting the landscape, he made no noise.

When she drew even with him, Chase gave her a sidelong glance. "What do you know of Rogan?"

"Only what my grandmother told me."

"He lives in a compound surrounded by a stockade of pine poles. The fortress sits on a shelf of igneous rock atop that cliff I mentioned. He was smart to put his castle up there," Chase said, leaping up onto a ledge of smooth, red sandstone, the first of many that rose like a staircase up the wall of the canyon.

"Okay."

"Your job will be to scale that three-thousand-foot basalt cliff. Then you have to enter the compound undetected. Your next task is to locate the Storm Pipe, grab it and get the hell out of there. All without being noticed."

"Okay…"

Chase cut her a glare. He seriously questioned whether or not Dana could do any of that. In his heart, he knew she couldn't, yet he'd given Grandmother Agnes his word to train her for just such a mission. Something deep and warm moved within his heart. Dammit, the last thing he needed was to care about her. Trying to see her only as a student, with no emotional connection, Chase snapped, "Okay? That's all you have to say? Do you realize what the hell is being demanded of you? How dangerous this really is?"

He jabbed his hand at the red sandstone wall

that rose above them. "If you don't kill yourself in the climb, then the possibility of being detected scaling that cliff is very real. Rogan has a team of twelve women, all of whom are metaphysically trained. You don't think any one of them couldn't detect your energy signature there? They're cosmic guard dogs, Dana. And they operate real well in the invisible realms, or Rogan wouldn't have brought them into his fold to work with the Storm Pipe."

Stung, Dana snapped back, "I don't know that much about Rogan. And if his women are metaphysically trained, well, so am I. I know how to cloak myself so my energy can't be detected."

Snorting, Chase growled, "Yeah, right. Just like you saw me waiting up here behind a juniper tree, ready to jump you."

Anger surged through Dana. She was huffing now as Chase effortlessly scaled the sandstone slope. He wasn't out of breath at all, while she was practically gasping as she clambered to keep up with his long strides. Finally, they reached the back wall of the canyon. Looking up, Dana eyed the red-and-white layers of rock that reminded her of a cake.

Chase dropped the canvas bag, opened it and pulled out nylon climbing ropes attached with aluminum connectors that he called carabiners. Rapidly, he went through the numerous pieces of gear, checking them over as he told her about them.

There were titanium pitons to hammer into the rock, angles, mallard wedge hooks, ibis hooks, cliff hangar and grappling hooks. He showed her a wall hammer, a drill holder and a rockpec, rapidly explaining what each was and its use in a climb. The array of equipment was dizzying to Dana.

"I'm going to put the climbing harness on you," Chase told her at the end of his lecture. "And then I'll get my gear on. Once we're ready, we're going to start climbing this wall—hammering pitons into it, for starters."

"What?" Dana stared at the black nylon harness he held in his hands. "I don't know anything about climbing. Can't you teach me some of the basics before we do this?"

"No. The Indian way is hands-on, in case you forgot that, too," he growled, motioning for her to step into the nylon trusses.

Dana reluctantly got into the harness. Chase brought it up to her waist and with swift efficiency locked her into her climbing gear.

"Tonight, when we get back to the hogan, you're going to take this off and put it on until you can do it without looking. You're going to have to climb that cliff in the dark. There won't be a flashlight available or anything else that could give away your position. So you have to know your harness and how it works as intimately as you know your own body. Got that?" He drilled her with a sharp look.

"Yes, I got it." No wonder they called him Iron Hand. They should have called him Steel! But Dana knew that the Iron Hand family was a very old and prestigious one within the Lakota nation. And steel had not been known about in earlier times. Iron was the metal of that age. If they were all like Chase, Dana thought, his family must be a warrior clan.

For the next hour, Dana absorbed the basics of climbing. By then, the sun was low on the horizon, the canyon swathed in shadows. Her arms hurt. Her joints ached. Chase had demanded that she learn how to pound a steel piton into the sandstone, and much harder limestone, with the hammer. She'd then had to fumble with the nylon ropes, put a carabiner on the piton and run the lines through it to hold her. By the time they were finished, she was halfway up the wall. Chase came down in a rappelling maneuver, and told her to do the same. Finding that if she mimicked his movements, she would be safe, Dana used her legs like springs and pushed away from the face of the cliff. Coming down was a lot more fun, and faster, than going up, that was for sure.

She landed with a thud and her knees buckled. If Chase hadn't grabbed her, Dana would have fallen off the narrow shelf. Gasping, she felt fear shoot through her. His hand was like steel as his fingers dug into her shoulder and he hauled her up like some lightweight doll. In seconds, Dana found herself pressed against his hard, unyielding body.

"Let me go!" she said, flattening her hands against his chest. His flesh was as hard as the look in his flashing golden eyes.

"And let you fall?" Chase grinned tightly and held on to her shoulder. There was something surprising and delicious about this unexpected contact, he decided. He secretly relished the crush of her breasts against his chest, the pressure of her hip against his. There was no doubt that he was drawn to her sexually. And that was one place he simply couldn't go.

"Grab on to that bush in front of you and I'll release you."

Quickly, Dana reached for a small rabbitbrush that grew from between a layer of red sandstone and one of white dolomite. Gasping for breath, her heart hammering, she stepped back, her grasp on the bush keeping her from tumbling off the shelf. Trembling badly, she gave Chase a glare and faced the cliff. Never had a man made her feel so feminine. Or so threatened.

Despite everything, she realized she'd like to tame this hardened warrior. Was he tamable? Dana thought not as she quickly readied herself to step down on a small outcropping. Chase was already off the shelf and down below on a wide sandstone skirt, waiting impatiently for her to descend.

Once she'd joined him, Dana wriggled out of her harness. Chase had already done so and put his equipment back in the canvas bag. She scrambled to catch up, feeling slow and bumbling in comparison. Heat radiated from his powerful body as he stood above her, hands settled imperiously on his narrow hips.

"You carry the bag down. You need all the workout with weights you can get."

Disbelief shot through Dana as she watched Chase leap down the slope and head toward the winter hogan far below them. The bastard! Zipping the bag closed, she fumbled to pick it up. The weight was surprising. What the hell else did Chase have in this bag? she wondered as she struggled to lift it onto her right shoulder. Every joint in her body ached. She'd injured her hands a number of times, trying to hammer in the pitons. With her knees feeling weak and unsteady, she started down cautiously, making damn sure she didn't fall. Within minutes, Chase had disappeared beyond the grove of piñon and juniper below. *Fine.* She wanted to be alone, away from that judgmental, bossy man.

Lips compressed, Dana ignored the beauty of the shadowed canyon. But the fragrance of pine wafting down from the rim was a sweet reminder that nature never smelled bad the way people did. As Dana struggled down the slope with her unwieldy load, she tried to convince herself that Chase smelled bad, too. But that wasn't true. No, whether she wanted to admit it or not, his scent was like a sensual perfume to her. And as she continued to descend, Dana wondered about his personal life. Her grandmother had said very little about him.

Well, Dana was going to find out tonight. They had to live in that hogan—together—and she wasn't going to be trapped with a total stranger.

OVER A MEAL OF LAMB STEW that Grandmother Agnes had sent up with them, Dana sat at an old pine table, Chase opposite her. He'd wolfed down two huge bowls of the stew, along with some fresh cornbread, saying nothing. So much for a polished dinner partner. After finishing her own stew, Dana set the bowl aside.

"I want to know who you are," she told Chase.

His chin lifted, his gold eyes resting on her. Instantly, Dana felt his power, his energy, move right through her defenses. Feeling uncomfortable, she added, "Grandmother didn't say much about you. If I have to spend five weeks with you, I want to know who I'm working with."

Pleased at her demand, Chase pushed his empty bowl aside. Taking another square of warm, home-made cornbread from the plate, he slathered it with melted butter. "I'll tell you what I want you to know," he agreed.

Dana wasn't going to be put off by the warning in his tone. She watched as Chase bit into the cornbread. Seeing how his eyes gleamed, she figured he must really like it. Usually, they were flat and hard.

Getting to know Chase a bit better would make her feel less intimidated, she figured.

"I'm ex-army. I was a captain," he told her. "I went to West Point when I was eighteen and graduated four years later. I put in my promised eight years afterward and here I am. Back on the res."

Raising her brows, Dana asked, "That's all you're going to tell me?"

"It's all you need to know."

"That's crap. You're from a medicine family, the Iron Hands. Are you trained in ceremony?"

"What do you think?" Chase popped the last of the cornbread into his mouth, savoring the flavors. Dana looked angry. *Good.*

"I think you are."

"You're right. My father taught me everything I needed to know before he died."

"You're a pipe carrier?"

"Of course. Personal, only."

That made Dana feel slightly better. Pipe carriers, personal or ceremonial, were supposed to be role models, having good morals, values and work ethics. Dana saw the parallel to the knights of King Arthur's time. They were supposed to be honest, and never lie, steal, cheat or do anything to harm others. They were there to protect anyone vulnerable. It was the same maxim for a pipe carrier, who was expected to utilize the pipe for the good of all their relations. A ceremonial pipe carrier had an even weightier responsibility: that of caring for the nation he or she belonged to.

"Enough about me," Chase said. "Here's your training schedule for the next five weeks. I'm waking you at 0400 tomorrow morning. You'll get on those boots and you'll run for five miles. I'll time you. When you return to the hogan, I'll make you a big breakfast, and you're going to eat all of it because food is fuel for strength. After breakfast, you're going to start lifting stones that I'll have waiting for you. Your shoulders and arms are weak. You need to build them up. The rocks will be of various weights, designed to do that. After an hour's workout, you'll go to the cliff wall and climb. You'll make it up to the top and rappel back down. I'll time you on that, too. At lunch, we'll come back here and you'll eat heavy. You'll rest for an hour after that, sleep if you can. Then you'll do a second five-mile run in the heat. When you return, you'll chop wood for the stove and then you'll make us dinner. By that time, you'll be exhausted."

"I'll be dead. I can't run five miles, much less ten."

Shrugging, Chase pushed away from the wooden table. He went over to the potbellied stove and picked up the coffeepot. Getting two mugs, he set them on the table and poured the boiling-hot coffee. "You will or die trying. I have five weeks to get you in shape for this gig."

The coffee smelled wonderful, but Dana's gut churned as she watched Chase put the pot back on the stove, away from the main heat. It was hot in the hogan, even with the door open, and dusk was falling. "I'll do my best," she muttered, defiantly.

Chase reached for some matches and lit the few kerosene lamps sitting on shelves nearby. The glow chased away the gathering darkness. The smell of kerosene was faint but present, so he opened a window to get rid of the odor. Electricity and phones didn't exist out here, nor any other modern amenities. Turning, Chase dropped the spent wooden matches into the stove, then grabbed the honey from the counter and brought it to the table.

As he sat, he noticed the open defiance on Dana's face. Spooning some honey into his steaming coffee, he smiled thinly. "You will stick to this schedule. It's real simple. And after the day's routine, we'll spend time each evening working with your psychic development, to strengthen your protective walls so Rogan and his team don't feel you coming." Chase slowly stirred his coffee. "You don't have a choice. You have to do everything I demand of you or you won't be ready to steal the Storm Pipe back before Rogan uses it to kill someone else.

"Right now, I'm sure everyone in the government is turning over every scrap of evidence to try and figure out what killed the vice president. Sooner or later, we can expect they'll figure out it wasn't laser-weapons created by Russia or some terrorist organization. I'm hoping we'll have five weeks of peace and quiet to get this mission completed. That way, we won't have the FBI snooping around on Indian land, or sticking their nose into our pipe ceremonies and other medicine."

Nodding, Dana sipped her coffee. "I don't want them nosing around, either. White men don't understand our world, our beliefs or our practices."

"Well, then," Chase rumbled, "at least we agree on one thing—we want white men to butt out of this mission. Let's hope like hell that the feds don't get wind of what really killed the vice president. If they do, it will only complicate what we're trying to pull off."

CHAPTER TEN

"YOU'VE GOT TO BE JOKING," David Colby said. He sat behind his desk at FBI headquarters and stared at the woman who'd just stunned him.

In her early forties, Annie Ballard was dressed in a conservative beige linen suit. She seemed the consummate professional.

"I told my superiors, Agent Colby, that you would have this kind of reaction to me." Annie smiled slightly. "Let me repeat—I'm a CIA agent assigned to the nonexistent Remote Viewing Department. If you take a look at my orders, you'll see that I'm a psychic and I've been working on behalf of our country for fifteen years." She handed him the paperwork.

Controlling his reaction, Colby took the papers and quickly read them. A psychic, of all things! It had been three weeks since the vice president had been murdered, and no clear enemy had been found. The Russians denied any responsibility, and even though they'd had optical and laser tech-

nology stolen, no Islamic terrorist group had come
forward to claim the heinous act.

As he sat up in his chair and set the papers on
his desk, Colby had no explanation for the murder,
not the slightest clue. Which wasn't making anyone in government happy. The military was jumpy.
The law enforcement sector was on high alert. The
president remained in hiding and had not come
back to the White House. Now, because there were
no leads, they were sending him a psychic?

He tightened his jaw in disbelief. "Have a seat,
Agent Ballard."

"Call me Annie. I'll call you David unless you
tell me otherwise." She turned and shut the door
to his small, neatly kept office. The opened vene-
tian blind behind him allowed in light and showed
a July-blue sky, a strip of grass and some white
granite buildings nearby.

"Okay," Colby muttered unhappily, watching
as she sat on the small leather couch to the left
of his desk.

Opening a black briefcase, Annie pulled out a
number of sketches. She set them on his desk.
"These are impressions of the man who killed the
vice president." With a long, thin finger, she tapped
the corner of one. "My job over at the lab is more
wide ranging than just remote viewing activity.
I'm sure you're aware of our department?"

"Vaguely," Colby said, looking down at the top

sketch. "You're quite an artist. Or did you have one of our FBI artists render this for you?"

She shook her head, her dishwater-blond hair sliding across her shoulders. "No, I did it. My mother is an artist. I think I got some of her genes."

"I don't believe in psychics and all that mumbo jumbo." Colby sat back and stared into her large blue eyes. She was about five foot six inches tall, rail thin, with triangular features. She was pretty in her own way, and Colby saw a wedding ring on her left hand. She didn't look like a psychic, more like an average working woman with all her ducks in a row.

"This isn't about you or me, David. The FBI has failed to come up with leads on the killer. My boss asked me to get involved. This is the face I kept seeing when I went into meditation. Does he look at all familiar to you?"

Shaking his head, Colby said, "No. But I'll run the sketch and we'll see if we get a hit."

"Whoever this is, he's very dangerous. He's a natural born killer," she said grimly. Showing him another sketch, she added, "I did remote viewing, and this is what came up. This guy is in or around the Carson City, Nevada, area. You need to run this against local criminals out there."

"Okay…" he muttered, looking at the sketch. How the hell could she get this kind of info? Colby didn't ask, because he didn't believe. It was all hocus-pocus to him. What they needed to break open this case was cold, hard, detailed work. Uncover the details and the puzzle would explain itself.

Annie pulled a third paper from the group and laid it on top. She leaned over Colby. "This last sketch is the impression of the weapon that was used to kill the vice president."

Frowning, Colby studied the L-shaped object— a long, vertical shaft with a much shorter piece jutting off at a perpendicular angle at the bottom. "Doesn't look like a laser to me."

"You're not a laser specialist."

Stinging beneath her softly spoken reply, Colby said, "That's true. So what is this? Do the science guys know?"

Annie stood and pushed her thin hair away from her face. "They don't have a clue, either. It's like nothing they've seen before. That's all I got when I asked during meditation to see the weapon that killed the vice president."

"I'll send a copy of this over to the laser specialist friend of mine here in the building. Maybe he'll recognize it."

"I've already asked around the CIA, and my people say it' s not a weapon they're familiar with."

Scratching his head, Colby took the papers. "Well, at least you came up with something, even if I don't believe in your work."

Grinning, Annie sat back on the couch. She retrieved a clipboard and pen from her briefcase.

"That's okay, David. You don't have to believe in what I do in order for me to get leads. I'm not interested in defending my abilities. I'm interested in finding the killer and stopping him from doing this again."

She was right. Colby called his secretarial assistant, Joan Stoneman, who quickly came and took the papers. They would be distributed to the proper people for analysis within the FBI. Colby privately figured no one else would come up with any hits or help, either.

"Now," Annie said brightly, "what lead have *you* developed?"

Leaning back in his chair, Colby said, "Not a thing. I'm sure you know that."

"I know some of the information through my bosses," Annie admitted. "But there are other things I wonder if you've analyzed or looked at."

"Such as?"

"Well, unusual things, you know? Things that are out of place for this time of year."

Rubbing his furrowed brow, Colby said, "We've done a lot of looking in the D.C. area and found nothing out of the ordinary."

"Can you swing your considerable assets to Carson City, Nevada? Take a look at any anomalies around there?"

"Of course." Colby decided that Annie Ballard, despite being a psychic, was pretty grounded and sharp. He'd expected a space cadet personality, but she was all-business. Brisk and efficient, even. Impressed, he picked up his mug and sipped the nearly cold coffee it contained, then said, "I'm going to bite. Do *you* recognize this man? Did you receive any other impressions about him?"

Annie shook her head. "No. As you may or may not know, being psychic isn't foolproof. I have good and bad days, which is par for the course for any emotional human being. I have good and bad reception, for whatever reasons. I can't control what I get, the depth or breadth of information. No one is a perfect clairvoyant." Annie shrugged and smiled. "We get puzzle pieces, as I like to call them. Hints. And hopefully, direction."

"I see…." Colby wondered about the L-shaped weapon.

"My general level of accuracy is ninety-five percent, by the way. What I get is solid intel."

"And we're all left to figure out what you're getting, and to interpret it accurately, right?"

"You got it. That's the fly in this particular ointment." She grinned.

Leaning back and lacing his hands behind his head, David murmured, "Okay, our bad guy is in the U.S., so we figure he's a U.S. citizen?"

"Why? He could be a terrorist operating in a cell out in Carson City."

"You sketched him as being darker skinned. A black? Middle Eastern? Hispanic?"

"I saw his skin as brownish, or deeply tanned. He had black hair, dark brown eyes. I don't think he's African-American. One of the other two, perhaps."

"Is he a terrorist?"

"I felt a fanatical energy around him."

"And he's operating out of the Carson City region." Colby leaned forward to make a couple of phone calls. He would find out what terrorist suspects might be located in that part of the country.

"We'll find out pretty quickly what Homeland Security has," Colby said, "about any cell activity."

"Good."

"So what's your next plan of action? More meditation?" Colby figured he might as well go along with this charade. It wasn't his nature to hurt anyone, and Annie Ballard seemed so genuine and caring that he really didn't want her to know he considered her work a blind alley.

"Well," she said hesitantly, "I get intel at odd times, David. I might be having coffee at Starbucks and I'll get a flash of something. Or it'll come through a dream. I have dreams that tell me a lot more than what I receive up here." She tapped her temple. "I can't control where, when or why the information comes to me. Sometimes it's just a hunch or intuition. I follow up on it and then something synchronistic happens to verify it." She opened her hands. "It's a mishmash of information, like puzzle pieces most of the time. I have to try and put the images together into some coherent, understandable format."

No kidding. But Colby kept that acidic thought to himself. The whole thing sounded harebrained. A wild-goose chase, for sure. "So, we just wait for the cosmos to contact you?"

"No, I'm authorized to take you to Carson City." Annie looked at the simple leather watch on her small wrist. "In fact, we're taking a flight out from Reagan National Airport in five hours." Looking up, obviously noting the surprise he felt. "Enough time for you to tidy up your business around here, go home and tell your wife you're leaving, and then pack a suitcase."

"I'm divorced," Colby said. "I live with a cat."

"Ah, that's why I saw a gray, long-haired cat around you."

Stunned, Colby felt his eyes bulge momentarily. "Why...Murphy is a long-haired gray Persian. How did you know?"

Chuckling, Annie wrote some notes on her clipboard. "I saw it. But I didn't know the cat's name. I knew it was a he."

"Neutered."

"Thanks for the confirmation. With you being FBI, and your buttoned-down look, I wouldn't figure you for a cat man. Most men are dog people."

"I like cats because they're independent."

"Makes two of us. My husband, Phil, and I have four of the curmudgeons. Oh, and we have a golden retriever named Rocky, too."

Scratching his head, Colby stood up and gave her an uneasy smile. "I guess you're going to have to convince me that a psychic is what this case needs."

"I'm ready to do that. But we have to get out to Carson City, where I can get a whiff, I hope, of a stronger lead. The only way I can do it is to be there. And since you're the special agent on this case, I need you along, too, in case we stumble onto something. The CIA wants this case solved just as quickly as the FBI does, for obvious reasons."

"You're right about that," Colby grumbled. He walked around his dark maple desk and opened the door. "I'll talk to my assistant and get a lot of balls in the air. Leave the flight info on my desk. I'll meet you at the gate, okay?"

Annie pulled out two airline tickets. She stood and dropped one on his desk. "Done. See you shortly. By then, you should have some info back on any known terrorist cells in that area, and maybe a confirmation on that face sketch." She crossed her fingers. "I hope we get lucky."

Smiling thinly, Colby stood aside as Agent Ballard walked out the door, briefcase in hand. A psychic who hoped to get lucky...

Shaking his head, he decided that doing something, even this, was better than sitting at his desk empty-handed. If the CIA had proved that psychics were useful enough to have their own department, who was he to sniff at the idea? Right now, his team had no leads, and he was hungry enough to grab at mumbo jumbo.

CHAPTER ELEVEN

"IS THE PIPE STRONG enough yet?" Rogan demanded of Blue Wolf.

It was before noon in the high Sierras, and they sat opposite each other in the cedar lodge. As he awaited her answer, he rubbed his hands together.

A scowl settled on the woman's face. Blue Wolf was Crow, a powerful medicine woman in her own right, which was why he'd chosen her. But Rogan didn't like her arrogance, which was heightened by the fact that only she carried the ceremonial pipe among the twelve women he'd selected.

"You know I work with the pipe at this time every day," Blue Wolf growled. In a protective gesture, she placed her hand over the stone bowl. "I don't like the fact that you come in here unannounced. You jar me out of my altered state. You cause stress on the pipe and me."

Shrugging, Rogan said, "I don't have time to dally. I've got to drive down to Carson City and pick up supplies." Who did Blue Wolf think she was? He was the leader, not her. Although, judging from the deep lines around her chocolate-colored eyes, she was truly angry over his intrusion.

Blue Wolf shook her finger at him. "Next time, wait, Rogan. I couldn't care less if you drive down the mountain to get food. That's *your* responsibility." She kept one hand over the pipe head, which rested in her other palm. Rogan's gaze had never left it. Damn him! She didn't like his careless disrespect toward the powerful object.

Rogan scratched his head and gave her a lazy look. "So answer my question! When will the pipe be ready to use again?"

"It's only been four weeks. We've never done this before, so how do I know how long it will take to recharge?"

"You said you knew everything about pipes," Rogan reminded her.

"This one's different! I can feel your impatience, but you're not going to push me or it to work prematurely. If we do that, we could harm the pipe forever. Is that what you want?"

"Of course not." He glanced around the dimly lit room, built of cedar as the rest of the lodge. Rogan liked its simple, clean design. The single-story building, a series of rooms each about twelve feet wide, reminded him of a caterpillar with segments. As a Native American connected deeply with Mother Earth, he realized the design reflected nature at its finest.

Rogan felt a glow of pride in the cedar shake roof and the vertical panels of the lodge, which he had designed himself many years ago. Each room had been thoughtfully laid out before he'd constructed it. The altar room, where the Storm Pipe was kept, was behind the meditation and prayer room, where Blue Wolf sat. There was a foyer in front, where cedar doors were carved with depictions of the rising sun and the full moon. Rogan's office was located here, along with a general meeting room. Yes, everything he'd done in the last seven years had been leading up to this moment.

Savoring the fact that he'd managed to steal the Storm Pipe, with Blue Wolf's help, Rogan smiled to himself. Things were progressing well. Still, he was jumpy and tense. He knew the government would be trying to find out who and what had killed the vice president. Rogan was counting on the fact that the stupid white men on Capitol Hill would never think of a pipe having such power, and would overlook that possibility. Linear thinking would keep him and his band of women safe from scrutiny.

Rogan grinned at Blue Wolf. "Yes, I am impatient. But with good reason. I want to see the white men suffer. They killed six million of us, on purpose. It's payback time."

Blue Wolf nodded. Rogan had to be spiraling

into one of his tirades, so she slipped the head of the Storm Pipe back into its pouch. "Genocide, pure and simple," she agreed. "The army deliberately handed our people smallpox-infested blankets, knowing that would wipe out an entire village. There should be revenge. Six million of us were murdered by them, by the white eyes."

In Rogan's mind, Blue Wolf looked like a mother holding a beloved child. The pipe was cradled in the crook of her left arm, her right hand resting gently overtop the two-foot-long bag.

"Well," he said, pleasure vibrating in his tone, "it has begun. Every one of us wants to see this retribution. So what if various chiefs of our nations have reviled me for my plan? Twelve women are with me. Twelve of the most powerful women from twelve different nations. I think we are being guided by the Great Spirit to balance the scales of karmic justice, so to speak. I'm glad to be a part of this."

Nodding again, Blue Wolf said, "Every one of us supports you in your vision, Rogan. Each of the women you have chosen is either a medicine woman or in training to be one, powerful in her own unique way. And we have seen what the white man has done to our people. Being forced to eke out an impoverished existence on a reservation is not right. Even now, in the twenty-first century, the white man's government dismisses us and our concerns. They don't care if our children starve, or we lack proper health facilities. Or education. No, they're very happy to see us continue to quietly suffer, as we've done since they forced us onto reservations over a hundred years ago."

"Well, that is about to change," Rogan reminded her, an edge to his modulated tone. He splayed his hand on the handsome handwoven rug they sat on. The wool was prickly and felt good to him. The rug had been designed and made by a Navajo woman who'd spent hundreds of hours on her labor of love. Only another Native American could truly understand what the weaver had gone through, could appreciate the untold hours she'd spent sitting before her loom. White men usually overlooked the weaver's laborious efforts and would try to get a rug for as few dollars as they could, once more stealing from Native Americans. Nothing had changed as far as Rogan was concerned. Well, it was going to now. Once and for all.

"You need to be patient, Rogan," Blue Wolf chided. "I am still learning about this pipe, its personality, its abilities, and how long it takes to recover after doing such powerful work. We have time. Let's not rush things."

Rogan rested his hand on his knee. "I feel things are unsettled, Blue Wolf. Don't you?"

"Why, of course they are! The federal government is in turmoil. They can't figure out who did this to the vice president. They're scared. They have no culprit. Of course things are in chaos, and as medicine people, we are very aware of that energy flux and flow."

Chuckling darkly, Rogan said, "A disturbance in the Force, to borrow from *Star Wars.* Now, there is a movie that deals with what we've always known about. Only we call it the Great Spirit, and we've been taught how to recognize it, tap into it and utilize it."

Blue Wolf allowed a faint smile to touch her weathered face. "Little did Luke Skywalker and all the rest know what he was portraying…. But we know, and that's enough. The white man's government doesn't understand our connection with all the invisible energies. Yes, you're right, Rogan, the Force has bit Washington, D.C., in the ass. Serves them right. It's been too long in coming."

Rogan had a narrow face with close-set, dark-blue eyes that reminded her of a weasel's. But then, she told herself, it would take someone of consummate cleverness to bring this particular plan to fruition. Just like the weasel, Rogan was rarely seen in public. Oh, medicine people from all nations knew him, but on the inner circle. No one had ever heard his name outside of the res. And that was one of many things he'd counted on as he brought his team of women together to forge his vision.

Unwinding from his position, Rogan stood and

gave Blue Wolf a pleased look. "I'll be back later this afternoon. I've got the grocery list from Wanda Running Deer. Anything special you need from Carson City?"

"Thank you for asking, but no." Patting the pipe bag gently, Blue Wolf murmured, "I've got everything I'll ever need right here in my arms."

"Well, keep working with the pipe. I feel like we're being stalked, and I don't know by who yet. It's bothering me."

"Stop worrying. It's only your nerves, Rogan. There's no way the government is onto us." Blue Wolf snorted. "They don't want to know that we even exist, so why would we ever be seen as the threat?" Waving her hand, her voice wry, Blue Wolf added, "No one else is psychically picking up anything. We all feel safe here."

Shaking his head, Rogan turned on his heel. "I don't know, Blue Wolf. I feel like we're being tracked by someone who wants that pipe back."

"The Blue Heron Society?" She spat, and laughed with derision. "They are nothing but a bunch of elderly, arrogant old women from different nations. The youngest is in her sixties, the oldest midnineties. How much of a threat do *they* pose?" Gesturing around the lodge, Blue Wolf cackled. "And tell me, Rogan, which one of them is going to climb a three-thousand-foot cliff to reach our compound? We have twenty-four-hour-a-day sentries on the only road into the area. And don't you think that, because we're all psychic, one of us would pick up on any attempt to steal this pipe back, even if someone did try? Do me a favor, Rogan? Go into Carson City and get our supplies for the next month. Stop worrying."

"You're right," he grumbled, turning away and heading toward the front door. "I'll see you later."

Still, as he stepped out into the pine-scented air, Rogan couldn't shake his uneasy feeling. The sky a light-blue, and robins were singing, yet someone *was* stalking them. But who? There was no question he could sense and feel it.

As he walked down the gravel path, he saw a few of the women hanging out laundered clothes on a cotton line near the kitchen. The compound was comprised of five buildings all enclosed within the ten-foot-high stockade, and the kitchen and dining facilities were in one. He headed toward the dirt parking lot, where his dark-blue Chevy pickup truck sat. There were five other vehicles there, all belonging to women who lived here with him. A couple of them spotted him as they hung up clothes, and lifted their hands in greeting. He gave a friendly wave in return.

Pulling out his keys, Rogan moved down the path to the parking lot, right inside the big double gates to the fort. Rogan made sure there was at least one guard on duty there twenty-four hours a day. He trusted no one. After waving to the woman, Ruby Tall Tree, who was opening up for him, he unlocked the pickup and got in.

Rogan drove out of the compound, carefully scanning the land around him. The road quickly dropped in elevation, until silvery sagebrush and a few straggly pines were dotting the barren landscape. For all intents and purposes, Nevada was desert. Only in the mighty Sierras, above seven thousand feet, where his compound stood, did tall, stately pines begin to flourish like a green army.

From the bumpy dirt access road, Rogan could see the main highway three thousand feet below. *Land of gambling,* he thought as he drove. Gambling, indeed. He was taking the biggest gamble of his life.

A smile cut across his face as he kept the truck in low gear during the steep descent. Like a thick smoke screen, billowing clouds of dust rose up behind him. A jackrabbit darted out in front, and he narrowly missed it. Rogan's reflexes were still sharp. Though forty-five, he had never felt more powerful or more happy. Hands wrapped firmly around the wheel, he kept his focus on driving. This was not a road that forgave someone who came down it too fast.

As he pulled onto the busy asphalt highway, Rogan still felt a niggling sense of foreboding. He wished to hell he knew what he was picking up on.

And *who*. After the nations spurned his plan to get even with the U.S. government, Rogan had told no one of his intentions. Back then, none of the chiefs or head medicine men would go along with his vision of revenge. They were peaceful and wanted only to live in harmony with Mother Earth, they'd told him. After being rebuffed and humiliated at too many council meetings, Rogan had devised a much different plan over time.

In the modern world, Native American women were no longer considered equal partners, as they had before the whites set foot on Turtle Island. Women were now treated like second-class citizens. In many of the nations, it had been fairly easy for Rogan to find disgruntled medicine women who wanted to reclaim their power and rightful place in the hierarchy. Rogan had mesmerized them with his sorcery and cajoled them to come work with him. He'd promised to give them back their power, as well as the respect they deserved. And they had agreed to help bring his vision to fruition.

Chuckling indulgently, Rogan opened a bottle of water and drank. All the while, he kept his eyes on the road. In the distance, he could see Carson City rising up out of the flat desert, all steel, glass and concrete. The white man's world was like an infection on the skin of Mother Earth. In his opinion, genetically speaking, most humans were little more than virus DNA. They *were* a virus, a blight on Mother Earth, Rogan believed, not the Native Americans. His mind flitted back to the members of his team. Hadn't Jesus Christ had twelve apostles? Look at what he'd accomplished. He saw himself in the latter role. His women were his disciples, and he was the powerful visionary with the talent to bend them to his will. He got intense enjoyment from being the only one who did understand it. That was enough for him.

The sun shone brightly into the cab and he switched on the air-conditioning. The traffic was getting thicker as Carson City came closer. The endless carpet of yellow desert dotted with sage was broken up by green pastures with Herefords grazing in them, or fields of wheat and corn. The flat land was a colorful patchwork quilt, Rogan decided. His spirits lifted, and he realized he actually felt happy. It was a foreign emotion to him, but he absorbed the light, airy feeling with gratitude. Yes, life was good. Very good. He was fulfilling his vision, and in another three weeks, the Russian ambassador to the U.S. would be the next target of the Storm Pipe.

Rogan smiled. That would completely unnerve the U.S. government. Rogan knew that top officials thought Russians had killed the vice president with laser equipment. Now, targeting the ambassador was going to stir up a hornets' nest in Russia. It would put the two superpowers into a deadly confrontational dance. Yes, life was good, and Rogan was happy. Happier than he'd ever been. No one could stop him, much less find out what he was doing. Being invisible had decided advantages.

CHAPTER TWELVE

A RAVEN CAWED NOISILY, dragging Dana out of a deep, badly needed sleep. The delicious scent of coffee teased her nostrils, pulling her awake. And then she felt strong fingers molding and massaging the aching muscles in her shoulders. A small moan of pleasure escaped her parted lips. Dana realized she was lying on her belly, face pressed against the scratchy wool of the Navajo rug she slept upon.

Caught between the arms of sleep and the gentle, delicious pressure of the strong fingers working on her shoulders, Dana absorbed the welcoming warmth and nurturing. She was so sore and tired…!

The harsh, loud croak of the raven brought her back to the here and now. She realized with a start that the only person who could be doing this was Chase Iron Hand. The fact galvanized Dana into action.

Pulling away from his wonderful, healing

touch, she scrambled into a sitting position. Her hair, long and straight, fell across her face, and she pushed it back. The last thing Dana had expected was to be touched like that by Chase. He was such a hard, brutal drill instructor, straight out of the Marine Corps tradition.

Dana brushed at her hair again and sleepily looked up. Chase was squatting a few feet from her, hands resting between his opened legs. A thoughtful expression came over his normally unreadable features.

"Time to get up."

Dana never woke up quickly in the morning. Ever. Right now, her shoulders were tingling pleasantly from his massage. Dana yearned for more contact like that with Chase, she realized, as she scrubbed her eyes, trying to force the grogginess away. His voice, always low, and reminding her of thunder in the distance, enveloped Dana like a warm blanket. After four weeks of nearly unendurable training, Chase seemed, well, nicer this morning.

Stunned by the change in his demeanor and touch, Dana hurriedly got to her feet. The hogan was pleasantly toasty. Outside the window she saw a gray hint of dawn. It was time to get going. Still, the thought wouldn't go away. Why had Chase touched her like that?

No time to think too much about it. Gathering her bathrobe from a nail on the wall, Dana wrapped herself in it. Even though she wore a long blue cotton shift, she still didn't like being the object of Chase's inspection. Hurrying outdoors, she headed to the privy. Over the last month, she'd toughened up her feet by walking barefoot except when jogging or climbing. Chase had demanded that her daily ten-mile run be done a week after she'd started that grueling routine.

The scent of fragrant sage covered in dew filled her senses. The raven sitting in a nearby piñon tree croaked and flapped its wings as Dana hurried by. A chipmunk scurried to the large pile of wood that she chopped daily to increase her shoulder and arm strength. The canyon was alive with creatures awakening, Dana realized.

Another day of brutal work lay ahead. Still, she was proud of herself. So far, she'd been able to do everything Chase had demanded of her.

As she stepped inside the old pine outhouse, which was weathered and gray, Dana thought of her grandmother. Agnes, too, was pleased with her progress. Dana had seen the hope burning in her watery eyes the last time she'd visited. Hope that Dana might really bring the Storm Pipe back to its rightful place within their sacred society.

After washing up at the well, Dana jogged back to the hogan and opened the door. Chase was at the potbellied stove cooking up a large skillet of scrambled eggs mixed with shredded venison. The smells made her stomach growl with anticipation.

There was little privacy here, but Dana had insisted upon some. Chase had built a paneled screen that she could slip behind to change clothes. Sitting down on the three-legged oak stool, she quickly put on a pair of socks to warm her feet.

"What's up for today?" she asked Chase from behind the screen.

"You're doing your ten miles this morning, an hour after breakfast. Between now and then, we're going to continue work to psychically strengthen your skills."

Dana always looked forward to their psychic training sessions. Quickly shedding her robe and nightgown, she slipped into a dark-red spandex T-shirt and a pair of comfortable gray sweatpants. The food smelled wonderful. Dana couldn't ever recall being as famished as she had been this last month. She hadn't wanted to eat much since the death of her mother and husband, and she'd lost thirty pounds. Now, her weight was returning to normal, despite the brutal physical training, which lasted twelve hours a day.

The coffee was perking away on the edge of the stove. As she often did, Dana stole a quick look in Chase's direction. He had a pot holder around the skillet handle, his concentration fixed on stirring the eggs, venison and onions. A month had worn down her objections to him. He was a firm teacher, Dana had come to realize. Not cruel or brutal as she'd first thought. And he remained very detached toward her as a woman. Most of the time, unless she hurt herself with more than a minor scrape or bruise, he never touched her. But when he did, Dana's heart opened up like a blossom to the warming rays of the sun.

Taking a deep breath, she hurried to the old dresser at the other end of the hogan. Its mirror was tipped back against the mud-caulked wooden wall. The glass had a lot of dark spots where the mirror backing had disintegrated over time. But she could see to brush her hair and twine the strands into braids.

From that vantage point, Dana could secretly absorb the intensity of Chase's features. He was handsome in a raw, uncut way. No pretty boy, that was for sure. With deep crow's-feet at the corners of his eyes, and slashes down either side of his sensual mouth, his face had been branded by harsh living conditions. When she asked Chase about his time in the army, he usually grunted a single-word answer. Something had happened to him, and it showed on his features.

Dana realized his eyes had the power to lift her spirits or crush her. When he was pleased with her efforts, they shone more gold than brown. If he was displeased, his eyes would darken and remind her of a coming thunderstorm. Chase never smiled, at least not completely. Dana ached to see his harsh mouth draw upward—just once. It would change his entire face, she suspected. But his serious expression remained constant.

Dana felt sad for Chase. He didn't joke or laugh. Had his life been so awful, so depressing?

After tying off her braids with red rubber bands, Dana went to the washbasin and quickly brushed her teeth. As she rubbed her damp hands down her thighs afterward, she turned, just in time to see Chase studying her.

Dana froze momentarily. Blinking, she couldn't believe what she saw in his probing eyes. Was that yearning? She nervously licked her lower lip and went toward the drain board to rescue the recently washed mugs for coffee. Her heart wouldn't steady its beat. When she glanced back at Chase, he was once again focusing darkly on the contents in the skillet. Dana wondered if she'd imagined it. She thought she'd seen the look a man gave a woman he wanted in every way, including sexually.

A shiver of anticipation wove through Dana's body and settled deep in her abdomen. Heat gathered and pulsed between her legs. Hands shaking, she grabbed two mugs. Was Chase reading her mind? Had he entered her sensual dreams, where she often felt him kiss her like sunshine kissed the warm earth? No, she had to be making this up.

Dana hurried to the small wooden table that sat

in the southern part of the hogan. After placing the mugs on the scarred surface, she retrieved flatware and paper napkins. The salt and pepper shakers were already on the table.

Chase set down two plates heaping with food. He saw Dana grab the loaf of whole-grain bread, along with a jar of strawberry jam. Without preamble, he sat down and silently said a prayer of thanks for the meal before them to the spirits who had provided it.

Happiness threaded through Chase. As he shook salt and pepper onto the fragrant breakfast, he felt Dana's knee brush his. Whether he liked it or not, he looked forward to this half hour every day with her. In one month's time, Dana had become an addiction for him. It was nice to wake up and see her, note the sparkle of life in her eyes and the huskiness of her just-waking voice. He couldn't ignore her natural beauty. Her smooth, high cheekbones usually were flushed with a hint of pink beneath the gold tones. Chase found himself mesmerized by her long, graceful hands, the way she held a fork, stirred cream and sugar into her coffee. Everything about Dana appealed to him, he realized.

As he ate in silence, wildly aware of their knees inches apart beneath the small table, Chase noted his mistake. He'd touched Dana this morning. He'd been fighting a daily urge to caress her glorious body. He wanted to ease the stiffness and tension in her muscles from the harsh training. She'd tried hard to please him, to meet his high demands, and she had a commendable work ethic.

He couldn't deny why his heart was hammering away: he was drawn to her as a woman. Why now? Why *her?* Chase understood the danger of the mission against Rogan. He wasn't sure that Dana could single-handedly carry it off. She was trying with all her heart to learn, and learn quickly, but she wasn't ready. At least, not yet. Was he sending her to her death?

His chest contracted violently at that last thought. The eggs turned tasteless in his mouth. Drawing in a ragged breath, Chase forced himself to eat. *Dammit, anyway.* Why couldn't Dana have been unattractive?

Groaning inwardly, he stabbed savagely at the food on his plate. Things weren't going right. He'd start the psychic training, send Dana on her ten-mile run and then report her progress to Grandmother Agnes.

"GRANDMOTHER," Chase began wearily as he sat opposite her in her hogan, "I'm worried."

Agnes nodded and passed him a mug of hot sage tea. Her hand shook badly and he quickly clasped his around it, then took the mug.

"Thank you. Age makes one shaky." She smiled, then tilted her head as if to listen.

Chase cautiously sipped the tea. "I think you know what I'm going to say," he stated.

"I do, but let me hear what lies in your heart, Chase."

He forced himself to hold her watery eyes. "I have concerns about Dana, about her ability to succeed in getting the Storm Pipe back to you. She is trying very hard to do everything I've taught her. It isn't that she doesn't have heart— she does. But frankly, four or five weeks just isn't long enough to get her trained to the level needed in order to take on Rogan and his band, Grandmother."

Nodding, Agnes sipped her own tea, both hands wrapped around the warm pottery mug. After setting it down in front of her, she wiped the corners of her mouth with her ever present cotton handkerchief. "The Storm Pipe gathers power again, Chase. We will be lucky if it isn't ready to be used again *before* five weeks are up."

"That's not good news," Chase growled. Rubbing his hands together, he stared down at the calluses, his brows knitting.

"No, it's not. If Rogan gets a second chance to kill someone, well, it may turn the world into chaos. And that's what Rogan wants—white men at white men's throats, to destroy their world. Only he's too blind to realize that as the white man's world goes, so go the rest of us."

"We're all related, whether we like it or not," Chase grimly agreed, his voice deep with worry.

"And," Agnes said gently, "I feel that you have made a personal connection with Dana. One that goes beyond being just a teacher to her."

A pang of guilt edged with terror lanced through Chase. He didn't think anything in his life could compare to the fear from his six months of torture in South America. But it had—unexpectedly. Rubbing his brow, he evaded Grandmother Agnes's stare.

"I know this is upsetting to you, Chase. I can sense it."

Lifting his head, he forced himself to hold the old woman's warm, understanding gaze. "I just never expected to like Dana on a personal level, Grandmother. I—well…it just sort of sneaked up on me. Not that she did anything to invite it. She hasn't flirted with me or done anything to make me think she feels similarly."

"But…?"

Glancing around the hogan, he noticed the morning light filtering through the windows and giving the inside a look of muted radiance. Nevertheless, Chase grimaced and finally muttered, "I worry for her. I just don't think Dana's anywhere near ready to take on Rogan. Oh, I'm sure she could climb that cliff without a problem. She's excelled at mountain climbing. And she's doing fine on her daily runs. But when I engage her in hand-to-hand combat, she falls short."

"Why do you think that is?"

Flatly, Chase said, "Because it isn't in her heart to kill. That's why. She's afraid to hurt me. She's a softy, Grandmother, through and through. She pulls her punches and kicks when I train her. She cries when she finds a butterfly with a broken, shredded wing. She can't stand to see anything hurt or wounded." Frustration rang through his tone. "Dana simply is not motivated to get tough and learn to fight back as hard as she can."

Sighing, Agnes blotted her mouth and gripped the handkerchief. "I was afraid of this. Dana *is* softhearted. But so was her mother. You know yourself that high-level pipe carriers usually are very heart centered. They know not to hurt anything. It's just a part of their heritage, their knowing and their spiritual advancement."

"I understand that," Chase replied heavily. "Ceremonial pipe carriers are spiritually more whole and balanced than the rest of us miserable two-leggeds. They've advanced beyond where most of us are still struggling."

"Well, then, we must give Dana reason to get more grit, to be prepared to fight and defend herself even if it harms someone else. Perhaps this is a lesson she needs to learn—that even though one hates violence and harming others, sometimes it must be undertaken for a higher cause."

CHAPTER THIRTEEN

"SIT DOWN," Chase told Dana. "We have some things to discuss." He handed her an old pink towel to wipe her perspiring features after her morning run.

She nodded and sat down on a huge round chunk of wood that was used as a chopping block. Blotting her face, she felt the soft breeze cooling her heated body. "I had a good run. Look." She showed him the time on the round dials of her stopwatch. "Seven-minute miles aren't bad for someone like me."

He nodded. "That's real good," Chase agreed. Her hair was plaited, with tendrils around her face loosened from the run. Chase tried to ignore the fact she wore a sleeveless, red spandex T-shirt that outlined her breasts and torso. The gray sweatpants that encased her long legs only emphasized the fact that Dana was shapely and desirable. Tucking away that heated reaction, Chase waited patiently while she took a good, healthy swig from her water bottle and wiped her face once more.

Dana wrapped the pink towel around her neck and shoulders, hitched one foot up on a piece of split wood, and rested her arm on her thigh.

"What do you want to talk about?" Her breathing was slowing down to a more normal cadence. Dana had noticed that running daily for a month had deepened her lung capacity. She felt good, and in the best shape she'd ever been. Seeing the darkness in Chase's eyes, she worried that somehow she was not meeting his demands. *What now?* As she tried to steel herself against his criticism, she nervously waited for him to speak.

"You've done well in four weeks, Dana. Considering you were a grade school teacher whose only exercise was walking to work and horseback riding, you've come a long way," Chase began. He saw surprise and then pleasure dancing in her eyes. How he wished that look had been reserved for him—a woman welcoming her man. But it wasn't. Rubbing his stubbled jaw, he said, "I just talked with Grandmother Agnes. She said that she feels the Storm Pipe is nearing the time when it can be used again."

"Oh, dear."

"Yeah. Not good news," Chase agreed grimly.

Rubbing more sweat from her brow with one end of the towel, Dana said, "Does this mean I have to go to Rogan's compound sooner?" Her heart skipped a beat in terror. Dana fought fear every time she thought about what she had to do. She wasn't about to admit it to anyone. Above all, she didn't want to disappoint her grandmother, who was counting on her.

"Yes, it may mean that." Chase continued, "You're strong and ready in your climbing and rappelling abilities. Plus, you've built up your wind and stamina. You've got better endurance now."

"That's good to hear." Dana managed a cautious grin. "Praise, finally, from the slave driver."

The warmth in her husky voice blanketed Chase. Dana's smile was rare. Her teasing him was new. She felt comfortable enough with him, trusted him enough now, Chase supposed. That was good. Because trust was something that couldn't be bought or sold. "Yes, you can bank on it," he told her softly.

His heart was heavy, and he tried to steel himself for what he was about to say. "Dana, you're weak in your combat skills. You don't have the heart to hurt someone if it becomes necessary. When I teach you the karate moves, you learn them, but you allow your emotions to blunt your drive. You need head and heart in hand-to-hand combat, or Rogan is going to kill you." Chase clasped his hands together and stared down at them.

"Look," Dana said, her voice tight, "I've told you time and again, Chase, that I don't like to hurt anything. Not even a fly. I was raised to know that everything, whether it crawled, flew or swam, was my brother or sister." Shrugging, she gave him a look of helplessness. "I'm just not the fighter or warrior you are. I'm trying, though."

She saw disappointment in the hard planes of his coppery face. Dana didn't like making Chase feel like that. From the beginning, something had driven her to try and meet his expectations. Now, she felt as if she'd failed. That hurt, and Dana pressed her hand against her heart. She didn't want to disappoint Chase.

"You are trying," he acknowledged, struggling to take the hard edge from his voice. Looking deeply into her soft cinnamon eyes, he said, "You don't have a reason to put your heart and soul into this. Oh, I know you're doing it because Grandmother Agnes asked you to. And you are the next one chosen to carry the Storm Pipe. But that's not *driving* you, Dana. You're doing this out of respect and tradition. And you need drive."

Frustrated, Dana said, "I don't know what else I can do, Chase. I'm willing to give my life to get that pipe back. Isn't that enough?"

Taking a deep, ragged breath, Chase said, "No, it isn't. Listen to me, Dana. Do you know who murdered your mother and husband?"

"Of course I don't know. I wish to hell I did. I've wanted to know for two damn long years." Her patience thinned. Her nerves were taut, and Dana felt the hurt eating her up inside. Confused, she whispered tautly, "What's this conversation all about? What's going on? Do you know who killed them?"

"Yes, I do." Chase straightened up and held her eyes, noting the surprise and shock in their depths. "Rogan Fast Horse stole the Storm Pipe from your mother. He has a partner, a woman named Blue Wolf. Rogan knew that he didn't dare touch the pipe himself or he'd die. So he had this woman come with him to pick up the pipe and steal it."

Gulping, Dana whispered, "Rogan murdered them?" Her heart galloped. She felt shaky. In shock. Dizzy.

Nodding, Chase continued in a low, pain-filled voice. "Grandmother Agnes has known this for some time, and she told me about it this morning. She felt you should know the truth now. The whole truth."

Chase saw tears flood Dana's eyes. His heart contracted with pain—her pain. "I'm sorry, I don't want to hurt you, Dana, but I know I'm going to. Grandmother said her guides showed her that Blue Wolf knocked on the door to your mother's house. Your husband answered it and let her in. Blue Wolf pretended to want to speak to your mother. As your husband turned away, Rogan sneaked in through the open door and stabbed him in the back of the neck. He was killed instantly. Then Rogan moved quietly through the living room and found your mother cooking in the kitchen."

Dana shakily touched her brow. "Oh, no."

Reaching out, Chase gripped her other hand and held it firmly. "Your mother knew of Rogan and distrusted him. The moment he came in, and she saw the bloody knife in his hand, she ran toward her bedroom. He followed her. Your mother saw your husband lying in a pool of blood near the front door. She tried to get to a dresser drawer where she kept a gun, but it was too late. Rogan stabbed her from behind." Chase's voice fell as he watched Dana sob, her hand pressed against her contorted lips.

"If it's any consolation," he told her wearily, squeezing her hand gently, "your mother, too, died immediately. Grandmother Agnes said they did not suffer."

Pulling free from Chase's grasp, Dana buried her face in her hands, sobs tearing from deep within. Agony and shock spun through her, churning up grief, questions, a sheering sense of utter helplessness and anger.

To hell with it. Chase rose swiftly and moved behind Dana as she sat hunched over and weeping uncontrollably. Crouching down, he settled his hands on her shaking shoulders and held her gently. "I'm sorry, Dana, so sorry you had to find this out." Damn, how he wanted to protect her, and yet he hadn't. Instead, he'd taken the invisible knife of truth and stuck it into her unsuspecting heart as surely as Rogan had struck and killed the people she loved. Swallowing against the bitter taste in his mouth, he moved his hands up and down her arms, trying to somehow soothe away her pain.

Chase enjoyed the contact far too much. His body responded, his heart opened. Somehow, he wanted to stop the brutal pain he'd just handed her. It had been a tactic to force her to connect more powerfully with her mission. To give her drive—a real reason to do this. Chase understood the need for it, but didn't like being the person who delivered the news. Right now, he didn't like himself at all.

"It's all right, Dana," he rasped, his mouth near her ear. Strands of her black hair slid across his lips as he spoke to her in a low, coaxing tone. He gripped her shoulders and absorbed her distress. "It's going to be all right. I'm here. Let me take away some of your hurt."

In that instant, Chase felt her slip from his grip and turn around. Dana's face glistened with tears. Her eyes were so filled with tortured agony that Chase automatically reached out to her. The moment his fingers touched her wet cheek, Dana moaned, closed her eyes and collapsed into his awaiting arms.

Heat mixed with shock and surprise as she pressed herself against him, her head buried against his neck, her arms wrapping tightly around his torso.

A ragged gasp escaped Chase's lips as he automatically swept her into a protective embrace. Dana was warm, soft and curvy against his own hard body. He inhaled the sweet sage scent of her hair. Her harsh weeping spread his heart wide open, and he had no protection against the pain he was feeling on her behalf. Nor did he want any. Feeling the wetness of her tears, he rocked her gently back and forth. What Dana needed—what he needed—was a safe harbor against the many storms that life threw at them. Eyes closed, Chase hungrily stole the moment like the emotional thief that he'd become. Everything about Dana appealed to him. Her kindness. Her inability to hurt others. Her sensitivity and awareness of everyone outside herself. In the greed-filled world they were forced to live in, he found her unselfishness an incredible breath of fresh air.

Without meaning to, Chase pressed his mouth against the side of Dana's face, and tasted her salty tears. Murmuring words of comfort, he felt her respond. In that silken moment, Dana turned her head. When his mouth unexpectedly met hers, a white-hot explosion occurred in his heart, then tunneled deep into his body. Groaning, he savored the sweetness of her lips.

A soft moan rose in Dana's throat as Chase returned her searching, tentative kiss. His mouth capturing hers in a sweeping motion, he held her in a firm embrace, her body crushed against his. He tasted her tears of pain and release, the sweetness of the honey she'd had in her coffee earlier. Even more heady was the taste of *her.* She was like no other woman Chase had ever kissed. His senses gloried in her full lips, the shy touch of her tongue to his, the taste of her as a woman.

As he deepened the kiss, Chase got lost in her fragrance, the tickling sensation of her hair against his cheek. The world ceased to exist. The danger he was putting her in faded to the background, superceded by all he was feeling. His hands itched to explore her.

Despite his wild desire, Chase knew he couldn't go further. Not yet. Maybe never.

There was such bittersweetness as their mouths clung hungrily to one another. Chase felt Dana's warm, ragged breath upon his face, felt the rapid rise and fall of her breasts against his chest. With a life of their own, her fingers slid across his shoulders, then touched his sandpapery face like a lover.

How he wanted to love Dana! Tearing his mouth from hers, Chase opened his eyes. He framed Dana's face with his hands and gazed into her face. What new emotion did he see in the haunted depths of her eyes? Chase didn't know what to call it. He was afraid to try.

"Chase…" Dana gasped. She blinked through the veil of tears beading her dark lashes. She was the only woman in the world and he, the only man. As he held her in his steely embrace, Dana had never felt more safe or more loved. Her lips tingled with the sensation of having that flat, hard mouth against hers. She'd kissed him!

Her heart thundered in her chest and made her feel shaky and tremulous. Dana could do nothing but cling to his golden gaze. She saw so much in Chase's face now. The change was remarkable. Breath-stealing. Frightening.

Dana didn't know what to do or say. Her hands rested against Chase's mighty shoulders and felt the tense play of muscles there. As he cupped her face, she closed her eyes and surrendered to him. Dana was so lost, so alone, and so hungry for the strength of a man in her life. After her five-year marriage to Hal, the desire for a man to sleep with each night, to share her life with, often over-whelmed her.

As she absorbed Chase's embrace, the feel of his hands moving from her cheeks to her shoul-ders, Dana trembled. She didn't want this moment to end. She didn't want Chase to stop holding her, because that eviscerating pain and grief would return. Hiccupping through her tears, Dana felt like a beggar stealing something that didn't really belong to her—Chase's touch. But after two long, barren years, she desperately needed to be held. Dana released a ragged sigh and leaned forward once more. Her brow came to rest against the thick, tense cords of his neck.

When he began to gently rock her, the rest of her lonely, ailing heart dissolved. Somehow, Chase sensed how badly she needed to be held, like a lost, hurt child. And that was how Dana felt after the news that Rogan had murdered her mother and Hal. Yes, she needed a safe harbor, and Chase had given it to her.

Before, she would never have thought him capable of such warmth and humanity, toward her or anyone. But she'd been wrong. Her hand stole down his chest, to rest against his pounding heart. Her nostrils flared as she inhaled his delicious male scent. How badly she wanted to stretch out on the floor and make torrid, passionate love with him.

As she trembled at the realization, she felt Chase's body tighten momentarily. His mouth was so close. So close…. Dana knew she could ease her head from beneath his jaw, look up and kiss him again. She felt his mouth open and then shut, felt him begin to gently rock her once more. The sensation was like that of a mother protecting a child. But it was also the gesture of a man who loved his woman and was trying to shield her from the atrocities of life.

For a moment, Dana wanted to forget everything. She pressed her face more surely against Chase and lost herself within him. He was the last person she had ever expected help, sustenance or support from. Yet she kept hearing his voice washing over her, comforting, warm and soothing. "It's all right, Dana. Everything's going to be all right. Just let your grief go, let it fly away from you."

Chase spoke those words in a husky tone that reverberated throughout her supersensitized body. There was no question that his voice was healing her bleeding, torn heart. She wondered if he realized the magical effect he had upon her. Dana had never experienced this from any man in her life. His vibrant warmth stole through her dormant, grief-constricted body. Suddenly, Dana wanted to live life once more—fully and completely. Chase was giving her a great gift, whether he knew it or not. She was ready to be present, not held a prisoner of her horrific past.

The awareness trickled through Dana like rain falling from Father Sky. That spark of wanting to do more than just survive burst through her and took root in her heart. The sensations were magical and shocking, in the best possible way. At the same time, old feelings warred with the newly birthed ones.

"Oh, Chase," Dana whispered, her voice shaky and unsure.

Easing Dana away from him, Chase found it was the last thing he wanted to do. But one of them had to be responsible. He had to put the mission before their own needs. Grimly, he realized he could no longer protect himself from the lush promise of Dana. She was like a beautiful flower—one that, if he wasn't careful, he could crush and destroy. The expression in her eyes tore at him. She was looking at him completely differently now. As if he was the man of her dreams. That realization shook him.

Chase did his best to sound hard. "Dana, this shouldn't have happened, I'm sorry. I couldn't help myself, you were hurting so much." He kept his hands on her shoulders, because she was trembling.

Her palm fell away from his chest, and Chase immediately missed her tender touch. What would it be like to have Dana explore his naked body with those long, wonderfully artistic fingers of hers? The thought sent a wave of violent heat to his core. No, he couldn't think of that!

The chances were good that Dana would be killed by Rogan and his women long before she ever found the Storm Pipe. Chase knew that, but he couldn't tell Dana. He needed her to believe that she could pull off this mission successfully. And he needed to detach himself.

His heart cried out that he shouldn't throw her life away like this. But the mission took priority. In the military, people's lives were sacrificed all the time for the good of the larger group. One life for many. Oh, yeah, he was more than a little familiar with that refrain. Chase had spent six months in captivity because of that belief. Now, he was putting Dana in the crosshairs to do the same thing: sacrifice a life to save many. It was a virtuous and courageous sacrifice, one that few people would ever know about.

"It's okay. It was my fault," Dana managed to reply in a hoarse tone. She forced herself to pull away, and sat back down on the stump. Wrapping her arms around herself, she tried to think clearly through the jumble of emotions. Her lips remembered his branding mouth upon them. She could still feel his power and tenderness as he'd swept his mouth across hers with strength and adoration. Oh! She'd felt so cherished in that moment.

Dana realized how starved she was to be loved once again. For two years she'd denied herself the longings of her body and heart. Now, one indelible kiss had brought her full circle: out of her grief and into a new awareness. And looking at Chase, his face dark with desire and disappointment, Dana knew he was the man she wanted. When had she fallen for him? She couldn't recall the exact moment. She realized she'd been unaware of so much—until now.

Chase slowly rose from his crouched position. His hands tingled with a burning desire to drag Dana back into his arms. She looked bereft, as if she'd lost another loved one. Grimacing, he shoved his hand through his short hair. Well, hadn't she?

He'd delivered the rest of the grisly story to Dana, of Rogan murdering her mother and her husband.

What kind of person was Chase to hurt someone as fragile and beautiful as Dana? His heart ached over what he'd told to her. He struggled to rise above his emotions and focus on the mission. It had to come first. But dammit, he wanted to keep Dana at his side, protect her and love her. What was he going to do?

CHAPTER FOURTEEN

"GRANDMOTHER," Dana began, her voice strained as she sat opposite Agnes in her hogan. "I have just found out the truth of who killed my mother and Hal."

Reaching out, Agnes patted Dana's hand. "Yes, I told Chase to tell you the rest of the story, child. You need to know the truth for many reasons. I'm sorry it had to be done like this. I withheld the information for so very long because I didn't want to hurt you any more than you had been already. I was hoping to tell you in another year or two, when you were more healed from the experience." She sighed heavily. "But that was not to be. Please forgive me for this poor timing."

Sniffing, Dana gently squeezed her grand-mother's thin fingers. "I—I would rather know than not know. Don't feel badly. I—it was just a shock. And of course I forgive you, Grandmother."

"You understand why you had to know?" Agnes

poured them sage tea and handed Dana a mug. The July heat of the noontime sun flowed into the hogan.

Nodding, Dana sipped the hot tea. "Yes, I think I do. Chase is worried I don't have my heart and soul invested in this mission."

"That's true, you don't. But now you have reason to fully commit yourself. I am not talking about being vengeful, for that is not the right reason to do this," Agnes counseled quietly. "Rather, you are here to right a wrong, which your mother and husband can no longer do for themselves. You will be the catalyst to rebalance the scales. Rogan will get what rightfully belongs to him, and you will return the Storm Pipe to the Blue Heron Society."

Pain flowed into Dana's heart as she sipped her tea. "Yes, I understand." Her lips still felt the molding strength of Chase's male, commanding mouth upon hers. He had urged her to go talk to Agnes after that life-changing kiss. Dana had left him at the winter hogan and walked down the canyon, in tears most of the way.

Holding the ceramic mug between her hands now, she cleared her throat. "I have only a week more before I try to get the Storm Pipe back, Grandma. I'll do my best. I know you're counting on me. The whole society is. I'm so afraid I'll disappoint all of you. And I don't want to do that."

"Listen," Agnes said gently, "we want the pipe back, that is true. But I do not want you killed trying to get it."

Shrugging, Dana stared down into the pale-green contents of the mug. "Right now, I don't know up from down. I'm so torn up over this information."

"Of course you are. When we are done with our tea, I want you to ask Chase to come down and talk with me."

CHASE GRIMLY LISTENED to Grandmother Agnes. As he sat cross-legged in front of her, his hands rested tensely on his knees. His heart twisted like an angry snake inside his chest. He wondered if Dana had confided the details of their hot, shocking kiss to the elder. Pushing the thought from his mind, he willed himself to be patient.

"I believe a change of plan is needed," Agnes was saying. "Dana simply cannot go into Rogan's compound and get the pipe by herself. I think you've known this all along."

Chase's heart churned. So did his gut. "Yes, Grandmother, I've known this from the time I met Dana. She has a good heart, but it's not in her to kill, if that's what she needs to do to defend herself against Rogan or his militant women. They *will* kill Dana if they find her in the compound."

"I have worried about this," Agnes admitted,

her voice soft and thin. "I don't wish to send Dana to her death. That is not what the society wants."

"Then the only choice we have is for me to join Dana. For us to go in as a team to retrieve the pipe," Chase said. "I *will* kill, if necessary. And I will protect Dana."

The passion in his tone was palpable. Agnes studied him for a long moment. Then she blotted the corners of her mouth with her handkerchief. "You have fallen in love with Dana."

He avoided her all-seeing gaze and stared down at his scarred hands. To Chase, the words felt like a crushing weight. Mouth tightening, he realized the elder had not posed it as a question, but a statement of fact. Medicine people were highly clairvoyant and knew things that most never would. Agnes was well aware of the chemistry that had rocked his and Dana's world less than two hours ago.

"I feel…" Chase began awkwardly, casting around for words despite the powerful emotions exploding through his chest "…that a window in my dark soul has just been thrown open, Grandmother. Kissing Dana was the most right thing I've done in my life, so far." There, the truth was out. It lay naked in front of the wise old woman. Chase tried to steel himself against what Agnes might say. He lifted his head and searched her wrinkled features.

"Love has its own way of making two people discover that they are bound to one another."

Nodding, Chase felt a weight lift from his shoulders. "I didn't know. Oh, I liked her, Grandmother. What is there not to like about Dana?" He gave the old woman a searching look. "She's all heart, and she wears it on her sleeve. Dana is kind, sensitive and mature. She sees the world in a way I never will." His mouth quirked. "I wish I could see it like she does. It would take away a lot of bad memories and experiences I've had."

Giving him a slight smile, Agnes reached out and gripped his hands. "My son, your heart yearns for her idealism and purity. She is, after all, the next woman in line to carry the Storm Pipe. We want to see that kind of heart in ceremonial pipe carriers."

"Yes, I know that. Dana's the right one to carry that pipe, Grandmother, no question. She will make the society proud of her, and she will use the Storm Pipe only for good, not evil, as Rogan is doing right now."

Patting his hands, Agnes said, "So you will be a team. You must leave next Saturday. I feel the pipe is near to full power now, and I have no doubts Rogan will want to use its lightning energy to kill again." Her hand tightened on Chase's. "You must stop him. At all costs."

Those trembling, hushed words weren't lost on Chase. He captured Agnes's work-worn hands and gently squeezed them. "I understand, Grandmother. We will do our best or die trying." Chase thought that if he had to die, at least he would die happy. He'd finally met the woman whom he dreamed of living with forever. And he'd found her in the most surprising of ways. Now that Dana was here, he'd damn well ensure that she wouldn't die. He would protect her with his life.

"I do not wish harm on either of you, but I know Rogan," Agnes murmured, her voice reedy with worry. "I wish there was some other way, but there is not. We must put your lives in jeopardy and win back the pipe."

Getting up, Chase leaned over, opened his arms and carefully embraced the tall, thin woman. She reminded him of a paper doll, her bones so old and brittle with age that he was afraid to put much pressure on her. Yet, for all her advanced years, Agnes was strong of heart and had an indomitable spirit.

"We will do our best," he promised her, his voice raw with emotion.

Now, Chase had to return to Dana and get her back on her training schedule. Just because she was hurting emotionally didn't mean she shouldn't continue to strengthen herself in every possible way.

As Chase said goodbye to Agnes and left the hogan, he wondered how he was going to handle all his powerful feelings for Dana.

DANA WAS ALREADY GOING through her series of exercises outside the hogan when Chase reappeared. The push-ups, the chin-ups always left her gasping for breath, but her muscles were taut and responsive after four weeks of effort. As she finished the last of her curls, Dana straightened and looked directly into Chase's dark, moody-looking eyes. His mouth was set more than usual. Squatting down in front of where she sat in the red sand, he draped his hands loosely between his thick thighs.

"You need to know that Grandmother Agnes wants me to go along with you to get that pipe back. I told her I would." Chase searched Dana's grief-stricken features, his gaze settling on those full lips he'd captured and cajoled less than two hours earlier. His body hardened.

Relief swept through Dana. "You will? I mean, that's great news."

Chase smiled briefly. "Grandmother feels better that I'm going along, too."

"And you, Chase? How do you feel about it?" Dana guardedly searched his face. Had their unexpected kiss changed things between them? Opened him up to her? Dana unconsciously held her breath.

"Truth be told, I didn't want to come along since the beginning, Dana." He gave a lazy shrug and looked past her to a hawk circling above the canyon. It was a zone-tailed hawk, with a white, horizontal band across its black, spread tail feathers. "I wanted this mission to be a one-person job. But Grandmother Agnes was running the show. I think she's realized you're going to need help." Chase carefully omitted the other factor: that he was falling helplessly in love with Dana, and he wanted to protect her from Rogan and the women who were more than ready to kill her on sight. It was a selfish reason, but a damn good one.

Perspiring in the hot sun, Dana stood up and moved over to the shade of a piñon tree. Chase followed, and she turned to look at him. How powerful he was, even when relaxed.

"And why are you doing this?" she asked. Was it the kiss that had changed things between them? Dana knew how she'd felt toward Chase all along, but she'd hidden it from him—or tried to. Until this morning. Oh, nothing was ever simple in life. There was so much overlay, so much complexity.

Chase cleared his throat and wrapped his arms across his chest. Dana looked beautiful with her braided hair framing her guarded face. But it was her cinnamon eyes that stole his heart. They were shining today. He could tell Dana liked him. How much? He didn't know, and was afraid to ask.

Dana was a widow coming out of two years of grief and loss. She'd just been told that Rogan had murdered the two people she loved most. So what was Chase seeing in her eyes? What emotion? And what fueled that feeling? He saw hope mirrored in Dana's expression, the soft parting of her mouth, those delicious, soft lips, calling to him once more.

Finally, he forced himself to speak. "I'm doing this because I don't think you can pull off this mission by yourself." Well, that *was* true. But Chase didn't want to confuse Dana any more. She didn't need to know that, on top of everything else, he wanted her, loved her. Wrong time, wrong place, as usual.

Swallowing hard, Dana nodded and looked away from Chase's intense gaze. "Oh, I see. Okay, that's fair. I don't feel like getting killed, to tell you the truth, and I'd welcome you along. You're the expert, really. I'm a bumbling novice in comparison."

His arms fell to his sides. "Listen, Dana, don't misunderstand. You've done well these four weeks. There aren't a lot of men or women who would have worked as hard or come so far. It's just that Grandmother and I believe, with me along, you'll be freed up to focus on finding the pipe. Once you get your intuition in gear and locate it, I can run interference and protect you while you recover it. You'll need a hundred percent concentration to tune in. If you're distracted, you can't focus and you won't find it."

It hurt Dana to think that the only reason Chase was coming along was to be her big, bad guard dog. But under the circumstances, she was grateful. In her heart, she had a dreadful feeling that she could be killed. She'd never spoken about that fear to Chase or her grandmother.

Dana nodded and gave him a quick smile, hiding her heartache. "I'm really glad you're coming, Chase, for many reasons."

"You're a good team member, Dana. We'll work well together. The rest of this week we'll spend in tandem, refining our skills and trying to establish a rhythm with one another. Particularly on the rock climbing portion."

Dana swallowed her disappointment. Well, what had she expected from Chase? One fiery, soul-melting kiss hadn't changed anything. She couldn't pick up on him psychically because he kept up defensive walls. For the most part, Chase was always armored, and Dana wasn't quite sure how he felt toward her.

She could still remember the feel of his blazing, branding mouth. That, she would never forget. But had it been just lust for him? Dana didn't know, and now was not the time to ask. Deep in her heart, she wished that Chase might desire her on all levels and not just for sex. She had been powerfully drawn to him from the beginning. Dana could admit that much to herself—but never to him. Not now, at least.

"Well," she said, more cheerily than she felt, "let's get busy, then. We need to learn how to work as a seamless team so Rogan and his women don't hear or sense us coming."

Pain was bright in her eyes, but her voice didn't reveal it. Chase savagely told himself not to reach out and touch the tousled hair at her temple. Dana was exceedingly vulnerable in that moment, and he saw her struggling to put her personal pain aside and focus on the mission.

Her unselfish quality only made Chase want her more. Giving her a rare smile, he said, "Let's go get our climbing equipment. We'll spend the rest of the day going up and down the canyon wall. It'll help us mesh as a team. We have to be fast and silent."

As they walked back to the hogan, his mind turned to Rogan Fast Horse. What was the bastard planning? Chase could sense that he was close to initiating the Storm Pipe once more. Would they be in time to stop him? Every passing moment pushed the world further into chaos and imbalance. The more entrenched they became, the more uncertain Chase felt. Everything felt tense. As if lightning was about to strike.

CHAPTER FIFTEEN

"DAMMIT!" Rogan yelled at Blue Wolf, who sat smugly with the Storm Pipe in her arms. "That pipe is ready! I want to gather the circle of women tomorrow morning and use it." Breathing hard, he towered over her. Blue Wolf's upper lip lifted in a sneer, and he itched to slap the bitch. How dare she refuse to use the pipe when he wanted it used!

"It's not ready yet, and I'm not about to let you abuse this pipe, Rogan." Her heart beat heavily in her breast. The Storm Pipe lay like a sleeping baby cradled in the crook of her left arm.

Blue Wolf saw the rage building in Rogan's dark eyes. Oh, she knew he wanted to hit her, no question. But he didn't dare. The pipe had bonded with *her*. Only her. The other women were merely catalysts to help move the pipe's gathering power around the circle. The energy would build up and up—eventually into a forty-thousand-foot-high thunder cloud that would be loosed upon Rogan's next target, Hornsby of the Bureau of Indian Affairs.

Frustrated, Rogan paced the room. The cedar floor shone in the dawn light filtering in the small window. His footfalls reverberated through the space. The door was closed, and Rogan knew most of the other women were still asleep. It was only 5:30 a.m. As he went toward the window, he struggled to get ahold of his anger. Clasping his hands behind his back, gazing out into the compound, Rogan steadied his voice.

"The pipe is ready. I can feel it, Blue Wolf."

Shrugging, she gently stroked the golden elk-skin bag in which it lay. "I don't agree. I work with this pipe daily. I meditate with her for an hour each morning and an hour at dusk." Blue Wolf lifted her chin defiantly and glared at Rogan's hunched back. "The pipe is *almost* ready. But not quite yet."

Turning on his heel, Rogan witnessed the defiant set of Blue Wolf's mouth. She was stubborn, and he had a dilemma. The pipe was bonded with Blue Wolf, not him. He couldn't even touch it for fear of being instantly electrocuted. *Dammit!* His hands literally itched to jerk the pipe bag out of her grasp. Instead, he fought for control. Eventually, he would have his way and Blue Wolf's power wouldn't be an issue.

The woman had weaknesses. Rogan's eyes were drawn to the carved turquoise wolf's head hanging from a thick leather thong around her throat. She was never without her namesake, the wolf's head crafted by her well-known artist father. Her late father had been creative, but an abusive alcoholic. Rogan couldn't understand why Blue Wolf continued to revere the drunken bastard who had knocked her around as a child. The medicine woman's long, hooked nose was crooked and bent, showing how many times her father had hit her with his fist. Maybe that's why she hated men, Rogan decided. He'd been beaten routinely and understood. Yet that turquoise wolf's head remained with her. As did the powerful and valuable Storm Pipe. Jealousy ate at Rogan.

"That pipe is ready to go, and you damn well know it. You're just being stubborn because I want to use it."

Nostrils flaring, Blue Wolf again lay her hand across the pipe bag. "Rogan, you're always in a hurry. You forget, I've known you since we were teenagers. I've seen your restlessness, your impatience with everything and everyone. You're right—I'm not about to let you tell me when the pipe I carry is ready for use." She patted it lovingly. "As I said, she is not quite there yet."

Rogan approached her and snarled, "Well, when *will* it be ready?" His voice sounded like the hiss of an angry rattlesnake.

"Soon."

Throwing up his hands, he yelled, "Well, when the hell does *soon* mean?"

Blue Wolf didn't cringe at Rogan's drama and threats. The other women did, but she refused to. No man scared her anymore.

Steadily, she held Rogan's blazing gaze. His fists were clenched at his sides. She sensed his desire to strike her, but he really *didn't* dare. If he ever laid a hand on her, Blue Wolf would disappear from the compound with the Storm Pipe, never to be found by this bastard again. And Rogan knew she'd do it.

"I will let you know when the pipe is ready to perform. Besides, you had the Russian ambassador targeted as the next victim. Why did you change your mind?"

Rubbing his stubbled jaw, Rogan muttered, "That's none of your business."

"I read the newspapers, Rogan. I see that the FBI and CIA are hunting for terrorists. Could it be that you've gotten cold feet? Are you afraid they'll find us?" Blue Wolf snorted. "Now is not the time to become cowardly, Rogan. So what if the feds are looking for something they don't even realize exists? No one will ever suspect a pipe capable of doing that kind of damage. I think you're wrong to target the head of the BIA. I think your original plan to take out the Russian ambassador is far better. That will create the world tension that we want."

"You've seen the papers," Rogan reminded her as he paced. "They hint at nuclear war. Russia and the U.S. are already on high alert with one another. Well, I don't want a nuke hitting us over here. Instead, I'm going to kill Hornsby, and then we'll send a letter to the FBI giving them our list of demands. They must improve all Native Americans' lives."

Blue Wolf sighed. "It's not a bad idea, but if you send a letter after Hornsby is killed, the FBI will know that some Native American is a potential threat. Worse, they may see all of us as home-grown terrorists. They'll start to tear up every reservation in the U.S., looking for us, even though they'll never realize who wrote the demand letter."

"Do you have a better idea of how to get the U.S. government's attention? The whites were wrong to imprison us on these reservations. We are the first Americans! We were here long before those bastards." Rogan punched his index finger in Blue Wolf's direction. "I want changes for the better for all of us, on every reservation. I want off the dole. I want our people to be respected and have industry come in so we can make a decent living, and not live in poverty as we have for over a hundred years."

"I don't disagree with your goal, Rogan. But I sense you need to be very careful about the letter and where you send it from. Once they get it, they'll have FBI agents crawling around here like ants."

"I'm not that stupid," he declared. "I'll write the

letter and have one of our women drive to California and drop it into a mailbox in Los Angeles. That will throw them off our scent. I'll warn the feds that if they don't give us the equality we demand within six weeks, we'll kill the president of the United States. And they will understand it isn't an empty threat."

Blue Wolf knew Rogan had spent years writing a document detailing how the U.S. government should release all Native Americans from the poverty of the reservation system. She'd read it, suggested changes and approved the subsequent draft. The only question was could Rogan push through changes this way? She knew that U.S. officials didn't negotiate with terrorists. Right now, newspapers were reporting that the vice president had died of a sudden, unexpected heart attack. Still, the terrorism warning level had been initiated, and there were articles in the paper hinting that the FBI was looking for a "terrorist sleeper cell." Well, Rogan's team *were* the cell. But Blue Wolf was positive they'd never be found, because white men simply didn't know the power of a ceremonial pipe.

"As soon as you decide the time to use the pipe, let me know," Rogan muttered, all his anger dissolving.

"I will," she replied. It was Tuesday. "I feel that by Saturday the pipe will be ready to go."

"Then we'll schedule the circle for Monday, because I want that bastard sitting in his office in D.C. when it happens." Gloating to himself, Rogan turned on his heel and left the meditation room.

As he did so, his scalp prickled, and Rogan sensed danger once again. But where was it coming from? Was it Blue Wolf herself? Or could the FBI have somehow found a lead? Scratching his head, Rogan moved out to the main area of the lodge, where two huge pillars, stout cedar trunks with the bark removed, supported the roof. Looking around, Rogan felt inexplicably jumpy. Who the hell was stalking them?

ANNIE BALLARD GASPED as she shot up into a sitting position. Her hand against her throat, she could feel her pulse bounding wildly. Light from the streetlamp leaked into her apartment window. She shakily wiped her brow and quickly got out of bed, grabbing the notebook and pen from a nearby stand. With trembling fingers, she recorded the horrific vision she'd just experienced.

For the next fifteen minutes, she tried to remember every detail, every face she'd seen, and the feelings surrounding the images. By the time she'd finished, Annie felt a terrible chill working up her spine. The Carson City apartment was warm, but she was cold. She pulled her yellow fleece robe from the end of the bed and shrugged it on. She had to have a cup of tea. No way could she go back to bed.

The clock read 4:00 a.m. Shaken, she walked on bare feet through the carpeted apartment to the kitchen. First thing this morning, she would call David Colby, the FBI agent, and let him know what she'd seen. It could be the clue they had been hoping for.

"THIS IS THE BIGGEST wild-goose chase I've ever gone on," David Colby griped to Annie Ballard as they drove down the main street of Carson City, Nevada. They'd flown in two days earlier. The FBI kept a few apartments there, and they'd each moved into one on a temporary basis. Annie had recounted the powerful dream she'd had the night before.

"The FBI provided us with a list of survivalist cells in the Carson City area," Annie reminded him. She looked up at the signs along the street. In her vision, she'd seen an Indian warbonnet on the front of a building on a busy avenue. There was something in that building that would possibly help them. "I gave good descriptions of the faces I saw in my dream to your FBI artist." She patted the leather purse in her lap. "We have more sketches now."

Colby wasn't optimistic. He crept along in the right lane, allowing the faster midmorning traffic to flow by them. The sidewalks had a number of tourists dipping in and out of the many trading posts along the avenue. All tourist traps, in Colby's opinion.

He'd asked Annie if there were trading posts with Indian warbonnets on the sign here. She'd said she didn't know, that they'd have to drive around and look for it.

Colby didn't put any stock in Annie Ballard's abilities. So far, none of them had panned out.

"There! Look! The warbonnet! Do you see it, David?"

Frowning, he squinted through his dark glasses. Pulling into a parking space, he turned off the engine. Sure enough, about half a block down on the right was a large sign with an eagle feather warbonnet. He shook his head and gave her a glance as he pocketed his keys.

Annie smiled triumphantly at him. "You think I got lucky?"

Colby grinned sourly. "You're reading my mind," he teased, easing out of the car. Annie was a nice woman, a kind person. She didn't brag about what she did; rather, she was like a quiet and unassuming mouse.

He joined her on the sidewalk, and they walked toward the establishment, the sign of which read Chief Eagle Feather Antiques. To Colby, it looked like a touristy trading post.

Drawing a deep breath of warm desert air, Annie

hitched her leather purse up on her shoulder. "We're looking for something, but I don't know what."

"A clue?"

"I hope. In my vision there was a powerful, threatening presence in this store. That's where I saw the man's face."

"Will you know where this thing is you're looking for?"

She shrugged. "I can't say. Being psychic doesn't mean I know everything. I just receive 'hits' or feelings, and then have to try and interpret them correctly."

"Hmm…" Colby opened the door and Annie stepped inside. "That and a lot of good ole gumshoe work," he said. "Nothing like going door-to-door to gather information and evidence." He heard Annie laugh and saw her nod.

Narrow and long, the place was much more an antique store than a trading post, he realized. There were stuffed buffalo, antelope and bighorn sheep heads hanging on the cream-colored stucco walls. Colby spotted a balding man wearing Ben Franklin–type glasses behind one of the counters. No one else seemed to be around. Colby smelled the scent of leather, and spotted several U.S. Cavalry saddles from the Civil War era on wooden stands, their brass shiny and the bull hide leather well cared for. Bridles from the same period hung on the walls behind them.

Annie wove her way between many rugs, antique tables, chairs and dressers, to the counter. She smiled at the man. "Hi, are you the owner?"

"Sure am. Joseph Spearling. What can I do for you folks? Are you interested in a particular antique or just browsing?" He adjusted his glasses on his bulbous nose and set down the pen in his pudgy hands.

Colby came over and offered a smile. "We're just looking, Mr. Spearling. Mind if we nose around?"

Shrugging rounded shoulders beneath his wrinkled short-sleeved shirt, Spearling said, "Sure, no problem. If you have a question, lemme know. I'll be glad to try and help."

"Thanks," Annie told him warmly. She caught David's eye as she turned on her heel and walked with him down the crowded aisle. "I'm just sensing," she told him under her breath, so that Spearling couldn't hear.

"Fine. Do your thing," Colby murmured, looking around. There were many glass cabinets filled with Native American objects—necklaces and silver bracelets inlaid with turquoise, beaded feather fans, deer-hide moccasins, beaded horse martingales, parfleche bags and other artifacts. Annie slowly ambled the entire length of the store, perusing the merchandise. What was she looking for? Colby didn't have a clue.

After many minutes of nosing around, she walked

back to the proprietor, who was busy doing paper-work. "Mr. Spearling, I think I need your help."

Looking up, he pushed his wire-rimmed glasses higher on his nose. "Sure. What are you looking for?"

Annie grimaced. "I'm not really sure." She pulled out a small notebook as Colby joined her at the counter. "Now, don't laugh at me, Mr. Spear-ling, but I had a dream and I saw this in it." Annie quickly drew the L-shaped object and turned the notebook around. "Do you happen to know what that might be?"

"Let's see." Spearling studied the sketch. "Why, I believe that may be an Indian pipe."

Colby frowned. "A what?"

"A pipe," Spearling told them. He led them past a long row of glass cases. "Come on, I'll show you one."

Annie followed him down the narrow aisle. At the very end, Spearling stopped. He dug in his pocket for a ring of keys, opened the lock on a cabinet and reached in.

"Here you go. This happens to be a Sioux pipe, circa 1890s." He put a rubber mat on the glass and then carefully laid the red stone pipe head on it.

Annie leaned over and studied it. "What is this, exactly? It's not L-shaped."

"Oh, sorry," Spearling said, and he reached for something else. "Here we go. If the pipe is going to be smoked, the wooden stem is fixed into this hole here. See?" He inserted the hollow wooden shaft into the base of the catlinite pipe. Holding it up, he said, "This is L-shaped, after a fashion. What do you think?"

Standing back, Annie saw that, indeed, the pipe had a definite L shape. She exchanged a quick glance with Colby, who seemed mystified. "Why, yes. That probably is it. Do you have any other Native American antiques that would resemble an L?"

Spearling gently placed the red stone head back on the rubber mat, after disconnecting the stem. "No, nothing else comes to mind. What do you know about pipes?"

Annie was drawn to the pipe head. The curious object was circular and plain, not decorated in any way, yet excitement riffled through her. Something about the pipe made her want to hold it. "I know nothing, Mr. Spearling. What can you tell us?"

He smiled and mopped his brow with a linen handkerchief. "Not much. You know, Native Americans don't talk about their ceremonial gear." He touched the bowl. "This is made of pipestone, a soft red rock found in a quarry in Minnesota. All the nations go there to get blocks of it to carve their pipes from. This is a nice one. You can see there are yellow spots throughout the pipestone, which is also called catlinite."

"I've heard of peace pipes," Colby said. "You

know, the ones in cowboy and Indian movies, where they pass this pipe around?"

"Yes, well, peace pipes certainly exist. Ones you saw in movies probably had a lot of beading, maybe some eagle feathers hanging from the stem, or they were wrapped in the fur of a wild animal. Symbolically, it all means something, but I don't know what."

"May I touch it?" Annie asked.

"Of course, but please hold it firmly with both hands. Pipestone is very brittle, and if you drop it, it may shatter or chip, for sure." Spearling gingerly picked up the piece and handed it to Annie.

"I'll be very careful," she promised. The moment he placed the ancient pipestone into her palm, she felt prickles of energy leaping up her arm, followed by a palpable warmth in the center of her chest. Then came a euphoric, expansive sensation of joy and lightheartedness. Stunned, Annie stared down at the pipe. "Oh, gosh, did you feel that, too, Mr. Spearling?" She gazed at the elderly man, wide-eyed.

"I was wondering if you were going to pick up on that or not. You must be quite sensitive."

"Call me Annie. This is David."

"Most folks call me Joe. Nice to meet you folks."

Colby leaned closer. "What did you feel?"

Annie explained it to him and saw the doubt on his face. "Joe? Is it okay if I let David hold the pipe?"

Chuckling, he said, "Sure, no problem."

Annie saw Colby's skeptical expression disappear about a minute after he'd grasped the pipe. He studied the piece, then gave her a confused look. "I don't understand this. I feel warmth, too. A lot more than the temperature in here."

Spearling chuckled. "That's why Native Americans guard their pipes so closely. They're alive, David." His eyes twinkled. "Holding this one makes you feel good, doesn't it?"

"It did me. Incredibly so," Annie whispered, hand pressed to her heart. "I'm still feeling it now. That's just amazing."

"Most people would poke fun at me for saying these pipes are alive, but it's true. They say each pipe has a spirit, as individual as you and me. No two are the same, apparently. Each is endowed with a unique personality, and talents or skills. And that's why the medicine people of any nation are real careful in choosing who carries such a pipe."

"What do you mean?" Colby asked, enjoying the soft, undulating lightness moving through him. He didn't want to believe a piece of carved stone could cause this. And yet, he wasn't just imagining this euphoric state. No way.

Spearling mopped his brow again, then walked back to the counter and turned on the air-conditioning. In moments, cool air began to circulate and chase out the desert heat. "Like I said, I don't know a whole lot about pipes, and the people who make and carry them aren't sharing, either," he stated. "As I understand it, a person chosen to carry a pipe has to have the utmost integrity. They're kind of like the Knights of the Round Table. They won't lie, cheat or steal, and are considered role models for their village and their nation. They help the elderly, feed the poor and generally do good deeds for everyone."

Colby reluctantly handed the pipe back to Spearling. "So what does a pipe carrier get out of all of this except responsibility?"

The proprietor placed the pipe head back in the glass case and laid the stem beside it. "Well," he grunted, leaning over and locking the cabinet door, "the community admires and respects a pipe carrier."

"That's all they get?" Annie said.

Straightening up, Spearling added, "When they smoke the pipe it is said to have magical powers."

"Oh?" she asked in an interested tone. "What kind of magic?"

Grinning, Spearling said, "No one's talking about that to me. But I've heard stories…."

"Tell us one," Colby urged.

"A pipe can kill or heal, is what I've heard. In the hands of a good-hearted person, a pipe can miraculously cure someone with a disease. In the wrong hands, it can be like a loaded revolver or weapon. I overheard a couple of Indians in here one time whispering about one pipe carrier who was into revenge. He smoked the pipe to send energy to his enemies, giving them chronic diseases as payback." Spearling's brows rose. "Now, you must understand, most pipe carriers are good, honest folks, but sometimes a pipe gets into the hands of someone who should never carry it. Sometimes people are jealous of true pipe carriers and they will steal a pipe because of its power. And they do damage with it."

Annie's eyes widened. "Oh, dear. What happened?"

"One guy is dead, from what I understood. Died of a massive heart attack, just like that." Spearling snapped his fingers. "Another has cancer and is dying more slowly."

Colby snorted. "A pipe can kill a person? Create a heart attack in them? Come on."

Annie bit her lip as she watched Spearling's round, jovial face grow serious.

"Listen, David, I know this seems far-fetched to you. I've been in this business, dealing with Native Americans, all my life. More than a few things I'd list as pure magic. On a few occasions where a pipe was smoked, I've actually seen someone either fall seriously ill or suddenly die. A bad person with bad intent who carries a pipe can cause those kinds of problems. Of course, just the opposite happens when a good-hearted person does. They use the pipe to heal and help others."

"Joe? May I beg a little more of your time?" Annie asked. "I know we're probably keeping you from work, but I had a dream a couple of nights ago and I'd like to share it with you. Maybe you can help me."

He glanced at his watch. "Sure. It's a quiet day and not too many tourists seem to be comin' our way. Tell me about your dream."

Excitedly, Annie said, "I heard drumming. Deep, beautiful drums beating slowly. And I saw twelve Native American women in a circle out beneath some pine trees. They were sitting cross-legged, their knees touching, and they were holding hands. As I moved around the circle, I saw this older woman with long black-and-gray hair. She was at the head of the circle and holding what I now realize was a pipe, just like the one you just showed us. Only it was different."

"No two pipes look the same. They can have the same shape sometimes, but if you look closely at the pipestone, you might see streaks of white, yellow coloration or other variations. And they're shaped differently, too."

"This pipe was red, just like the one you showed us, but much larger. The woman held the head of the pipe in her left palm and her arm was completely outstretched. The wooden stem had black-and-yellow beading, and I saw a long, yellow lightning bolt." Annie frowned and glanced at Joe. "Does that sound familiar?"

"Indeed it does. You said the woman's arm was outstretched as she held it?"

"Yes, in my dream it seemed she was straining as she held it because the stem was so long." Annie motioned to the glass cabinet. "This pipe stem was short in comparison to the one I saw in my dream."

"It's probably a ceremonial pipe you saw, then," Spearling guessed.

"What's that?" Colby asked.

"I understand there are two types of pipes carried by chosen Native Americans. One is a personal pipe, which usually has a shorter stem. The other is a ceremonial one, which has a very long stem. And if you're short, as many women are, compared to men, then your arm may not be long enough to hold the pipe."

"Yes!" Annie exclaimed. "The woman looked like she was really straining to hold it. The pipe head was in her left palm, and the long stem was the full length of her left arm."

"Most likely ceremonial, then. Go on."

Swallowing, Annie continued, "I saw a man standing behind this woman. He had his hands resting on her shoulders. They were singing a song, in some language unfamiliar to me. I saw smoke, white and thick, as the woman smoked the pipe. But the smoke poured out and began to form a huge, dark, roiling cloud above them. Lightning flashed, and the rumbling thunder was so loud it seemed to go through me, as if we were having an earthquake."

Annie opened her hands. "And then things got crazy in my dream. The drums started beating harder and louder and faster. The storm clouds enveloped all of them. I was standing in this swirling mass of lightning and thunder, with winds screaming around me. In the distance I could hear the women's voices, rising and falling in a very impassioned chant. I heard the drums, too, but the power that I felt...! It was amazing. Then I saw this face." Annie quickly opened her purse and put the sketch on top of the glass case. It was the same sketch she'd showed Colby at his office in D.C. earlier. "This man's face. His image kept appearing and disappearing in the clouds and storm. And I saw the woman who was holding the pipe, too. She would glare at me and then disappear. And then this man's face would rush at me, trying to scare me away. I was seeing something he didn't want me to see. I felt like he wanted to murder me." Annie managed a short laugh. "I jerked awake at that point."

"Hmm," Joe said, studying the sketch of the man's face, "this gent looks familiar." He tapped his fingers on the case, deep in thought.

Colby watched the antique owner intently. "He does?"

Scratching his balding head, Joe said, "Yes, vaguely. Give me a moment and maybe it will come to me." He looked over at Annie. "That was quite a dream you had. Do you know this guy?" He pointed down at the sketch.

"No. I don't know any of them. I didn't even know that I was looking at a Native American pipe until you showed us that one." She pointed to the glass case.

"Interesting. Ah, wait! I remember who this might be!"

"Who?" Annie asked anxiously.

"Rogan Fast Horse. I'm not sure, but it could be him."

"Who is he?" Colby demanded.

"A Cherokee métis medicine man. He lives up in the Sierras just above Carson City. I've seen him down here in the city from time to time."

"A medicine man. Wow." Annie shook her head. "And to think it was just a dream."

Colby nodded. He scooped up the drawing and handed it back to Annie. "Mr. Spearling, do you know where this guy lives? An address perhaps?"

"I can give you directions. He'd be an excellent contact if you're interested in pipes. And who knows? Annie, if you share your dream with him, he might even be able to give you an interpretation of it. After all, he is a medicine man."

CHAPTER SIXTEEN

WHAT THE HELL WAS WRONG with that bitch, Blue Wolf? Rogan paced along the stockade around the Eagle's Nest compound. It was a name he'd come up with many years ago. Rogan had for a long time dreamed of having a place high in the Sierras, in the arms of the mountain spirits, where he was safe and no one, white men especially, could find him.

The damp morning air was filled with the calming scent of pines, which grew on the craggy basalt clifftops. Dawn had just arrived, tinting the sky a pale peach color. Two women guards carrying M-16 rifles slowly walked the quarter-mile perimeter of the compound. They were young and tough, and they respectfully acknowledged Rogan as he strided on by them, hands behind his back. Security was always on his mind. He trusted no one. Not even Blue Wolf now.

Chewing on his lower lip, Rogan watched the sky turn from peach to a pale-blue as the sun inched above the horizon. The morning was cool without being cold. Absorbing the pine fragrance, the healing stillness and quiet, he found his thoughts returning to Blue Wolf. She'd been his partner for quite some time. Once, they had been inseparable, obsessive lovers, but over time, sexual encounters became less frequent. But they shared something else, Rogan knew. Something that kept them together. Blue Wolf wanted power. Absolute power. So did he. It was always a battle between them.

And Blue Wolf knew she had *real* power now that the Storm Pipe had bonded with her. Damn that twist of luck! Rogan thrust out his chin and glared up at the cloudless sky. A cardinal flew overhead, toward a tall pine growing just outside the compound on the cliff edge. Blue Wolf had power now and she was wresting more from him. She'd just confronted him boldly, insisting the pipe wouldn't be ready until Saturday. The bitch was the one in charge—not him.

A bitter taste coated the inside of Rogan's mouth as he considered the vile, undeniable truth of it all. Wiping his lips with the back of his hand, he stared up at the impenetrable, ten-foot-high wall of redwood, pine and Douglas fir. The different hues of the timbers, from deep red, to white, to corn yellow, served to remind him of the ongoing fight between red men and white.

What to do? How to get the power back from Blue Wolf? Rogan folded his arms across his chest and stared down at the powdery umber dust beneath his booted feet as he felt his way through this unplanned predicament. The Storm Pipe could not just be arbitrarily handed to another, more acquiescent of his students. When a pipe like this one formed a bond, it was for life…until the woman died. Whoever took the pipe next became the owner.

Maybe, just maybe, Rogan thought, running his index finger across his bearded chin, Blue Wolf needed to die. Then the Storm Pipe would be free to bond with the next woman. Someone more malleable, someone he could control. Lifting his head, Rogan heard sounds of stirring. There were two dormitory-style buildings that housed the women. Rogan inhaled the delicious smell of coffee being perked in the kitchen. Whoever had cooking duty today must be starting breakfast. The fragrant scent of bacon frying soon followed.

Rogan sighed. He'd planned for so long, for years, for this place to become a reality. To have a ceremonial pipe that would give him the power to change the lives of all his people. Now, his vision was in jeopardy because Blue Wolf was taking his power away from him. If she got pissed off, she'd disappear with the pipe and he'd have nothing.

Rogan knew he'd have to be subtle, cloak his real feelings, and play the game with Blue Wolf until the time was right.

Looking toward the gates, he saw one of the

women on guard duty testing the wooden bar across them. They were locked tight. No one could get in without him knowing about it. A wonderful sense of security blanketed Rogan, and for a moment, he truly felt safe here. This compound was impregnable. He'd purposely built it on this huge basalt outcropping, a cliff that dropped three thousand feet into a rocky canyon. The only way in and out of Eagle's Nest was an old dirt road, and his women controlled access 24-7.

Feeling safe was important to Rogan. He all too poignantly recalled growing up in a household with a father who had fetal alcohol syndrome. Don Fast Horse was a mean drunk with a low I.Q. Red-nosed and ornery, he would seek his kids out and beat the hell out of them with an old leather strap. Rogan still bore scars where the thin leather had bitten into his tender young flesh. Whip marks still crisscrossed his back, and every time Rogan tugged on a pair of socks, he could feel the ridge of scars on his ankles and calves, a constant reminder that power had been wrested from him as a child.

Don Fast Horse had been an artist of sorts. When his creative efforts with leather went well, he was a nice man, and happy. But when his pieces didn't sell and money was tight, he'd start drinking. It was at those times that Rogan had become a shadow, hiding from all that focused rage.

Sighing, Rogan unfolded his arms and continued to walk, more slowly now as those unbidden images from his childhood welled up within him. Oh, Great Spirit, how he wished he could get rid of those memories! Just forget about them! But how could he? At age sixteen, after being beaten with that strap, Rogan had stood up and fought back. He'd taken his father's whiskey bottle and struck his out-of-control parent in the head with it. Don Fast Horse had died instantly; a large wedge of glass had penetrated his skull and lodged deeply into his alcohol-saturated brain, or what was left of it.

Smiling slightly, Rogan watched the women begin heading to the cookhouse for breakfast. Some were yawning. Others were brushing their long, black hair or braiding it as they walked. One thing they all had in common was abusive backgrounds. These women had come from alcoholic or fetal alcohol families just as he had. And they'd suffered more or less the same as he.

Except none had gone into juvey hall for killing their father, as Rogan had. Only, as a teen, he couldn't be placed in prison, so the judge had made him stay in there for two years. That was fine with Rogan; it was a helluva lot safer than being at home, and he'd taken advantage of the white man's education available while he'd been incarcerated.

His mother, a meth addict, came to visit him once or twice, early on. Her face scarred from meth use, she was little more than a bumbling idiot, as far as Rogan was concerned. On the res, no one had intervened on behalf of himself or his younger brother and sister, both of whom had run away. Out of some stupid idea of protecting his mother, he'd been the only one to stay at home. What a fool he'd been!

Exhaling slowly, Rogan watched as more of the women tumbled out of the dorms and headed to breakfast. He could smell pancakes on a hot griddle, and his stomach growled. But he didn't feel like company this morning. He preferred to focus on the past and how it had shaped him.

After escaping the toxicity of their family home on the Tahlequah, Oklahoma, reservation, his sister, Sally, had gone into prostitution in Los Angeles. Rogan had discovered her fate when the cops came to juvey hall to tell him his sister had died of a drug overdose. Dead at age fifteen, at the hands of her unhappy pimp. Rogan recalled sobbing alone in his room. He'd been put in solitary confinement because he'd gotten into a fight with a bully, busting the white kid's nose and taking out two of his front teeth. Rage over his father, who had sexually molested Sally from babyhood onward, had sickened Rogan. He hadn't blamed her for running away; he'd wanted to leave with her. But who would take care of their mother? He was the oldest, so it was up to him.

218 HEART OF THE STORM

And then, six months before his release from juvey hall, Rogan had gotten word that his brother had been murdered in New York City. Eagle Wing had become a mule, someone who willingly swallowed plastic bags of cocaine and brought them from South America to the U.S.A. Only Eagle Wing had been found with a bullet hole in his head, his body gutted, his intestines pulled out and the plastic bags of coke removed. Eagle Wing was tough and combative, but the weekly beatings by their angry father would make anyone that way. Rogan had cried then, too.

And when they'd given him his freedom on his eighteenth birthday, Rogan had gone back to the res to see his mother. She was still hooked on meth, looking like a leper, the sores on her body discharging terrible odors. And her mind was almost eaten up by the terrible drug. She'd barely recognized Rogan when he came back to the house—a house that held nothing but nightmarish memories for him. Rogan recalled his mother looking at him as if he were a stranger. Only after they'd talked awhile did she remember him. To Rogan's sorrow, she didn't seem to recall Sal or Eagle Wing at all.

Rogan had left, completely depressed, and angry at the white man's world. He would do better for himself, he'd vowed. One thing Rogan had learned from his life was that whoever had the power had control. And that was something he'd

sworn *he'd* have: control and power. No one would
ever abuse him again. No one would take control
away from him, either.

Spotting Blue Wolf, Rogan scowled. She was
wearing tight jeans that did nothing for her thick
body. And she was walking with her dearest friend,
Alice White Elk, a woman from another tribe.
They chatted and laughed, the sound carrying me-
lodically across the empty yard.

Hatred welled up in Rogan. She was taking his
power away from him now as surely as his father
had taken it away from him as an innocent and un-
protected child.

Moving his lips to form the word *bitch,* Rogan
leaned against the stockade wall, feeling the rough
bark through the fabric of his long-sleeved cotton
shirt. He unbuttoned the cuffs and rolled them up
to just beneath his elbows as Blue Wolf disappeared inside. Now, the familiar smells of frying
bacon, hot cakes and coffee mingled in the cool
mountain air, but Rogan scarcely noticed them.

Blue Wolf *was* like his father, he decided. How
could he have been so blind to her real ambitions,
and chosen her to carry the Storm Pipe? Although
his father was an idiot, he'd known how to wrest
control from Rogan and his siblings.

Blue Wolf was far more sneaky and subtle about
it, and Rogan had recognized that fact far too late.
She was not a product of fetal alcohol syndrome,

but she did come from a family of drug users. And she'd done cocaine as a teen. Later, she'd been slapped into a women's federal prison for ten years for selling the drug.

Facing the acid truth of his faulty judgment, Rogan began to amble along the wall again, hands clasped behind his back as he mulled over his complicated relationship with Blue Wolf. They'd been together nearly thirty years. She'd been his lover, his guide, and had never taken power away from him before this. Yet now, with her being the keeper of the ceremonial pipe, Rogan was seeing huge shifts in how she worked with him. Blue Wolf was no longer obedient. No longer the follower. No, she knew she had a special pipe and that she was in total control.

Bitter over that admittance, Rogan scratched his head and walked toward the closed gates of the compound, where one woman soldier was always on duty.

What to do about Blue Wolf? Rogan couldn't just kill her outright. Visions of tossing her over the wall and down that three-thousand-foot cliff warmed his knotted gut. But who would then carry the Storm Pipe? Who among his other eleven women would obey him and not get ideas of power and control in her head as Blue Wolf had?

Rogan thought about Star Woman, who was forty. She was half-Cherokee and half-white. But she was willing to please and grateful to be involved in his quest for power. She'd been a pock-marked kid and her face permanently scarred when Rogan had lured her into his arms. She was ugly, that was all there was to it. She'd come out of a home of ten children, and being one of the youngest, she'd been ignored. Star Woman lapped up any attention. Perhaps Rogan could manipulate her to take on the handling of the Storm Pipe after he got rid of Blue Wolf.

Yet did Star Woman have the necessary grounding, the ability to handle the power of the pipe as Blue Wolf did? Rogan pondered that tricky question. Not everyone could manage the raw, universal energy. There was a recipe, if Rogan could call it that, to handling such a pipe. Carriers had to be completely grounded and in their body. They had to have unshakable focus. They were, body and spirit, the receptacle for a pipe's energy. Most of all, maturity was essential. Did Star Woman have the necessary qualities?

Rubbing his chin, Rogan wheeled around and headed back along the wall. She was the youngest woman, dammit. Too malleable. Handling the invisible energy of a ceremonial pipe would be too much for Star Woman. Yet, she was the easiest to manipulate from his band of women....

For some reason, Rogan looked up just then into the ever brightening sky. When he spotted a huge, black raven flying overhead, croaking raucously, he scowled. He hated ravens and crows. They were the tricksters. The magicians. When one showed up, it meant something was about to go wrong. What the hell was it this time? Birds were always messengers. Who was coming? Rogan didn't like unwelcome guests appearing at their compound. It happened from time to time.

Stupid white folks on vacation, lost and unsure of how to get back to Carson City. Off-roaders who'd taken their four-wheelers in the wrong direction. *Damn.* Rogan didn't want tourists intruding on the busy agenda he'd laid out for today. They had a test run as a group scheduled for later that morning. Blue Wolf would have the Storm Pipe, coddled to her ample breast. It would not be smoked in these trainings. The other women would sit in a circle, knees and hands touching, to form a funnel through which the energy of the pipe could pass. Such training was essential so that nothing would go wrong during the actual ceremony.

The raven croaked again, grating on Rogan's already sensitized nerves. Lifting his hand, he gave the black, shining bird the finger. *Go to hell.*

"I THINK WE'RE LOST," Annie Ballard told Agent David Colby. She looked at the scribbled directions to Rogan Fast Horse's compound that Joe Spearling had given them earlier. Up ahead, the dirt road they were on forked into a Y. Which branch to take?

Colby grimaced and pulled off the road. Around them, sparse pines grew interspersed with sagebrush and prickly pear cacti. The east slope of the Sierras wasn't moist or verdant like the western side. The sunlight was bright and lanced through the windshield of the Toyota Land Cruiser. He punched up the air-conditioning and then ran his finger across his sweaty upper lip.

"Okay, let's look at the map," he told Annie. She handed him the open road map she held. Frowning, Colby traced their route from Carson City up into the Sierras. "The problem is this map isn't going to show all the back roads crawling over these mountains," he told Annie.

She nodded. "Plus, Joe's directions aren't exactly clear."

"That's because he's a local. He knows the roads up here. For him, the map made sense, but for us out-of-towners, it doesn't." Colby removed his sunglasses and glanced around. The road was crossing a long, sloping meadow dotted with chunks of black basalt, cactus and yellowing grass.

"My intuition tells us we're near Eagle's Nest, where Joe said this medicine man, Rogan Fast Horse, lives." Annie pointed to the left fork, which meandered upward across the rough terrain. "That's the way. I feel it in my gut."

David folded the map and handed it back to her. "Hey, you have a fifty-fifty chance of being right. Let's take the high road. We're on an adventure." His watch said it was near 11:00 a.m. They'd eaten breakfast earlier at a Denny's Restaurant. Annie had packed them a lunch, and now he was glad she had. The sky was an intense blue, with high, filmy white clouds that resembled strands of a woman's hair. The day was beautiful, and he found himself enjoying Annie's company as well as the rugged natural surroundings.

Chuckling, she put the road map away, but continued to hold Joe's map in her hand. "Lead on, Macduff! I'm excited about meeting this medicine man. I'm hoping he'll be able to help us."

"Don't get your hopes up," David murmured. "The FBI has a jaded history with Native Americans. Wounded Knee pretty well killed any goodwill between us and them—not to mention trust."

Annie thought about the incident on the Sioux reservation decades before, in which an FBI agent had been killed. A Native American had been charged with the crime, but Annie had read enough about it to realize that maybe, just maybe, the wrong Indians were in prison. Colby was right that the event had forever changed how Indians saw the FBI.

"Okay, I'll try not to get my hopes up too high," she promised the agent. Still, she was eager to meet a real medicine man. What an honor and an opportunity!

CHAPTER SEVENTEEN

WHAT WAS SHE GOING TO DO? Dana sighed and sat on a flat boulder. She was five miles from the winter hogan. Wednesday morning's sky was apricot-colored, infusing her pounding heart with awe and appreciation as she cooled down from her daily run. Wrapping her arms around her drawn-up legs, she studied the orange ribbon of light silhouetting the mountains in the distance. The strong, steadying scent of sagebrush filled her lungs.

As beautiful as the morning was, Dana felt as if a proverbial nest of snakes had moved into her heart and gut. No matter what she did, how much she tried to forget Chase's kiss, she couldn't do so. Couldn't escape it or hide from it. Since that incident, Chase had been quiet and painfully distant. Was he sorry he'd kissed her? More than likely.

Dana watched a black-eared jackrabbit hop from sagebrush to sagebrush, always alert for a nearby coyote. She felt much like the long-eared animal. She'd been playing hide-and-seek with Chase since that sudden burst of intimacy. Rubbing her damp brow, she closed her eyes and tried to steady her heartbeat. Why did Chase have to kiss her? Did he realize he'd awakened her, made her want to live again? More than likely he did, being a metaphysician like herself. They were far more sensitive to other people and their thoughts than most individuals. Dana was sure Chase could read her mind if he really wanted to, although she was certain he respected her enough not to go there. At least, most of the time. Otherwise, how had he known she needed to be held, kissed, protected?

In the distance, she saw movement. To Dana's delight, it was a herd of about twenty tan-and-white-coated antelopes, foraging on cactus and dried tufts of grass. She was sure they knew she was here, and didn't seem at all threatened.

Absorbing the healing qualities of dawn's stillness, Dana contemplated the new day. It was yet to be written, yet to be acted upon. Dawn was a symbol of birth. Father Sun rose in the east, and on the medicine wheel, that was the direction of giving birth on some level of one's self.

The apricot color intensified as the sun inched closer to the horizon. Dana loved this moment, where Mother Earth herself seemed to hold her breath as Father Sun rose to announce the day.

Whether he knew it or not, Chase had birthed a

new era for Dana. And right now, with the mission bearing down on them, something good stirred in her yearning heart. Her grief still held her captive to the loss of her loved ones, but not as much as before. If Chase could see her aura now, her fields probably looked like a witch's brew of conflicting energies.

Focus on the positive, she told herself.

As she continued her daily morning run, the pronghorns came within a quarter mile of her. Dana appreciated their small, gazellelike bodies, their spindly legs so thin they looked as if they could snap. Their coloring helped them blend in perfectly with the desert plains. What she liked most about them were their huge, shiny black eyes, which missed nothing. They would reach down, grab some grass, then quickly lift their head again, looking around as they chewed. They were always on guard and wary. And so must she be on Saturday morning, when she and Chase would scale the cliff to Rogan's compound.

Slowly rising, Dana dusted off her gray sweatpants and turned around. As if knowing she was no threat, the antelope kept on eating. She had another five miles to jog, back to the winter hogan. *Good.* It was so tough to face Chase, to look at him and avoid gazing at his sensual mouth. Maybe, in that five miles, she could build up enough resistance against him and his masculine charisma to focus on the mission. As she began to lope down the sandy trail between the sagebrush, Dana wondered if Chase was at all disturbed by their hot, incredible kiss. He seemed absolutely impervious, as if it was in the past, done and completely forgotten. Was it? Did Chase consider the intimacy with her as part of his "duty" to Grandmother? To do whatever he must to prepare her to retrieve the Storm Pipe?

Determined, Dana focused on the path and picked up her pace.

CHASE SENSED Dana's return from her morning run. This was his favorite time of day—early morning, when dawn and quietude blanketed Mother Earth. The sacred silence was pregnant with life, and as he stood over the small woodstove, stirring scrambled eggs, Chase absorbed the healing energy with pleasure.

Already it was Wednesday. Tomorrow they'd leave for Carson City, Nevada. They'd arrive Friday morning, and go check out Rogan's Eagle's Nest compound. And then, early Saturday morning, under cover of night, they'd climb that cliff, enter the compound and steal back the Storm Pipe. It sounded so easy.

Frowning, Chase added chopped-up Bermuda onion, diced ham and slices of red and green peppers to the heaping mound of scrambled eggs in the iron skillet. As he stirred the colorful mixture, the smells stirred his dormant sense. He had biscuits rising and browning in the oven. He enjoyed cooking. It wasn't a task to him. Cooking was about life, about appreciating the colors, the fragrances. It was about eating the food that plants and animals gifted to humans so they could continue to survive, with gratefulness.

Chase sensed rather than heard Dana's approach. The door to the hogan was open, rays of sunlight slanting in silently. Though his heart sped up, he focused on making breakfast. Trying to ignore Dana after their kiss was like trying not to breathe.

He picked up the handle of the skillet with a pot holder, walked over to the small table and put half of the Denver mixture on Dana's plate, and half on his. As he set down the skillet in a basin filled with dishwater, it sizzled and spat, sending steam roiling upward like angry clouds. He grabbed some sliced sharp cheddar cheese and plopped it on top of the eggs.

Hearing Dana's footfalls, Chase went to the oven, opened it and retrieved half a dozen browned biscuits. As he put them on a plate, she entered. Her hair was in braids, with runaway tendrils around her face from the run. Her golden cheeks were stained pink, her cinnamon eyes dancing with life. When she smiled tentatively, Chase put a choke hold on his body, so he wouldn't respond to her.

"Come on, you're just in time," he growled.

After setting a jar of honey on the table, he retrieved the percolator and poured steaming coffee into the chipped mugs.

"Smells wonderful, Chase. Thank you." Dana quickly got out of her running shoes and padded over to the table. She'd already taken off her sweatshirt, the white tee beneath it clearly outlining her lean upper body. Sitting down, Dana cast a quick glance across the table as Chase sat opposite her.

"You're welcome," he said, then dived into the hot, steamy food. "How was the run?"

Dana ate the delicious scrambled eggs with relish. "Fine. I saw a herd of antelope this morning. There were some cute babies at their mama's side."

Chase slathered butter and then drizzled honey across a biscuit. "Good sign. Antelopes always bring a sense of peace."

Far from it, as far as Dana was concerned. She nodded and continued to eat. Because the table was so small, their knees would sometimes touch. Chase seemed uncomfortable with the contact, but Dana enjoyed the physical connection with him. "I'm hoping for peace after we get the Storm Pipe back," she said wistfully.

Chase quirked his mouth and took a sip of coffee. "I wish that, too, but we don't know what Rogan will do once he finds it missing. I'm worried he'll try to track us on the Other Side, find our energy trail and come physically to take it back. He'd do it, too."

"I keep reminding myself Rogan is a sorcerer and that's what he does best—hunts and follows trails of unsuspecting prey."

"Before we climb to his compound, we need to cloak ourselves and our energy very carefully. I'm assuming there are guards inside the fortress. As I mentioned earlier, you'll have to travel astrally to check out the layout inside and find where the pipe is hidden."

The flaky biscuits were Dana's favorite. She followed Chase's example with melted butter and honey, then sank her teeth into the warm, sweet bread, as she thought about astral travel. The skill came naturally to her, passed down through the family lineage. She had the ability to leave her physical body and travel at will through the world, to a different galaxy or even to another dimension. It took years and years of dedicated practice to perfect astral travel. What made this attempt worrisome for her was the danger she'd be under in the process. Chase seemed to have confidence in her skill, but Dana had misgivings. If she couldn't astral travel, which was very possible under such stressful circumstances, that would leave them wide open to discovery. And she couldn't do it beforehand for fear of Rogan or his women being tipped off to their plan to scale his stronghold. Scaling the cliff would be damn stressful, not to mention life-threatening. Dana wasn't sure she could focus enough to accomplish the feat, but she had to try.

"I'm worried some of Rogan's medicine women are just as good as we are, metaphysically speaking. There might be one who sounds the alarm even if I astrally travel into the compound." Dana knew that a person with strong clairvoyant talents or skills as a medium could detect her presence or actually see her. And that would ruin their cover and sound the alarm.

Raising his head, Chase saw the worry in Dana's expression. He could spend a lifetime just watching her eat. The way her lips glistened, the way her eyes darkened when she became lost in thought… Groaning to himself, Chase felt helpless with Dana so near. She was so damn touchable. And he wanted her. All of her. In every conceivable, pleasurable way.

Focusing on her concerns, he cleared his throat. "It's doubtful. Rogan has certain skills. I don't believe he'd work with anyone, especially a woman, who is better than he is."

"Do you think he will sense me coming?"

Chase shook his head. "Grandmother seemed to think his skills in astral detection are not that well honed. I hope she's right." He turned back to his scrambled eggs. Before cooking for Dana, Chase hadn't paid much attention to food, especially since his release from that hellish South American prison. Oh, he ate, that was for sure. But now, in her gentle, soothing presence, food tasted delicious to him as never before. Dana's energy made Chase feel so alive, more sensitive to his surroundings. She was like a rainbow in his life. His favorite times of the day were when they ate together. Dana was his dessert, even if she never realized it.

Chase was glad she didn't know how he felt. She'd been hurt enough; he didn't want to wound her any more than she already had been.

"When you move astrally into the compound, everyone except the guards should be asleep. You'll cloak your energy trail to keep the possibility of detection to a minimum. In the astral, you'll see the colors and glow of the Storm Pipe. You'll be able to locate it pretty easily, I'd think."

Nodding, Dana finished off her mountain of scrambled eggs. Daily ten-mile runs left her famished. "I worry a little about getting out of my body, Chase." She got up, put her empty plate in the basin and returned to the table. Picking up her coffee, she said, "The stress, you know? I've never attempted astral projection under a situation like this."

"I know," Chase agreed, hearing the anxiety in her tone. He put his own plate in the dishwater, then picked up the coffeepot and refilled their cups. "It takes intense focus," he agreed, sitting back down. Holding her guarded gaze, he added, "Focus and nonstop concentration. You've trained all your life for this moment, whether you realize it or not."

"You're right," Dana admitted sourly, sipping the hot coffee. Her nerves sizzled as Chase gave her that hooded look that made her blood race and her heart pick up in beat. The man was so ruggedly good-looking, and Dana felt she could drown in his eyes. Right now, all she wanted was to melt into him and be one with him. Wrestling with her selfish desires, she managed to say, "I'll probably do it, because I'll be so scared for both of us that I won't dare lose focus."

Chase smiled lazily. The way his mouth quirked drove Dana crazy with the yearning to kiss him again. Did he want to kiss *her?* Had it been a one-time deal only? She hoped not, but she understood that the mission came first. And as Chase had warned her many times before, they might not survive.

"Being scared is good," Chase assured her. He picked up the last warm biscuit, opened it and offered her half. Dana took it and smiled in thanks. When their fingertips met, Chase felt an electric current leap up his hand and into his arm. That was the kind of effect Dana had on him: electric. He was sure she felt it, too.

"I have a lot of fear to work through," Dana admitted as she buttered her half of the biscuit. "You have a lot more training in that area than I do." She grinned as she dripped honey on top. "My mom used to call me 'scared little rabbit' when I was young. She threatened to name me that." Dana recalled the teasing that her mother had given her over her fearful reaction to many things around her.

"How old were you then?" Chase tried to imagine Dana as a child. She would have been pathetically thin, like a greyhound.

Shrugging, Dana laughed. "Five, maybe. I was afraid of my shadow at that time. I used to have such scary, violent and frightening dreams."

"Hey, any young child is naturally going to be frightened," Chase declared, enjoying the biscuit. "The world looks pretty big through a five-year-old's eyes, don't you think?" He liked the way Dana licked the honey from her long, elegant fingers. He had to place a steel clamp on his desire when he felt his body tightening.

"I suppose," she sighed. "But the nightmares really fueled my fears."

"What were they about?" Chase wondered if Dana's mother had held her, rocked her and made her feel safe after some of those hideous dreams. He was sure she had. The woman had carried the Storm Pipe, after all. She must have been an exemplary mother.

"Fighting." Dana finished off the biscuit and wiped her hands on the paper napkin. "Blood, gore, screams, dying, stuff like that."

"What did your mom say about them?"

Picking up her coffee cup, Dana said, "That they were past-life memories that I still hadn't disconnected from. She told me I had been a warrior in many lifetimes. My mother would hold me on her lap. She'd explain to me that over time, the past would shut off like a faucet, and the flow of memories would finally leave me alone."

"Did they?"

"By the time I was nine, they were gone." Shivering a little, Dana held his intense gaze. "I still find it hard to believe I was a warrior. I killed a lot of people, from what my mom told me. What I saw back in the Middle Ages was gruesome. The Crusades… I get a lump in my throat just thinking about it. I can't even kill a fly or an ant in this lifetime. I'm glad those memories are walled off in me, because they would be too overwhelming."

Without thinking, Chase reached out and gave her hand a gentle squeeze. Dana's eyes grew huge with shock and then something else that started his heart thudding. He quickly released her fingers and castigated himself. Once more, Chase found himself wanting to protect Dana. She deserved protection. Maybe she wasn't a warrior in this life, but death had followed her anyway. "I'm sure it was overwhelming."

Feeling tense, Chase pushed his chair away from the table. He had to create space so he wouldn't reach out and touch her again. "Do you recall other lifetimes or just those?" While desperate to get on another topic, he couldn't help but notice the disappointment in Dana's eyes when he'd released her hand.

"I've had glimpses of other lives when I meditate," she admitted. "Peru is a place I have lived many times. And in the Far East. I've had lifetimes as a Chinese man and woman. I was a Chinese herbalist when I saw the British sail into our bay for the first time. Later, I went through the history books and found that event had really happened." Her hands still tingled wildly from Chase's touch. The contact had been so unexpected, but so wonderful.

"That's a good way to double-check those past-life movies, as I call them." Chase pointed to his forehead. "My movies often show me snippets of my many thousands of lifetimes."

A wry smile crept across Dana's lips. "Same thing happens to me. It really is like a movie. Sometimes I cringe over some of the things I've done."

"None of us have had stellar lifetimes," Chase agreed. "How could we? We reincarnate in order to learn right from wrong. We commit many mistakes to learn morals and values. And it's damn painful most of the time."

Finishing off her coffee, Dana smiled. "Yes, but with each lifetime we accrue more knowledge through experience. Over time, that *does* make us a better human being. We make progress. At some point, we transcend the animal side and become more spiritually minded, more compassionate."

"And that," Chase said, grinning as he scraped the chair back and stood, "is when you get tests like this one. This one life has come about because of the hundreds you've lived before."

Dana looked up at him, appreciating his masculine power, the hard angles of his body. "Yeah, but I'd really like to get past all this blood, gore and life-death stuff. Wouldn't you?"

"Sure," Chase said, picking up the flatware and taking it to the basin. He grabbed a cloth and began to wash the dishes. "When we've evolved so much that we no longer need to reincarnate into third-dimensional bodies, we'll cease to fight, or to attract life or death matters. This is one time, Dana, that our lives are worth the cost of going after the Storm Pipe."

Rousing herself, she watched as Chase busied himself at the sink. "I know. I just hope I can overcome my fear and perform. I don't want to let you or Grandmother down." She saw Chase's questioning glance. For a moment, Dana felt as if she'd been blanketed in an invisible energy of the most wonderful kind. He had sent an energetic gift to her. Accepting the embracing warmth, which carried with it such peace, she gave him a small smile. "With your help, I know I can do it."

"That's the spirit," Chase murmured. "And even if you don't believe it, you are a warrior, Dana. It's inside you. You may not look or feel like one, but believe me, there's a warrior woman inside of you." And he prayed to the Great Spirit that Dana would never have to tap into it.

But on their mission, she just might have to. Chase had real concerns. What if Dana saw someone die? What if she saw him kill one of Rogan's women, or Rogan himself? Would her disgust with him drive her away? That thought scared him ten times more than scaling that cliff or climbing into Rogan's compound.

"I like the idea of Grandmother having both of us go on this mission," Dana said. "You make me feel safe, Chase." She felt such relief to share that tidbit with him. She tried to steel herself against any negative reaction he might have to her truth. Instead, Chase turned, wiped his hands with a nearby towel and leaned back against the counter. There was such care and thoughtfulness in his expression. Usually, he kept what he was really feeling from her.

"I'm glad, Dana. Because if anyone deserves protection and care, it's you." And the Great Spirit knew how badly he wanted to give her those things—for the rest of their lives. Only one roadblock stood in the way of that dream: Rogan Fast Horse.

CHAPTER EIGHTEEN

ROGAN WAS ENJOYING an early lunch in his room when there was a sharp knock at the door. He'd made it clear he wanted no interruptions. His Wednesday-morning quiet had been broken.

"Come in!" he snarled, setting the plate of eggs and bacon aside on the bedstand.

Jeanne Bright Sun appeared and gave him an apologetic look. "Rogan, I'm sorry to bother you—"

"I gave orders not to be disturbed, dammit!"

She scrunched up her brow. "I know, but a couple of people are down at the gate asking for you."

Rogan wiped his hands on the thighs of his jeans. "Me?" He looked at his watch. It was 11:30 a.m. "They must be lost tourists. No one is looking for me."

"Um, I don't think they're tourists. The woman, an Annie Smith, said she needed to talk with you. She sounded like it was urgent."

Rogan didn't know the name. Instantly, he

went on guard. "What kind of identification did they present?"

Shrugging, Jeanne said, "The man, a Ron Connolly, said they were sent up here to the Eagle's Nest by Joe Spearling."

Joe he knew. But Joe understood Rogan didn't want unexpected visitors. The trading post owner was rich and powerful, and Rogan had curried favor with him for over a decade. Sometimes he would give him a gift, some insignificant ceremonial item, and Spearling would almost swoon with joy.

Rogan gave no one his phone number, which was unlisted. So these two people, whoever they were, had had no way to contact him beyond coming up here without an appointment.

Studying Bright Sun, who was in her early forties, Rogan noticed her shifting nervously from foot to foot. Though she wore camouflage and boots, her black hair was in braids and tied off with red yarn and eagle feather fluff. "Who did they say they were?" he asked.

"The woman, Ms. Smith, said she's a psychic. She showed us a sketch of details of a dream she had. She'd shown it to Mr. Spearling and he suggested they come up here to talk with you."

"Damn. That's all I need—some ditzy space cadet dreamer right now."

"I don't trust the man, Rogan. I felt his energy. It's closed and he's hiding something."

"Oh?"

"Yeah. Blue Wolf happened to be at the gate when they drove up. She told me to tell you the dude looks like an FBI agent."

Rogan's gut knotted. Had the FBI found him out? Did they know he'd nailed the vice president with a ceremonial pipe? Sweat popped out all over Rogan's body. "This doesn't make sense! A psychic with an FBI agent?"

Jeanne shrugged. "I know. It does seem strange. Do you want to see them or do you want me to send them on their way?"

"Take them to my office. And while I keep them busy, you and Blue Wolf search their car and see what you can find. If anything raises suspicion, bring it to me." Rubbing the back of his neck, Rogan stood. "I feel bad about this. The energy is off."

"Blue Wolf feels the same way. She doesn't trust the guy."

"Act like nothing's wrong. Escort them to my office. Smile and be friendly."

"Right away." Jeanne turned on her heel, thudded down the wooden steps of the porch and headed for the gate.

Rogan inhaled deeply and slowly. He automatically cloaked himself in a bubble of protection, so that if this woman really was psychic, she wouldn't be able to pierce his energy field and find out anything about him. On the other hand, he sure as hell was going to look into their auras to see who *they* really were.

ANNIE NEARLY GASPED when Rogan Fast Horse entered the small office. She was using the fictitious name of Smith to protect her identity. He looked very much like the man she'd seen in her upsetting dream. Alarm spread through her, though she suppressed her reaction. This was a powerful person.

The medicine man was tall and lean, in his forties, his black hair interspersed with silver, pulled back in a long ponytail that grazed his shoulders. He wore jeans, cowboy boots, a black leather belt with an oval of turquoise on the front, a white shirt with pearl buttons and a deerskin vest.

The colorful beading designs on the vest intrigued Annie, but she didn't have time to absorb it all. Around Rogan's neck was a dark-brown necklace. He had a long, narrow face, and his eyes were a brilliant blue, large and close together. His nose, hooked and crooked, told Annie that this man had been in a scrape or two. She could tell it had been broken at least twice.

"Welcome," Rogan purred as he reached across his immaculately kept oak desk, hand extended to the woman first. "I'm Rogan Fast Horse, and you are…?"

Annie had been sitting beside David in the visitors

chairs, and quickly got to her feet. She felt dizzied by the power around this medicine man. Rogan's voice was mellow compared to the fractious energy she felt swirling around him. As she gripped his long, lean hand, Annie noticed that his nails were carefully manicured. She found his palm firm, but without calluses or any hint that he did hard work on a daily basis as a cowboy would. This was a man who liked the finer things in life. So, was he a wolf in sheep's clothing? Did he wear cowboy duds to hide behind? And if so, who was Rogan Fast Horse?

"A pleasure to meet you, Mr. Fast Horse," Annie said. As she quickly released his hand, she had the maddening urge to wipe off his energy.

"Please, call me Rogan," he insisted, giving her a slight smile.

Annie felt a swift change in the air around the medicine man as he smiled perfunctorily at David, who was using his undercover name, Ron Connolly. The medicine man's eyes narrowed just a hint, nothing obvious. His voice was smooth and welcoming as he pumped Colby's hand. She sensed Rogan did not trust the agent. They needed to get their information and go.

"I hear from my friends at the gate that you wanted to see me?" he asked Annie, focusing on her. "That Mr. Spearling sent you up here to find me?"

Eagerly, she sat down again, drew out the sketch and handed it across the desk. She made sure to prevent physical contact with Rogan. "Yes, I did." She filled him in on the dream that had prompted the drawing. The moment Rogan looked at the sketch, his smile dissolved. His thick, dark brows drew into a V. As she finished her story about the vision, Annie gave him a hopeful look. "Does this mean anything to you, Rogan? Mr. Spearling said it was probably a pipe. We know nothing of pipes, so he felt you might be able to help us."

"I see…." Rogan dropped the sketch on his desk. His heart was pounding like a sledgehammer. But a long time ago, he'd learned to keep a perfectly calm expression. If his drunken father didn't see any reaction, he'd leave Rogan alone. The moment he revealed any feelings, his father would explode and beat him up.

Propping his fingers together, Rogan leaned back in the chair as if in thought. "It could be many things, Ms. Smith."

"Oh, call me Annie, please."

"Of course," he murmured, giving her a sweet smile meant to lull her into a vulnerable state. At the same time, he started emitting golden threads of energy that had hooks attached. He consciously sent them into her chakras. When they fastened there, Rogan could start sucking life energy out of her aura without her ever knowing about it. Symptoms were generally mild—sudden tiredness at the same time every other day or so, for example.

Most people thought it was fatigue and not a sorcerer pumping energy out of them.

But Rogan got a rude surprise when all the lines of energy suddenly boomeranged and snapped back toward him. Whatever or whoever she was, she had a hell of a defense system up and in place, aurically speaking. Keeping the frown off his face, he destroyed the hooks before they reached his own field. Did Smith know what she was doing? Bright Sun had said she was a psychic. Maybe she knew enough to protect herself around a stranger. Or maybe she knew a lot more.

"This sketch…have you had dreams like this before?" he prompted.

"Uh, no." That was a lie, but Annie wasn't going to tell him the rest of the story. She saw Colby shift uncomfortably in his chair. Even though the FBI agent wasn't psychic, Annie was sure he was picking up on the energy around Fast Horse. The man was like a power station. And a person with that kind of energy had to be watched—carefully.

"I see. Well…" Rogan cleared his throat and idly gestured toward the sketch. "I suppose it could be a Native American pipe." He gave her a dazzling smile. "Whatever possessed you to put a lightning bolt on the long end of the L shape?"

"I saw it in my dream."

Rogan kept his unease to himself. The wooden stem that fitted into the Storm Pipe *had* a yellow lightning bolt running the length of it. This woman's psychic abilities were more than alarming. "Interesting," he murmured. "And this dream just came out of nowhere?"

"Yes, that's how I receive information." Annie smiled and tapped her temple. "I have no control over this, of course. I get what I get."

Rogan moved his eyes to appraise Connolly, who seemed relaxed but alert. The man wasn't saying much of anything, and Rogan wondered why he was there, if not in some official capacity. Moving his gaze back to Annie, Rogan said, "And this dream had to do with what? There must have been a reason for it?"

"I don't know, Rogan," she said. Another lie. She sensed it had to do with the death of the vice president in some way. Pointing to her drawing, she asked, "Can you tell me if a Native American pipe could kill a person?"

Rogan's mouth went dry. "I think you've been reading too many Indian mysteries written by white men," he joked, laughing.

"I guess so. I really don't mean to insult your ways. We know so little about them, and Mr. Spearling felt you might be able to help us sort truth from fiction."

As he sat up, Rogan's hands came down on his desk. "No problem, Annie. Though I'm afraid I can't tell you much about a pipe, because it's sacred and secret knowledge."

"You're a pipe carrier, Mr. Fast Horse?"

Rogan's gaze riveted on Connolly, who was studying him intently. "Why, yes, I am. Which is why I can't tell you much. We're sworn to secrecy." He relaxed back into his chair. "You could consider pipe carriers sacred, who took an oath to defend and protect the vulnerable." He slanted a glance at Annie, who seemed disappointed. "So, I'm sure you can understand my position."

"*Is* the sketch of a pipe?" Connolly asked.

"I really don't know."

"Do the stems on the pipe ever carry drawings or carvings?"

The man was beginning to get under his skin. Rogan didn't like him at all, didn't like the look in his eyes or the feeling around him. "I wouldn't know, Mr. Connolly. As I said before—sacred is secret." *It's not for dumb white folks like you to know,* he retorted silently.

A sense of danger flooded the room. Annie could feel it. Rattled, she realized Rogan disliked David Colby. Maybe *hated* was a better word, but Annie couldn't logically go there. The medicine man was studying the agent as if he were a rattlesnake that should be killed. "Well, listen, we won't take up any more of your time, Rogan. We appreciate that you tried to help us."

Annie heard a disturbance behind her. The door to the office opened and she recognized the woman at the gate, Jeanne Bright Sun. Her round face, once smiling and friendly, was filled with rage. What scared Annie was the fact she had an M-16 rifle in her hand now and wore what looked like a Kevlar vest.

"Rogan, Blue Wolf found this in the glove box. Look." The woman tossed him a black leather identification wallet.

Rogan caught the case and opened it.

Annie reeled from the sudden energy change. Bright Sun waited at the door, the M-16 in hand, her face grim.

"Son of a bitch," Rogan snarled, dropping the case on his desk. He glared up at Colby. "You're an FBI agent." Without a thought, he pulled a pistol out of a drawer, cocked it and aimed it directly at the man who represented everything he hated.

"Wait!" Annie said, rising out of her chair.

Bright Sun stepped forward, gripped Annie's shoulder and shoved her violently back down. "Sit still, white woman. I'd like nothin' better than to blow your head off." She snapped a look at Rogan. "Is she FBI, too?"

"No," Colby growled. "Only I am." He held Rogan's black, glittering gaze, the barrel of the 9 mm pistol staring him in the face. "She's just a psychic, someone I hired."

Bright Sun snorted and pulled out two pairs of handcuffs from her military web belt. "Here, Rogan. You want to do the honors or should I?"

"You do it," he ordered. His gaze never left the agent's pale face. "So, why are you here, Mr. FBI man? You lied. Your real name is David Colby."

When Colby said nothing, Rogan's face turned from tan to red. The pistol never wavered.

Annie felt Bright Sun grab her wrist and cinch the metal cuff around it. "Wait! You can't do this! Let us go!"

"Shut up," Rogan barked, without looking in her direction.

"What do you want done with them?" Bright Sun demanded after she'd cuffed the agent, too.

Rogan lowered the pistol. "Put them in the main lodge. Chain one to each of the two main poles. They can sit there and think about why they really came here." He suspected this whole thing was a setup, that the U.S. government had somehow figured out that they had killed the vice president. He saw Annie Smith's mouth fall open. Was she for real? Or just playing a role, as the agent had done?

"Blue Wolf found no identification papers for this woman?" he asked.

Shaking her head, Bright Sun said, "Give me her purse. I'll check it out."

Rogan grabbed Annie's bag from beside the chair and tossed it over. He lifted the pistol as

Bright Sun opened it and shook out the contents onto the floor. After rifling through them, she crowed, "An ID badge case." She flipped it open. "Oh, shit, Rogan…she's CIA! Look." She passed the badge to him. "And her real name is Ballard, not Smith."

Rogan eyed the identification. "A CIA remote viewer?" Nostrils flaring, he glared at Ballard. "You're good. But not good enough. Now I know why you had that energy shield up around you. You damn well know what you're doing."

Gasping as Bright Sun jerked her out of the chair, Annie cried, "We're not your enemy! You have no right to keep us here! Let us go!"

Rogan snorted. "Since you're a remote viewer, then you oughta be reading my mind to know what I'm going to do next to your white asses."

CHAPTER NINETEEN

"READY?"

That one word sent a spasm of raw fear through Dana's gut. Chase had mouthed the word quietly as they stood in their climbing gear below the Eagle's Nest. It was Friday night; darkness had come and they had to make the ascent into Rogan's lair. Flexing her fingers in the light, thin leather gloves that would protect her hands, she whispered, "Yes. I'm ready."

Just having Chase at her side imbued Dana with the courage she needed. The wind picked up, whipped around and then ebbed away. Below them, on the Nevada plain to the north, lights sparkled like colorful jewels. That was the capital, Carson City. Dana could hear the highway traffic passing far below them.

Chase double-checked his gear. Lightning flashed nearby, and he scowled. They wore radio headsets, the microphones near their lips so they could quietly communicate with one another as they climbed. "Looks like the thunder beings are coming our way." He pulled his night goggles into place so he could see through the darkness. Everything took on a grainy, green appearance.

"The storm spirits know we're going to try and rescue the ceremonial pipe," Dana told him. "My mother would always see them come and be present just before she used the pipe."

Chase settled the night goggles gently over Dana's eyes and made sure the strap was firm around her head. "I have a feeling it's going to pour. If it does, that'll make our climbing even more dangerous."

Her scalp tingled where his fingers brushed her hair. "They're our friends. They aren't here to harm us, Chase."

Snorting softly, he automatically checked Dana's climbing harness. They were dressed in black spandex from head to toe. The material was no protection against the wet and cold, should it rain. "You're ready to go. So am I. The only problem is every time there's a flash of lightning, our night vision is destroyed for a minute or two until our eyes readjust. Can you ask them to move away so we aren't blinded every few minutes?" Chase knew the thunder beings could be talked with, pleaded with, but ultimately, these huge sky spirits would do as they damn well pleased.

Giving a soft laugh, a nervous one, Dana said,

"They don't usually listen to me, Chase. You know that. But they know the Storm Pipe is in trouble, in the wrong hands. They know we are going to try and save it. They're around to help us."

Planting the first titanium piton, with rubber coating on the top of it to prevent noise from occurring, into the basalt, the hammer looped around his thick wrist, Chase began the slow, arduous task of leading the way up the cliff. "Just plead with them not to rain on us, eh?" Chase knew this was impossible. He'd said it in jest, to ease the tension he'd heard in her voice.

Dana moved behind Chase as he began to put the pitons in place, like a ladder leading up the vertical cliff. Here and there on the rock face were ledges where small junipers or other vegetation tried valiantly to survive. They reminded Dana of some people's lives, so precarious and harsh.

There were four trees along the route of their three-thousand-foot climb. Chase had planned that at each one they'd rest, recoup, drink water to stay hydrated, and then move up to the next one, until they reached the compound wall at the top. The lightning flashes momentarily exposed his shadowy shape and then temporarily blinded her. Dana shut her eyes, realizing how dangerous the lightning was to her night vision. Hanging in the harness, her boots planted firmly against the basalt wall, she touched her night-vision goggles and waited impatiently for her eyes to readjust.

Silently, Dana sent a plea to the approaching thunderstorms to veer away from them and their route. She felt Chase heft himself upward. The nylon rope between them grew taut. They were climbing a few feet at a time. Swallowing against a dry, constricted throat, she found purchase with both hands and followed him up the craggy face.

The wind was erratic. Gusts pounded against them as they inched their way upward in the blackness of the night. Dana's hopes fell as she realized the thunder beings seemed to be ringing the area where they were climbing. She sensed their impatience. The storm clouds seemed not only to grow larger and more powerful, but the sky spirits started to move in—toward them.

As Dana climbed, trying to focus intently on each handhold, her fear grew over the possible run-in with Rogan Fast Horse. Were he and his band of women waiting for them? Dana and Chase had taken great precautions to cloak their energy, so they could not be detected by even the most psychic within the group. But things happened and mistakes could be made.

Another flash of lightning shattered the darkness. Dana heard Chase curse softly beneath his rasping breath. Pressing herself against the jagged cliff, Dana closed her eyes. She knew now to wait at least a minute before opening them and moving on.

As she clung to the cliff, the wind buffeting and slamming against her, Rogan's leering face suddenly loomed in front of her. Dana gasped, totally unprepared for this vision of his lean, angry features. What the hell was going on?

"TELL ME WHAT YOU KNOW or I'll slit your throat," Rogan rasped into Ballard's bloodied, bruised face. He saw her blackened eyes open to slits in response to his guttural threat. His fist ached from the blows he'd delivered. Not wanting to break his hand on the CIA bitch, he breathed, "Tell me or I'll—"

"I don't know *anything!*" Annie cried, blood leaking from her split lip. She was bound to a chair, her hands behind her, the ropes cutting off their blood supply. She had to protect David Colby!

Heart pounding, she saw Rogan's mouth open in a snarl, revealing his yellow, pointed teeth. Her stomach ached where he had repeatedly hit her, and tears leaked from Annie's eyes. "I don't know anything!" she repeated. "I told you what I know." Bloody spittle spewed from her contorted lips, which were fat and swollen from him slapping her. Her head spun. What was happening to Colby? Was someone beating him up like Rogan was her? This was the last thing Annie had expected. She was a remote viewer, who spent her days sitting in a nondescript room with a table and chair. That was all. She wasn't trained as a spy. Nor trained to endure interrogation. Now, with Rogan's face inches from her own, his fetid breath spilling over her like that of a bull in a rage, Annie realized she was probably going to die.

"You had that dream about that pipe."

"Y-yes. I didn't know it was a pipe, though. I—I just saw the shape of it."

"And you saw the lightning mark on the stem."

"Y-yes, but honest to God, I didn't know what it was!" she screamed into Rogan's face, her fear mixed with rage. "I still don't!" Annie wasn't a fighter by nature. She believed in peace, and desperately wanted peace for this world. And yet she was facing a medicine man who had murder written in his blue, shining eyes, and he was going to kill her.

Blue Wolf jerked open the door to the small inner office in the lodge. "Rogan!"

Snapping his head up, he growled, "What?"

Blue Wolf glared down at Ballard, then shifted her focus to her partner. "We got storms coming. A lot of them."

"So what?" he demanded, taking a cloth and wiping the blood off his knuckles. Ballard's blood.

"If we think the FBI knows about us, about our plans—"

"Shut up!"

Taken aback, Blue Wolf slammed the door and crossed her arms. "Don't you tell me to shut up!" Her breathing became raspy and uneven. "We haven't gotten anything from Colby. He's playing dumb. I know he is." She jabbed a finger toward the white woman bound in the chair. "You got anything more out of her?"

"Not yet." Rogan made a cutting gesture toward the door. "Let's talk elsewhere." He glanced down at Ballard, whose eyes conveyed terror. As they should.

Spinning on her heel, Blue Wolf left the room. Once Rogan joined her, they walked down the corridor toward the ceremonial area. The lights in the hallway flickered as lightning lit up the darkness outside the glass doors. "Damn storm," she growled. Turning, she glared up at Rogan. His hair was disheveled and he was nursing his right hand. "The Storm Pipe knows something's up."

"I think the FBI is onto us," Rogan rasped in a low tone. He didn't want his voice to carry back to Ballard. "Isn't Colby telling you anything?"

"Nothing. We're beating the shit out of him and he's not talking. The FBI could know about us, about the pipe."

"Ballard is holding to the story of having a dream about the Storm Pipe," Rogan said unhappily. His knuckles were bruised and swelling.

Never mind that the CIA agent had lost a couple of teeth; his knuckles throbbed with pain and he wanted to put ice on them.

"Colby is hiding something, but I don't know what. Every time I try to get into his mind, he repels me. He's stronger than I thought. Have you been able to get into Ballard's head?"

Rogan scowled. "Not yet. But I'm close. I wanted to soften her up. She's pretty scared. And when a person's scared, they lose their focus, and their protective shields drop. I'm close."

"Well, get it done. Colby's a trained agent, but I don't think Ballard is. As a remote viewer, she probably sits in an empty room with a pad and paper, and astrally travels to wherever she's sent." Blue Wolf winced as a bolt of lightning struck very close to the compound. "Damn, the thunder beings are restless."

"Well, of course they are! I've decided tomorrow we're going to use the pipe instead of Monday. They're excited. I think this is a good sign. Don't you?"

Blue Wolf looked at him. "They've never done this before. These are angry thunder beings, Rogan. I don't know if they're friend or foe tonight. I've tried to talk with them, but my pleas are falling on deaf ears."

"The Storm Pipe is secure, though?"

"Of course. On the altar gathering force in the

middle of the lodge," she said, pointing down the hall.

Rubbing his face, Rogan muttered, "I think our best chance is through Ballard."

"Then go back in there and read her mind, dammit! If the FBI know about us, we need the information *now*. That means we gotta get out of here and drive for the Mexican border. Tonight." Her mouth thinned. "And if you aren't up to it, I'll dig into that white bitch's brain. She can't be that strong."

Rebuffed by Blue Wolf's arrogance, Rogan growled, "You should talk. You can't even get into that FBI agent's head. You leave Ballard to me. Let's go back and probe their minds." He looked at his watch. It was near midnight. "Meet me here in thirty minutes. We'll compare what we managed to dig out of them."

"Good plan." Blue Wolf turned and quickly walked down the hall.

As Rogan turned the other way, another bolt of lightning slammed into the ground, shaking the building, though it was sturdy as a Quonset hut. Frightened by the nearness of the strike, Rogan paused. A pissed-off thunder being could hurl a bolt and easily kill a person. What was going on with this storm? This had not happened before when they used the Storm Pipe. What was different this time?

Angry and anxious, Rogan stalked down the

hall, determined to try and get into Ballard's mind. One way or another, he had to learn what the FBI had planned. As he walked, he felt a sizzle of warning, of danger, shoot up his spinal column. Halting, he jerked his head up and looked around.

Rogan knew that signal. *Danger!* Danger was near. Was it the FBI coming for them with specially trained SWAT teams? Rubbing his neck, he picked up the radio from his belt and depressed the switch. "Bright Sun?"

"I'm here. What do you want, Rogan?"

"You've got four women on guard duty tonight around the compound?"

"Of course, just like you asked. It's quiet. It's starting to rain, the wind is awful and lightning is everywhere. I've never seen a storm like this before."

"Keep your eyes and ears open, in case we're being stalked by the FBI. They could be out there. We hope to have more information from our prisoners in a little while. In the meantime, stay alert."

"This night is hellish, Rogan, but we're like wolves with our ears up. Don't worry, we're making sure no one can get near the compound without us knowing it."

"You got your night-vision goggles on?"

"Of course. But the damn lightning destroys our sight for minutes at a time. There's nothing we can do about that."

"I understand," Rogan said, frustration in his

tone. "Okay, keep checking in with me every fifteen minutes, like before. Out."

As he jammed the radio back into his belt, Rogan couldn't shake the feeling of being stalked. Certain that it was the FBI, he jerked open the door to the office. One way or another, he was going to get information out of this bitch of a white woman.

THE WIND WAS VIOLENT, shaking and pummeling Dana as she clung stubbornly to the slippery, wet basalt. The storms had begun in earnest near midnight. She and Chase were halfway up the cliff. Above her, she heard his labored breathing as he worked to set the pitons, one after another, into place. The sounds of the hammer were further muffled by using a rubber mallet. They didn't talk much. Chase was afraid that Rogan might have radio equipment that could pick up their conversations. If Dana needed anything, she was to jerk twice on the rope strung between them.

Another bolt of lightning flashed above them. Closing her eyes, she heard Chase grunt. Had he reached the second shelf, jutting out of the side of the cliff? Dana hoped so. The nylon rope tightened. Yes, he had. The silent signal meant "climb" and that's what she did. Her vision was still foggy, but she brushed the basalt with her fingers until she found solid handholds. Shifting her right foot upward, Dana found purchase. Her rope tightened more. It was good to know that Chase was at the other end. He wouldn't let her fall. That gave Dana confidence in the midst of the violent storm.

As she finally lunged onto the flat rock shelf next to Chase, the rain began again. Only this time, hail pummeled them, as well. This shelf was much smaller than the first one they'd discovered on their climb. Shivering, Dana pushed the night goggles up on her head and scooted into Chase's extended arms. The ledge was less than four feet wide and three feet deep. There was barely room for one person, much less two. As the lightning flashed, she saw his grim features, his mouth a slash, his own night goggles pushed up on his head. It was hard to tell whether his face was gleaming from the sweat of exertion or from the deluge.

Feeling suddenly safe in a chaotic, unsafe situation, Dana huddled against his hard, warm body. She slipped her right arm around his torso and absorbed the heat he emitted like a furnace. His arm closed comfortingly around her shoulders, drawing her near. Dana moaned with relief. She felt his lips, his hot breath, against her ear.

"Okay? Turn off your radio. We can whisper back and forth and no one will hear us."

Nodding, Dana did as he instructed. Lightning zigzagged across the heavens and for a second she saw the turbulent, churning clouds. There was no question that the thunder beings were upset. Dana prayed that the spirits were aligned with them on their mission. Otherwise, they could hurl a bolt and kill them in an instant. So far, Chase and Dana had been left alone.

"Why such a violent storm?" Chase asked near her ear. He selfishly absorbed the feeling of Dana's strong, graceful body pressed against his own. She was shivering, and that wasn't a good sign. The temperature had dropped when the storm had broken. They were at an 8,500 elevation, and cool weather was the norm even in the summer months. Dana would have to concentrate later on her astral traveling, once they reached that fourth shelf about thirty feet below the cliff top.

"I don't know, Chase. I've tried to talk to the thunder beings, begging them to leave, but they aren't listening to me. It seems we have four or five storm cells around us, and they just keep circling." The hail continued, slashing downward. Dana held up her hand to protect her eyes from the onslaught. "I don't know what's going on."

With his face turned away from the raging wind, Chase whispered, "I think they're pissed. But at us? With what we're doing to get the Storm Pipe back? That doesn't make sense. Were they ever like this when your mother worked with the pipe?"

Closing her eyes, Dana shook her head. "No. Oh, the thunder beings always showed up before Mom was going to use the pipe, but never like this. I don't understand it, and they're not talking to me."

The hail stopped as suddenly as it had started. For a moment, the rumbling of thunder eased. Chase caressed Dana's shoulder. She was soaked to the skin. "How are you doing? You're shivering."

"I'm cold, Chase. All our climbing, night and day, we did in good weather, not rain. I sure wish I had a fleece jacket to put on about now." Dana gave a slight, strained laugh.

Chase kept rubbing his large hand up and down her arm to increase circulation, to warm her. "I know. Makes two of us. Damn, this weather is weird." Chase glared up at the roiling heavens.

Dana felt like a sponge magically absorbing Chase's warmth as he rubbed her arm. "Maybe something else is going on that we don't know about. The thunder beings always mirror what we two-leggeds do. And it feels like they're really upset. I don't think at us, but maybe that Rogan is going to use the Storm Pipe very soon."

"Could be," Chase agreed. The rain began again, the wind pushing it horizontally. Turning, he tried to protect Dana from the pounding spray. He held her in his arms, hoping his body heat would warm her and his bulk shield her from the driving deluge.

Moaning softly, Dana took off her night goggles and held them as Chase pulled her into a tight embrace. Being able to nestle her head beneath his strong jaw, his body a wall protecting her from the worst of the rain, was wonderful. "Thank you. You're the best fleece jacket a girl could have," she whispered. When he laughed, Dana felt some of her stress and anxiety dissolve.

"Hell of a place to tell the woman I like that I care a lot for her. I have to get you up on the face of a cliff, on a tiny shelf, to let you know how I feel."

His words warmed her even more than his body did. Chase's courage fueled hers. Leaning upward, her mouth near his ear, she said, "I feel the same, Chase. Something happened when you kissed me last week. At first I was in shock, but later, your kiss somehow helped free me from the past. It let me know I had a present and a future for the first time since I lost Hal and my mother." There, the truth was out. Dana held her breath after her confession. How would he react?

Closing his eyes, Chase hungrily absorbed her soft admission. "Listen, after this is all over, Dana, I want our relationship to change. I don't want to be your teacher or a hard-ass. I want to have the time, the right, to get to know you as the beautiful heart-centered woman you are." Gulping as the rain sheeted down on them, Chase added, "More than anything, you've got to know you hold my heart in your hands, Dana." It was as close as

Chase could come to telling her he was falling helplessly in love with her. And he was sure the Native American expression would not be lost on her. She would understand exactly what he was saying to her.

The lightning flashed savagely above them, so close Chase swore he could smell the ozone released. Only this bolt struck inside the compound above them. Wincing, he felt the shuddering vibration not only through the air around them, but through the cliff, as well. That was close! What the hell was going on up there?

All Chase knew was that Dana was in his arms, as he'd dreamed of so many times, clinging to him. Closing his eyes and resting his jaw on her wet hair, he prayed to the Great Spirit that both of them would survive this hellish night. He wanted a life with Dana. He wanted the time to explore her, get to know her in so many sweet and wonderful ways. As the thunder shook the mountainside, Dana clung to him. He clung to her. The world was turning inside out around them. Chase had no explanation for all this commotion. He knew two things: first, that they had to find the Storm Pipe and steal it back. Secondly, that he loved Dana.

Would the Great Spirit allow them to celebrate their love for one another? Would they be discovered and killed? Chase was uncertain. As the rain ran down his hair and face, he wanted more than anything else the chance to love Dana. And there was no guarantee he'd ever get it.

CHAPTER TWENTY

DAVID COLBY WANTED to scream. He had no control over the horrific events that were rapidly unfolding. Rogan Fast Horse had dragged Annie Ballard into the main lodge, where David was cuffed to one of the huge lodgepole pines. The woman, Blue Wolf, smiled as Rogan hauled the badly beaten psychic in and hurled her to her knees in front of the agent.

"Now," Rogan snarled, holding the gun to Ballard's skull, "you either tell me why you're really here or I blow her head off. I'm giving you to the count of three. One…two…"

Colby croaked. His gaze was riveted on Annie's swollen face and blackened eyes. "Don't hurt her, for God's sake! We came here because of her dream!"

"Liar," Rogan snarled, his finger squeezing the trigger.

With that one movement, Colby's world up-ended. His shriek of helplessness coincided with the gun going off. In shock, he watched Annie's lifeless body drop in front of him, blood and brain matter splattering everywhere. Breathing chaotically, he cried, "You didn't have to do that. Annie's innocent. She had a dream. Just a damn dream, you son of a bitch!"

Blue Wolf rushed him, drawing back her fist, encased in brass knuckles. He was in such deep shock over Annie's murder, that he didn't brace for what was coming. Seconds later, his head exploded with pain.

Simultaneously, a bolt of lightning struck just outside the lodge, illuminating the room with ten million watts of light. His vision graying, Colby fell to the side, his arms taking all his weight because he was cuffed around the pole. The last thing he felt was the lodge shaking with thunder.

Wincing, Rogan held up his hand against his eyes as another bolt of lightning struck. Blue Wolf cried out and sank to her knees. The lodge trembled violently. Breathing hard, blinded by the light, Rogan stumbled, tripping over Ballard's lifeless body. The revolver flew out of his hand as he braced himself for the fall, hitting the cedar floor with a thud and rolling to absorb the blow. Long moments later, Rogan got to his hands and knees. Rain was coming down in a deluge the likes of which he'd never seen. The cedar shakes were banging as if a million hammers were pounding it.

Cursing, Rogan struggled to his feet, dazed.

What the hell had just happened? His gaze cut to Blue Wolf, who looked stunned and frightened.

"What's going on?" he screamed above the unending noise. Moving swiftly, he recovered his pistol and thrust it into the holster at his side. He barely gave Ballard a glance, instead training his gaze on his partner. "Dammit, Blue Wolf, snap out of it! What the hell is happening? Why are the thunder beings hurling bolts at us?"

The wind rose, shrieking like a banshee. The cedar lodge quaked and rocked. The rain pounded down from the heavens.

Blue Wolf scrambled to her feet, terror sizzling through her. "Rogan, you shouldn't have killed her. I thought you were just threatening her, dammit." Jabbing her finger toward one of the large, square windows, the medicine woman screamed, "They're pissed off at you, Rogan! The thunder beings don't like what you just did! Now we're really gonna pay for your stupid move!" She scurried to the door and yanked it open.

"Hey!" Rogan yelled. "Stop! Where are you going?"

Jerking around, she shouted, "As far away from you as I can get! I'm telling the women to go to the dorms, and we're waiting this out. You stay the hell away from us until this weather blows over."

"Go to hell!" Rogan shouted back, shaking his fist at her. How he wanted to pull his pistol out and shoot her in the head. But he couldn't do that. He needed Blue Wolf to work with the Storm Pipe tomorrow.

He watched the woman run out the door, leaving him alone. Breathing harshly, his chest rising and falling, Rogan looked around. He was frightened that a bolt of lightning might rip into the lodge and snuff out his life. How the hell could he know the thunder beings would be pissed off at him for shooting Ballard in the head? She was only a white woman! Didn't the sky spirits know that? Wiping his mouth with his trembling hand, he felt perspiration dotting his brow. His hand was bloodied with bits of Ballard's brains. He decided to go wash up. This storm would blow over soon.

Turning jerkily, Rogan stalked across the lodge to the bathroom at the other end. By the time he washed up, the FBI agent would have regained consciousness. And Rogan would interrogate him personally. If the bastard wouldn't talk, he was going to meet the same fate Ballard had. Then Rogan would have his women go dig two graves high up in the Sierras, a long way from Eagle's Nest, and bury them. Where no one would ever find them.

THE STORMS NEVER STOPPED. Dana continued to climb in the blinding rain, the night-vision goggles protecting her eyes. Despite the cold, whipping wind, the nonstop deluge, she felt warmer. Hope spiraled giddily in her heart. Chase's words had warmed her spirit and energized her physical body. She was no longer shivering. Whatever magic had occurred on that ledge was like a healing balm to her wounded soul and heart. Chase wanted a relationship with her.

With each step upward through the flashing lightning and rumbling thunder, Dana felt safe and hopeful. Hope was a protection all on its own. So many good things had happened despite the fury of the thunder beings.

Dana had never seen such a storm, but she knew they were wanting her to steal the Storm Pipe back. Return it to the Blue Heron Society, where it rightfully belonged. She felt this was the spirits' way of protecting them. In such a storm there would surely be no sentries out on guard duty, Dana thought optimistically.

Water ran in rivulets down her face. Her thin leather gloves were soaked and her fingers began to go numb. That wasn't good, because she couldn't feel the handholds on the sharp basalt. Dana was afraid of falling. Oh, it was true her nylon harness and rope were hitched to Chase, but if she fell it was doubtful he could hold both of them on the side of this cliff.

When would it end? They were headed for the last ledge, about thirty feet below Rogan's compound. Dana felt fairly confident no one would be out in weather like this.

Once Chase reached the last stone shelf, which jutted out in a point, almost like an arrowhead, he hauled Dana up and into his arms. He heard her soft laugh of relief as he held her.

Chase gave her a swift hug and reluctantly released her, so she could sit beside him. It was 4:00 a.m. With the angry thunderheads rumbling around them, dawn would come late, and Chase was glad. They needed the cover of darkness. After taking up the ropes, keeping them neatly coiled, he pushed the goggles off his face. He wiped his eyes and turned toward Dana, who was doing the same.

"Catch your breath, woman of mine. You're going to have to get quiet, go inward and travel astrally now." Fumbling, he found her hand and squeezed it gently. When Dana returned the squeeze, Chase's heart opened with such joy that all the pain from the brutal, demanding climb momentarily left his limbs.

He hadn't meant to say "woman of mine." The words had slipped out before he realized it. But if Dana minded the endearment, she didn't say so. Instead, Chase saw the white flash of her teeth in the darkness. Her smile was an unexpected gift to Chase as he sat on the cold, slippery ledge, huddled next to her.

"Okay, Chase, let me get centered." Dana handed him the rest of her nylon rope. Water was running down the cliff face in small cataracts. The rain had slackened, thank goodness, and suddenly even the winds hushed.

As she closed her eyes, her heart pounding and her body trembling from exertion, she felt Chase's hand again wrap around hers. The connection made Dana feel loved in a night fraught with danger. Chase knew enough not to speak. To try and astral travel with thunder and lightning dancing around them was worrisome enough. Another human voice, a jarring touch or an unexpected sound could snap her out of her focused state. If that happened, her astral body would come slamming back into her physical form, shocking and stunning her for an hour or more. It could leave her partially paralyzed, feeling nauseated or dizzy. No, it wasn't a pleasant experience to have one's astral form snap like a rubber band back into one's body.

Inhaling through her nose, Dana took the first of three breaths, drawing air deep into her abdomen. As she slowly released the inhalation, her breath became her focus. She performed the breathing technique and simultaneously visualized silver tree roots gently twining around her ankles, the tips of each going down through her feet and then diving deeply into the soil of Mother Earth. This was to keep her grounded, a necessary precaution to anyone attempting astral travel. Whatever Dana viewed with her astral eyes had to be sent back to her physical body and brain, to be noted and remembered. She'd spent ten years practicing this technique, with her mother's instruction and support. Now it was all going to pay off, Dana hoped.

A dizziness washed through her as she exhaled the last deep breath. With her eyes closed, she began to see a flickering purple light in the center of her forehead—at her brow charka, or third eye. As the color swirled, moving like a whirlpool in a clockwise direction, Dana became less and less aware of her physical surroundings.

Dana no longer felt Chase's warm, rough hand around her own. The thunder became distant. The wind no longer ruffled the damp, stringy hair plastered to her face and neck. Moving into the whirlpool of purple hues, Dana sensed lightness. The heaviness started to dissolve. And then she heard a vague popping sound. Suddenly, she was buoyant, like an escaping balloon, and ready to astral travel.

Dana got her bearings and switched to seeing through her astral eyes. Instead of the grainy green smudges of her night goggles, she saw the shapes and outlines of objects, including the living electromagnetic energy that throbbed around them. And she saw them four-dimensionally. The colors were many and varied, and it took her moments to recognize the wooden wall of the compound. First things first, however. Dana cloaked herself in a silver-white bubble of light for protection. It was energy armor that no one could penetrate. If there was a clairvoyant in that compound who was awake, he or she would not discover Dana skulking quietly among them.

Floating upward, she headed over the wall and drifted toward the buildings. She was searching for a particular energy signature, and she found it. The Storm Pipe had a blue auric field, to denote Father Sky and the thunder beings. Blue sky, blue energy. It was really very simple. Dana hovered near the wall and noted a bluish-white light flashing like a beacon within the compound. Moving forward like a feather in the breeze, Dana followed the light until she was just above the main lodge's cedar shakes.

Dana scanned the area, but saw no one out on this miserable night. At least in astral form. Even though rain continued to fall more gently than before, she was impervious to it. The lightning had waned, too, although Dana saw cloud-to-cloud forks and flashes.

She could feel her heart beating hard, pumping heavily as if it were a pulsing cord connecting her physical body and her astral one. She felt no fear. Just anxious to see exactly where the pipe was located.

Because she was in a pure energy form, Dana was able to drift down through the roof of the lodge into the building. Walls were no deterrent to her entry or exit. As she did, Dana froze near the ceiling. Below, she saw Rogan Fast Horse with a man who was handcuffed to a large, central pole. Rogan struck him repeatedly with his balled fist. Dana watched as blood spurted out of the man's broken nose and from his split lips. To her horror, she saw a dead woman nearby, her blond hair soaked in blood. Terror sizzled through Dana. There was nothing she could do to help the man, whoever he was.

She struggled with her shock and turned away from the traumatic scene. She couldn't be diverted from her main goal. She had to find the Storm Pipe! Moving like a silent apparition, she floated through several walls, one after another, the blue light becoming brighter and more intense. As she slipped silently into a room halfway to the other end of the lodge, Dana finally saw the pipe. When she entered, it blazed with intense and swirling turquoise and cobalt colors, as if welcoming her.

Hovering over the pipe bag, the same one her mother had held and used for so many years, Dana felt a surge of raw emotion. The Storm Pipe was resting on an altar, the stem next to it. The door to the room was unlocked. Rogan must have felt very safe to allow it to be exposed like this, Dana thought.

She dared not speak to or touch the pipe. Dana knew it had bonded with someone in this compound. And if she did anything to trigger it, the owner would know and sound the alarm that an intruder was in the room. No, best to leave now.

She could hear Rogan's shouts, flesh striking flesh, as she floated away from the lodge, and her stomach turned violently. She had to concentrate hard to memorize the layout of the buildings, and her head was beginning to ache. Where were the sentries? She saw none. There were no guards at the main gate, either. Chances were the awful weather had driven everyone inside.

Moving quickly, Dana left the compound and descended the cliff, very slowly and gently slipping back into her body. When her astral feet were locked into place with her physical ones, Dana let out a long, tremulous sigh. She squeezed Chase's warm hand to let him know she was back.

Carefully turning toward him on the narrow ledge, Dana quickly shared what she'd seen. She spoke in hushed tones, her lips occasionally brushing his ear.

Chase scowled as she finished her report. The wind was starting to pick up again. In the distance, another thunder cell advanced down the mountain toward them. Cupping his hand to Dana's ear, he asked, "Who were the man and woman with Rogan? Did you recognize either of them?"

Dana leaned against him, her hand resting against his damp chest. "I don't know them. She's dead, Chase. Half her skull is gone. It was awful."

Slipping his arm around her, Chase drew Dana close. "Rogan did that. He's damn dangerous," he growled. "I'd sure like to know who his victims are."

"I don't know. I wish I did, but I don't, Chase."

"It's okay. We need to move *now*. Maybe we can save this guy from Rogan. The pipe is first, though. We need to scale the wall, drop down on the north side of that main lodge and slip in the back door. While you're retrieving the pipe, I'll go and try to save this dude's life."

Dana gulped. Her heart was slamming into her rib cage. She was shaking—the aftermath of seeing the murdered woman and the bloody, violent scene, she was sure. "Y-yes. I'm ready. Are you?"

"It's a go, woman of mine." Chase turned to her. In a flash of nearby lightning, he saw her large, beautiful eyes. Dana's lashes were thick, and he felt like spiraling into her lustrous gaze. "I want to kiss you…" he rasped. "For luck. For love…"

"Yes…." Dana met his mouth with a hunger that surprised her. As Chase's lips joined hers, the restless, stormy, chaotic world around them ceased to exist. His strong fingers moved across her cheek, threaded through her damp hair and cradled her head. His breath was hot, his mouth hungry and restless as it melded with her own. Moaning, Dana matched the ferocity of his need for her. Chase's returning groan vibrated through her like the rumble of thunder. It was a wonderful, sizzling sensation, and Dana absorbed it like the thirsty earth in need of rain.

For two years, the idea of sex and sharing herself with a man had never entered her consciousness. Not until now. Not until Chase Iron Hand had entered her life. As the wind rose, whipping around them, Dana realized how intense, yet how momentary, their kiss really was. They could be killed. Shuddering as she recalled the astral view she'd had of Rogan, Dana concentrated on Chase's searing mouth, his lips taking her places she'd never been before. Her body ached to mate with him.

But it wouldn't happen now…and maybe not ever. For they had a mission to carry out. As Dana broke their kiss, their breathing ragged, she understood the fragility of life as never before. This could be the last kiss they ever shared.

CHAPTER TWENTY-ONE

WITHIN FIFTEEN MINUTES, Chase was up and over the high wooden wall. The timbers were each set in concrete on the edge of the cliff. Inside one wall, there were bracings every five feet to keep the wall upright and strong. When he jerked the knotted rope, Dana quickly followed and heaved herself upward. She had left her safety harness behind, which made the last few feet the most dangerous. They could not risk having the pitons being hammered in this close to the fence. Another storm was breaking over them, the wind tearing at her clothing. The pack on her back made the climb more difficult as the wind caught it. Dana ignored the buffeting. She had to focus. If her wet gloves slipped on the rope, she could fall three thousand feet to her death. As she tried to put that terrifying possibility out of her mind, she twisted the rope around her arm and pulled herself upward, closer and closer to the top. Time had halted. Rain slashed into her face, but the night goggles protected her eyes. Just a few more feet…

A powerful gust slammed Dana against the rough wooden palisade. One of her hands slipped off the rope and she dangled precariously. The wind slapped her to the right and then the left. She was on a slowly moving pendulum, the dark chasm below illuminated by lightning flashes. A croak escaped her as she twisted.

"Dana!"

Chase's harshly whispered command roared into her frantic mind. Gulping, Dana knew what she had to do. She had trained for this. She had to stop panicking! But as her fingers slipped down the knotted rope, Dana felt as if she was going to fall to her death. *No! Oh, Great Spirit, no! Give me strength! Help me!*

"Turn around!"

Chase's deep, implacable order shattered through Dana. Another gust of wind struck, turning her so that her belly was flat against the wall. With a grunt, feeling her right arm weakening by the second, Dana threw her left hand upward. Her wet glove met the rope. *Grab the knot!* Groaning, her right shoulder burning like fire, Dana curled her fingers around a knot in the nylon. *There.*

She caught her breath and pressed her feet together on a lower knot, so that they took most of her weight. Her right shoulder burned so badly she felt it going numb. Had she torn her rotator cuff? Chase had always warned her about climbing with both arms, never just one, for fear of injuring a shoulder.

"Dana! Are you okay?"

His urgent tone now was like a slap in the face. Gasping and choking, the rain dripping down into her open mouth, Dana gurgled, "Yes! Give me a second…."

"Climb up now! You can't hang there!"

Dana sprang into action. She knew if she didn't get off this rope soon, she'd fall. Grunting, she made it up the last ten feet to Chase's extended arm.

The moment his strong, steadying hand wrapped around hers, he hauled Dana up to the top of the wall, as if she were a leaf in the roaring wind.

She would have fallen off the narrow ledge of four-by-fours that braced two feet inside the wall so that the sharp points could deter visitors. The ledge ran the length of one wall as a strengthening device to keep it strong. And yet Chase perched easily upon it, his balance better than hers. Relief sheeted through her as he slid his arm around her waist. She carefully turned around on the narrow shelf. The wind howled, keeping her off balance. As she gripped Chase's shoulder, her own right arm aching, Dana choked down her fear.

He dropped some coils of rope into the compound. "Squat here," he rasped. "I'll go down first. Then you come."

Dana nodded, knowing they shouldn't speak unless absolutely necessary. She crouched and gripped the top of the wall with her left hand. This allowed her right shoulder a brief respite as Chase dropped the rest of the rope and shimmied down inside the compound.

Thunder rolled and the stockade wall shivered. Chase held the rope taut. Maneuvering carefully, Dana made quick work of getting back to solid ground. The earth had never felt so good or stabilizing to her as she landed next to him. He quickly released the rope from the gaff hook that held it solidly on the top of the wall. They ran the short distance to the side of the cedar lodge.

Breathing raggedly, Dana rubbed her right shoulder, which was aching in earnest. But she couldn't dwell on the pain. Flexing her fingers, she shucked off her wet, slippery gloves and stuffed them into a thigh pocket. Chase quickly pushed the coiled rope back into his pack, retrieved two pistols and handed one to her.

The pistol was heavy in Dana's numb, wet fingers. Chase had schooled her for weeks on how to handle it, but her stomach turned at the idea of shooting someone. After seeing the murdered woman, and the man being brutally beaten, Dana knew Rogan would kill her if he caught her. She had to be ready to use the firearm.

Chase tiptoed along the edge of the building a

ways, then lifted his hand. With her night goggles in place, Dana saw the signal and quickly moved forward to where he crouched.

"Okay," he whispered, "let's enter the back door of this lodge. We don't know if Rogan is still in there. Can you feel his energy?"

Dana tried to concentrate. She hoped Chase didn't know how much pain she was in. "I... Wait..." She made another attempt to focus, but it was impossible. Opening her eyes, she murmured, "I'm sorry, Chase, I can't concentrate enough to find out for sure."

"It's okay." Chase swallowed his disappointment. Psychic functioning hinged on many factors, and was easily blocked by stress. He knew Dana was upset over what she had seen—the murdered woman, and realizing the danger Rogan truly presented to them.

Chase reached out and squeezed her hand. "Okay, we're going in. You get to the pipe. You get it in your pack and meet me at the gate."

"But what about the man in there?" She strained to see Chase's darkened features. Only when lightning flashed could she see the thin set of his mouth—a sign that he was all-business, all-military at the moment.

"I need to find Rogan. That's my priority. We need a clear shot at getting to the front gates of this compound and then making a run for it down that road. That's our plan. This guy—if he's still alive—will slow us down."

Sickened, but aware that Chase was right, Dana gave a jerky nod. They must get to the pipe immediately. She crawled along the edge of the lodge toward the door. When she wrapped her hand around the brass doorknob, it turned easily. Chase slipped inside and on down the narrow passage. Focusing her senses, and trying to ignore the pain in her shoulder, Dana started toward the area where she'd seen the pipe during her astral travels. When Chase headed in another direction, toward where she'd seen the man and the dead woman, she swallowed against a hard lump in her throat. Dana knew she had to concentrate on her part of this rescue.

The door to the small room, too, opened easily. The moment Dana stepped inside and saw the blue glow on the altar, she gasped. The Storm Pipe throbbed with such vibrancy that joy washed over her like a wave from the ocean. Quietly closing the door, she tiptoed forward. Just as she had seen in her astral travels, the pipe lay next to its wooden stem on the red cloth of the altar.

Dana shucked off the backpack and crouched before the altar. With shaking fingers she unzipped the bag. She could feel the pipe's response to her being here. She knew it must recognize her as the daughter of a woman who had once carried it proudly for three-quarters of her life.

A memory flashed within Dana's brain. She'd been barely ten years old when her mother, after meditating with the Storm Pipe one day, had come and settled the pipe bag into Dana's thin, spindly arms. Cora had smiled and instructed her on how to carry the pipe—as if it were a much loved baby. Dana recalled the happiness and warmth she'd felt washing over her like a rainbow after a storm. It was the first time her mother had entrusted her with the ceremonial pipe. And even as a ten-year-old, Dana had realized the honor of even getting to hold it. Very few people ever got such a privilege.

She slowly unwound from her crouched position. Would the woman who'd bonded with the Storm Pipe feel her here? Would she come running for it? Panic joined fear as Dana's hand hovered for a split second above the sacred object. She counted on it seeing her as a friend and not sounding the alarm. Would her mother's years of caring for the Storm Pipe be enough for it to trust her, the daughter, now? She prayed to Cetan, the pipe she left at the hogan for safekeeping during this raid. Feeling the personal pipe respond energetically to her prayer for help, Dana steadied herself.

Closing her eyes, Dana focused her intent, mentally communicating with the pipe. She begged the spirit within it to remain quiet and not give away her position.

To her relief, Dana felt the pipe promise its

silence. She imparted her next steps: rescue the pipe and bring it home. The moment she communicated the idea, a wave of delight seemed to roll through the room. That instantaneous, glad response brought tears to Dana's eyes. Yes, the spirit would entrust itself to her; after all, she was the daughter of the woman who had cared for her for decades.

With the pipe's allegiance settled, Dana wondered about Rogan's whereabouts. And was Chase safe? Feeling suddenly vulnerable, Dana gently slid her fingers around the pipe head. She retrieved a special, protective pouch from her pack and sheathed it inside. As she did so, a feeling of warmth moved through her fingers. Then a bolt of heat shot up her right arm and exploded through her shoulder.

For a moment, Dana was staggered by the sensation. The heat was so intense, she gasped. She realized belatedly that the pipe was sending healing energy to her aching shoulder.

She dropped to her knees in front of the open pack. But just as she felt relief, the lodge trembled from nearby lightning and thunder. It was a clear warning that she had to act. Her hands shook as she placed the pipe and pouch into an insulated pocket of her pack.

As she rose, she reached for the stem and slid it into a long sheepskin pouch. She tightened the drawstrings and settled it within her backpack for optimum protection.

Rain pelted the cedar of the lodge. Dana couldn't hear anything except the pinging roar of the downpour. Was the current pipe carrier aware she had the Storm Pipe now? Dana knew that the owner of any pipe had an energetic link to it, an open line strung between them. Had the Storm Pipe turned off that connection?

As she zipped her pack shut and hefted it upward, Dana realized there was no more pain in her shoulder. Stunned by the unexpected miracle, she settled the straps into place.

She took a deep breath and opened the door. The hall was empty. Her first instinct was to help the man she'd seen. She wanted to, but knew she couldn't. It sickened her that someone was suffering like that, but she remembered Chase's directive: rescue the pipe and get out. Dana closed the door and ran on tiptoe down the hall. As she went, she felt the warmth of the pipe continuing to roll through her.

At the back door, lightning flashed. Thunder followed moments later, and the instant Dana stepped into the night, rain assailed her. It felt as if the thunder beings were attacking the compound. She kept her head tucked and repositioned her night goggles.

Where was Chase? Her mind whirled over the possibilities. Had he run into Rogan?

Keep going, Dana willed herself. Turning, she ran stealthily along the edge of the lodge. From here there was a clear path to the gates, which appeared to be unbarred. That meant Chase had arrived already. Getting through the gates had been his job. She did a quick scan of the area and saw no sentries. She had to make a run for it!

The rain had turned the ground into slippery mud. Puddles were everywhere, and in places, streams of water gushed. Across the yard, Dana recognized the dorms where the women stayed. They were dark, as if everyone was asleep. But who could sleep in this hellacious storm?

Uneasy, Dana edged along the last side of the lodge. Her nerves screamed when her boots nearly slipped out from under her. The ground was like black ice, and her speed put her at risk of falling. She kept her hand against the side of the building as she ran.

She was less than eighty feet from the entrance. There were no guards out there that she could see. Who *would* be out on a night like this?

Blue Wolf jerked open the door of the dorm. The electricity had gone off during this last storm. The building was hot and muggy and she desperately wanted some fresh air. Standing out on the porch, out of the pouring rain, she winced as a flash of cloud-to-cloud lightning occurred. Because she lived in fear of being struck by an angry thunder being, Blue Wolf raised her hand to protect her eyes from the light.

As she did so, she saw a shadowy figure trotting down the side of the main lodge. Who was that? Turning, Blue Wolf wondered if Rogan had ordered whoever was supposed to be on guard duty back to the gates. Because that was the direction the figure was running.

Something wasn't right. Blue Wolf felt it in her gut. She darted back into the dorm.

"Guards, get out here! There's someone in our compound!"

Chase waited tensely near the gate. When he'd gone into the lodge, Rogan was nowhere to be found. The stranger was unconscious in the main room, handcuffed to the pole. Chase could do nothing to help him, even though he'd wanted to.

He finally spotted Dana slipping and sliding through the mud. He'd already pulled off the massive board that held the gates closed. Rain made it hard for him to see her clearly.

"Are you coming?" he rasped into the mike situated against his mouth. He stepped out of the shadows and stood at the opening, a hand on each gate so the wind wouldn't swing them open prematurely and tip off the guards.

"Y-yes...coming!"

Chase heard the panic in Dana's breathless voice. She had only ten feet to go across an open stretch. His heart clutched in his chest. Chase knew this was the most dangerous part of their operation. Dana would expose herself to anyone who might be watching from these buildings. They'd see her running hard for the gate and know it wasn't one of their own people. Pulse accelerating, Chase realized he, too, was exposed to view. He watched as Dana awkwardly started her sprint across the open gap.

In that moment, he heard the shriek of women's voices raised in alarm. Jerking his head to the left, Chase saw through his night-vision goggles three women, all armed, running toward him. *Dammit!*

"Dana! Three sentries coming my way! They're armed. Hurry! I'll open the gate and you slip out. I'll take care of them."

Danger! Dana felt it sizzle through every screaming nerve in her body. She lunged and slid through the heavy rain toward the gate. If not for her night goggles, she wouldn't see anything.

Chase's warning rolled through her like a tank. Glancing to the right, she saw armed figures running toward the gates, where Chase stood. *Oh, no!* She dug her muddy boots into the wet ground and tried to listen through her headset as she ran. What was he saying? That he'd stay behind? No, he couldn't. It was three against one!

Sobbing for breath, Dana reached the gates. Chase opened them just enough for her to pass through. She started to slow her pace.

"Get out of here, Dana! Follow the mission!"

"Chase…"

"Get the hell out of here!" He shoved her roughly so that he could shut the gates behind her.

Giving a cry, Dana heard the gates slam shut. Lightning flashed, revealing the road before her. The one she needed to run down to escape. But what about Chase? There were three armed women running toward him!

Her mind whirling with indecision, Dana lurched down the road. Like any dirt road in a rainstorm, this one had turned into an oozing mire, winding like a snake across a high meadow of cactus and sagebrush. As she trudged through the mud, Dana twisted to see if Chase had come out yet. That had been the plan: he'd meet her at the gates and they'd run away from the compound together, to a car parked two miles away, near the highway.

A gust of wind tore at her. And though the rain slackened, Dana slipped and fell on her butt. She landed hard, managing to throw out her hands to stop herself from falling onto the pipe. Covered with mud, she scrambled back to her feet and glanced around. Having rounded the first curve that was dropping slowly in elevation, she couldn't see the compound any longer. Where was Chase? She readjusted her headset, trying to hear him, but couldn't.

"Chase! Chase, do you read me?" Dana begged as she ran awkwardly down the road.

No answer.

A horrible feeling flooded her. Something was terribly wrong. She had to make sure Chase was still alive. The breath halted in her chest at the thought of being alone. She'd just found him. Had the women shot and killed Chase? Taken him prisoner?

On instinct, Dana leaped off the road. About fifty feet down the shrubby slope, she spotted several large sagebrush growing close together. Approaching quickly, she knelt by them. Looking them over, she made a decision. Dana shook off the pack and placed it in the bushy clump. No one would see it from the road.

Kneeling in the grass, her heart pounding unrelentingly, Dana tried to gather her wits. Focusing on the Storm Pipe, she mentally telegraphed that it would be safe here. She asked the spirit of the pipe not to answer the last carrier. She explained that she needed to go back and find her partner.

As soon as she'd relayed the message, Dana felt confident the pipe would remain silent. She saw a faint blue glow pulse around the pack, then fade and vanish. Grateful, Dana leaned down, pressed her palm momentarily on the pack and whispered, "Just stay quiet. I'll return for you soon."

The storm was now moving away. Dana gathered her deteriorating resolve, turned and trotted back up the slope. With night goggles, she managed to avoid the murderous thorns on the hundreds of cacti that dotted the meadow. And as she ran back to the muddy road, she sensed that Chase was in trouble—either captured or dead. Memories of this man, so warm and cajoling, so powerful and beautiful, slammed into her pounding heart. Hot tears clouded Dana's vision, and her goggles grew misty. Taking them off, Dana halted. She wiped her eyes, sobbed once, then dived deep within herself. Now wasn't the time to cry, even though she wanted to. She had to stay together. She had to *think*. Chase was in harm's way. And she had to go back and try to rescue him. But how?

Settling the goggles into place, Dana realized she'd never felt so helpless. But the closer she got to the compound, the more she felt a new strength threading through her. She recognized the feeling as love. Love for Chase.

She didn't try to deny it. Not now, not ever. As she climbed back up to that dark, threatening place, Dana knew her life was nothing without him.

Tonight, she was either going to live or die. But she could not leave Chase behind. He wouldn't have left *her,* she was sure. Somehow, she would have to use all the knowledge Chase had imparted to her over the last several weeks, get back into the compound and find him. Find out if he was alive or dead…

CHAPTER TWENTY-TWO

IN A HAZE OF PAIN, Chase slowly awakened. He tasted blood and discovered his wrists were bound around a wooden pole in the lodge. Sprawled out, his head throbbing, he caught the sound of far-off thunder. Movement to his left made him more alert. But his eye was nearly swollen shut, he found. Chase remembered having a shootout at the gate with the three sentries. They'd fired simultaneously. A bullet had grazed his left temple, and Chase remembered nothing after that.

It hurt to move from his position. Rain was drumming softly on the cedar shake roof of the lodge. As Chase fought to regain full consciousness, he looked over and saw the man Rogan had been holding prisoner. His face, badly swollen and bruised, was a bloody mess; his eyes, what little Chase could see of them, looked haunted. Chase stared at him for a long moment and saw his unshed tears.

Where is Dana? Closing his eyes, Chase forced

himself into a sitting position to relieve the pain and tension placed on his arms and shoulders. No one else was present in the large, dimly lit space. Had Dana escaped? Chase wanted nothing more than that. He flexed his hands, his fingers numb because of the tight cuffs. Dana *had* to be gone. She had to have followed their escape plan to get the Storm Pipe to safety, back where it belonged.

"Who are you?"

Chase raised his head. It hurt to move, but he looked up to meet the stranger's eyes. "In trouble. Like you."

The man's mouth moved slightly. His lower lip was split open, and blood had dribbled down his chin and onto his rumpled, filthy clothing. "We're both in more trouble than we ever wanted to be in."

"Yeah…" Chase muttered, scanning the room. The windows showed it was still dark outside. How long had he been unconscious? "What happened?" he asked the stranger, who was tied to the next pole.

"I heard gunfire. Must have been you. And return fire. About five minutes later, a couple of women dragged you in here. Rogan Fast Horse came in and cuffed you to the pole. And then all hell broke loose. There's a woman named Blue Wolf, and she came shrieking out of the room over there." The man lifted his elbow to point. "She was saying the pipe was gone. And then she switched languages and I couldn't understand anything else."

"So everyone's out looking for this missing pipe?" Chase kept the terror out of his tone. The man, whoever he was, was trying to be helpful. Right now, Chase had to try and figure out how to escape. Sooner or later, Rogan would come in here and try to pry information out of him. If he couldn't, he'd put a round in his head, just as he had that woman. Rogan was a cold-blooded killer who thought nothing of wasting a life to get what he wanted.

"I think so."

"Have they found the person who took it?" Automatically, Chase held his breath, his fingers flexing.

"I don't believe so. Blue Wolf had nearly a dozen women out running around in the storm earlier." He looked at Chase. "They know you're part of a team," he warned him in a low tone. "And from what Fast Horse said, you had better prepare yourself...."

"I think we're on the same side," Chase told the stranger. "My name is Chase Iron Hand. I'm here to help you."

It must hurt the man to talk, Chase figured, since some teeth were missing from his mouth. "I'm David Colby, FBI."

Frowning, Chase felt his head clear. "FBI?"

"My partner, Annie—" Colby choked on her name "—had a vision. She is—I mean, was—psychic. She was murdered by Fast Horse." Colby couldn't stop the tears from forming in his eyes. Feeling shattered from the inside out, he managed to croak, "Annie had a dream about an L-shaped object. We tracked it down to an antique dealer in Carson City, who said it was a pipe. He suggested we drop in and visit Fast Horse, who might know more about it." With a grimace, Colby said, "That was one hell of a mistake."

"Yeah, it would be," Chase whispered roughly. The blood from the wound on his temple had dried, and now it pulled the surrounding flesh. "I'm sure he thought you were after the Storm Pipe." In Chase's mind, there was nothing more to hide about the pipe. If he died, the FBI agent would know the truth and be able to prosecute Rogan—provided he survived.

"Fast Horse and Blue Wolf kept asking us about it," Colby said. "We don't know what it is. All I've ever heard or read about are the peace pipes from history books, when I was a kid in high school."

Managing a grimace, Chase said, "There's a lot more to pipes than that." He glanced around the room once again. "We've gotta get out of here or we're both dead men."

"I know that."

Chase heard a sound and turned his head. Instantly, his eyes narrowed. Heart banging in his throat, he couldn't believe what he saw: Dana!

Dana held her finger to her lips as soon as she spotted Chase. He and the other man were cuffed to the two center poles. She quickly shut the door and looked around. Her throat was tight with fear, her heart pounding so loudly it scared her. She almost cried out when she noticed Chase's bullet wound. If that missile had sliced even an eighth of an inch deeper, he would be dead.

Hurrying to his side, Dana squatted down and gripped his arm. "Chase! Are you okay?"

'I'm fine, Dana."

"Where's the key for the cuffs?" she whispered urgently.

Never had Dana looked more beautiful to Chase. "I don't know—"

"It's over there," Colby called to her. "See it? On that wood table opposite us." The agent gave Dana a pleading look that spoke volumes. "Get it and free us?"

Chase nodded. "Dana, this is Colby. He's an FBI agent. We need to take him with us."

FBI? Dana's mouth fell open as she stared over at the badly beaten agent. She had questions, but swallowed them for later. Had the murdered woman been an FBI agent, too? "Right." Dana sprang up and ran across the room to the table. Despite the dim light, she found the small key. Just as she reached for it, the door at the other end of the room opened. Whirling around, she gave a gasp as she saw Rogan enter. In that split second she recognized him as her twin soul. Only he was the dark half. Dana realized then that a death spiral dance would now take place. Would she die? Or would he?

The door slammed shut with a terrifying finality.

Rogan eyed the woman at the table. His gaze cut to the two men, who were still cuffed. "Well, well," he said, smiling slightly, "the fox comes back to the henhouse. Welcome, my dear. You must be Dana, the daughter of Cora Thunder Eagle, who used to carry the Storm Pipe. You are my twin soul." Rubbing his hands together, he walked slowly toward Dana, his grin fixed. "Now, why didn't I think that you might try to retrieve the Storm Pipe? Why indeed?" Rogan looked at Chase. "And you brought this big brute with you. Your guard dog, eh?"

Chase was helpless. He saw Rogan's eyes glitter with hatred. Dana had turned, her face pale. She was no match for this brutal man, and yet there was nothing Chase could do. His heart clenched with anxiety and terror. Rogan had already killed one woman. He'd kill Dana.

Choking, Chase called to Fast Horse, "She knows nothing. I know it all. You want me, not her."

Rogan kept his gaze trained on the woman in the black spandex suit. She was tall and strong. And beautiful. "I can see how much you look like your mother, Dana."

Hatred and anger replaced her terror. Dana closed her fist and crouched, knowing Rogan was going to attack her at any moment. "You son of a bitch, you murdered my mother and my husband!"

Rogan chuckled. He felt confident he could grab her, haul her to the pole and tie her up with her accomplice. "Oh, come now. All's fair in love and war. Your father was already dead years earlier. And you know the Storm Pipe is all about power. It was a power I wanted, and your mother just didn't see it that way." He raised his hands and shrugged. "What was I to do?"

Adrenaline coursed through Dana so powerfully that her head became clear, chasing out the fear. She went for her pistol. The strap was over it and Dana fumbled with a shaky hand to release it. It was kill or be killed. She had to act.

There was a baseball bat on the other side of the room. This had obviously been Rogan's weapon of choice on the FBI agent. Perhaps she should use it on Rogan. If she was fast enough.

In that moment, the medicine man leaped forward. With one swift kick, he knocked the weapon out of her hand.

Dana had been taught the rudiments of karate by Chase. As she lashed out with one booted foot, she connected solidly with Rogan's narrow chest. He seemed surprised as her sole slammed into him, hurling him backward.

Dana was knocked to the ground, as well. Scrambling to her feet, she realized she was no match for Rogan, who was a black belt in karate. Racing across the room, she heard him curse, then turned to see him getting up. She ran on, but his footfalls were heavy, coming closer and closer. Her pistol had slid beneath a cabinet and she couldn't reach it.

Reaching the corner, Dana grabbed the handle of the oak bat, spun around and lifted it with both hands. Rogan was charging so fast he couldn't stop his forward momentum. With her one slicing movement, Dana got lucky. The bat slammed into Rogan's head in a grazing blow. But it was enough!

Rogan crumpled like a felled ox to the floor, unconscious.

With a cry of relief, Dana dropped the bat. She raced back across the room, her hands shaking so badly she could barely pick up the key.

"Hurry!" Chase called, watching as Rogan lay unconscious on the floor. "Hurry!"

A peal of thunder sounded nearby, closer than any others had been in the last half hour. Dana skidded to a stop and dropped to her knees. She tried again and again to work the tiny key in the handcuffs. Finally, one side opened up. Chase quickly pulled free. In moments, the second cuff opened.

"Thanks," he declared, a look of pride on his face. "Now get Colby free. He's coming with us."

"Okay," Dana said breathlessly, glancing once again at Fast Horse. He could awaken any moment. If he did, he'd come for her. She ran to Colby, knelt and repeated the process of releasing the cuffs. The man groaned as he slowly, with stiff, robotic motions, tried to move his arms.

Chase was already on his feet and heading toward Rogan. Reaching him, he pulled the man's limp arms behind his back and snapped the cuffs in place.

Dana brought over the second pair. "Cuff his ankles, too. I want to make sure he doesn't follow us."

Grinning, Chase did as she asked. "Throw away the key when we leave, Dana. He and his women can sit here figuring out how to release him while we make a getaway. Get your pistol. They took mine and I don't know where it's at."

"Right."

Chase stood. He was dizzy but fought it off. "The pipe safe?"

"Yes." She looked up into his glittering, narrowed gaze. Even though Chase had been wounded in the head, he looked wonderful. Dana turned. "I found a way to sneak in here without being seen. Come on, we gotta leave." She looked at her watch. "It's 5:00 a.m. We have an hour before dawn."

Chase nodded. He went to where Colby was standing, near the desk. The FBI agent could barely walk. He'd been beaten repeatedly, and chained to that pole for a long time.

Despite his battered state, Colby opened a drawer of the desk. "There are more pistols in here." Picking up two, he handed one each to Dana and Chase. "Any way you can get me out of here?"

"We will," Chase assured him. "Can you walk?"

"I'll make it," Colby muttered. He eyed Rogan, who lay motionless, far less lethal-looking than before. "I need to contact the FBI office in Carson City. I'll need backup."

Chase nodded. "I'm sorry for the loss of your partner. Come on." He gripped the man's shoulder and propelled him toward the exit. "Dana? Can you lead the way?"

Already at the door, she opened it. Of the three, she was the only one who wasn't injured. The person with the least experience was now responsible as never before. Adrenaline still coursed through her system, keeping the fear at bay. "This way! Hurry!" At any moment, Blue Wolf and her women could find them.

Colby shuffled along with a decided limp, his left leg dangling as if it were broken. What pain he must be in! Chase put his arm around the man's waist and hurried him along, half carrying him. They hustled through the door. Dana gestured for them to enter the room on their left. "There's a side entrance to this lodge, through here. It opens with the compound wall three feet away. We can sneak between the lodge and the stockade to the gates."

"Good going!" Chase whispered. He was worried about the agent, who was barely able to walk. Fast Horse had probably broken his bones with the bat as he'd interrogated him. Anger churned through Chase. He'd like nothing better than to take Rogan prisoner, but right now, the odds were against that. Those women guards were killers and there were a lot of them. No, best to get out of here and plan for another time when he could find Rogan and bring him to justice.

The darkness was complete, and the rain came down at a steady pace. Slipping out the side door, Dana quickly led them to the end of the lodge. Another building six feet away was her next objective. She pulled on her night goggles and looked around. She saw no one. Beckoning for the men to follow, Dana leaped forward. Because the mud was slippery, she nearly fell, but caught herself just in time. From the shelter of the next building, she turned and saw Colby floundering along, with Chase's help. With each step, they were moving forward, out of this nightmare.

The rain was cleansing and cold, from yet another storm cell approaching. Dana almost dared to feel hope that they might actually get out of here, when she suddenly heard voices. She froze. Holding up her hand in a silent signal for Chase and Colby to halt, she sneaked to the end of the building. In the grainy green glow of her goggles, she saw two women bearing M-16 rifles standing at the open gates. Two more ran toward them, re-entering the compound from outside. There was some kind of argument going on, their voices rising in anger as the four of them shouted angrily at one another.

A lightning strike just outside the gates stopped the four women's screaming. Instantly, they scattered and ran back into the compound. The gate was now unguarded! Dana silently thanked the thunder beings, who were clearly helping them. Gesturing again for Chase and Colby to follow, Dana raced across the next space. There was a log cabin next to the gate. When she'd come back in, she'd dived behind it and worked her way between the buildings and the stockade to the main lodge. Now, she was retracing her tracks.

The wind picked up, pushing against her, but she surged forward to the end of the cabin. The men weren't far behind. Dana could hear the agent gasping in pain, and suspected he was rapidly weakening. That wasn't good. But given how badly beaten he was, Dana figured he was doing remarkably well.

Closing her eyes for a moment, she prayed to the advancing thunder beings.

"My brothers, please aid us. We need your

cover. Hide us from these women who would take our lives. Please, have pity upon us." She added, "Thy will be done."

Chase felt as if he were falling forward, a result of his head wound. Despite this, he kept his arm around Colby. His job was to get the agent out alive. The man was in bad shape and needed the nearest emergency room. "Hang on, Colby," he urged. "Once we get out of the compound, we should be safer." Or so Chase hoped.

He watched Dana turn and gesture to run for the gate. But before she moved, Chase heard a loud, thunderous *crack*. The reverberation of lightning striking the center of the compound shook the ground beneath his feet. On instinct, Chase glanced over at Dana to make sure she was all right. And that's when he saw her white teeth glitter in the dark. She was smiling.

He realized belatedly that Dana had prayed and asked for help from the thunder beings. He watched her burst from behind the building and head for the gates. Chase gripped Colby and gathered his strength. "Hang on, we're going for it."

The sharp smell of ozone permeated the air as Dana raced for freedom. Just as she passed the gate, she glanced back. Chase was running hard, Colby flapping along beside him like a puppet, without control of his legs. She knew Chase was strong and that Colby wasn't extremely heavy.

Once they were outside the compound, the rain began to fall in sheets, making it nearly impossible to see three feet in front of them. Dana joined the men, moving close to the agent and draping his free arm across his shoulders. Together, she and Chase hurried down the slope, the badly injured FBI agent between them.

The storm was violent now. Water ran down the road in a river, making it impassible. Sliding and stumbling, they continued at a trot along the shoulder. When they reached the bend near where she'd halted and turned back, Dana stopped them.

"I've got to get the pipe, Chase!" she shouted through the teeming rain. She released Colby and hurried across the meadow. Once she reached the clump of sagebrush, she was relieved to find the pack was still there. The moment Dana picked it up, she felt the pipe's warmth thrum through her shaking hands. Mentally welcoming it and asking it to remain silent, she quickly donned the pack, strapped it tightly to her body and hurried back up the hill.

Colby hung off Chase Iron Hand like a wet rag. His legs were numb. He could barely stand, he was so weak. Yet the Indian's strength, his ability to keep Colby on his feet, was amazing. Relief started to thread through the agent. For the last several hours, he'd thought he was a dead man. "You have a plan? A car?" he asked Chase.

Chase divided his attention between Dana, who was scrambling up the hill, and the agent. "Yeah, about a mile from here, down at the base of the mountain."

"And a cell phone?"

"That, too. But we're taking you straight to the nearest hospital. You're in bad shape, Colby. Besides, cell phones don't work out here. You're gonna have to wait until we get closer to Carson City."

"I want that son of a bitch," Colby growled weakly. "Drive me to the FBI office in Carson City. Can you do that? I'll get medical help later."

Chase watched as Dana moved quickly back to them. He was proud of her abilities. She'd saved their lives. All that training had paid off, more than he ever would have realized. Dana had the heart of a warrior. And any doubts Chase had had earlier about her abilities under fire were gone. The deep love he felt for her welled up in his heart and spread through him. That feeling eased the throbbing pain at the side of his head, at least momentarily.

"Got it!" Dana yelled through the cacophony of the rain. She quickly took up her position again.

"Great!" Chase grinned at her and they continued their descent, with the injured agent between them. All the way down the mountainside, the thunder beings kept up their work, hiding them from Rogan and his women. Chase breathed a grateful prayer of thanks. Clearly, Dana had her mother's abilities, for few medicine people could work with these powerful sky spirits.

The rain lightened as they spotted the rental van parked off the road in a grove of pine trees. Dana ran ahead to the vehicle. By the time Chase arrived with the agent, she had opened the side door so he could put Colby inside. His legs barely working, the agent groaned and grunted, but managed to gamely haul himself inside it. After shutting the door, Chase followed Dana around to the driver's side.

"You take the wheel, woman of mine." He gripped her by the shoulder after she'd shucked off the pack. Dana had pushed the goggles off to hang around her neck. Her hair was plastered to her scalp, her eyes shining with triumph—and something else that Chase didn't have time to decipher.

Dana gripped her pack as Chase opened the door for her. She saw the glint in his narrowed eyes. A thin, gray dawn was beginning to creep across the eastern horizon, and the rain slacked off completely. Thunder rolled in the distance, moving away from them. As she wiped her wet face, Dana held Chase's warm gaze. His intimate expression spoke volumes, and his hand felt so comforting. She began to tremble in earnest now from the adrenaline letdown. And cold. "Chase…"

"Not now, woman. Let's get this FBI agent back to his people. After that, we're hightailing it to a nice, comfortable hotel to lick our wounds."

Did that ever sound good. Dana slid in and Chase shut the door. Once he climbed into the passenger seat and strapped in, she handed him the pack that contained the pipe. "I want you to hold her," she confided, her voice quavering with feeling. "You've earned the privilege, Chase." Dana knew that a man could hold a woman's ceremonial pipe bag. He just couldn't open it or handle the pipe itself. She saw the shock registering on Chase's drawn, glistening features. Reaching out, he took the pack as if it held the most fragile treasure in the world.

Once the handoff was accomplished, Dana started the van and turned on the heater. They were all wet and cold from their experience. Hands shaking, she slowly drove out of the pine grove. In a matter of minutes, they were on the highway heading toward Carson City.

Relief started to leak through Dana. They'd done it! They'd rescued Colby. They'd located the Storm Pipe, stolen it and now it was going home. *Home!* Oh, how wonderful that word sounded to Dana. Hot tears welled up in her eyes. She tasted the salt as they slipped silently down her dirty face. Home… It held so many more meanings to Dana than before. Most important, Chase was here, beside her. He had been her teacher, her partner and now she wanted nothing more than time to talk to him, about her and him, and a possible future together....

CHAPTER TWENTY-THREE

COLBY FRANTICALLY WORKED the cell phone as Dana drove toward Carson City. Having lost several teeth, he could barely talk. Not to mention his jaw was broken and his lip split in several places. Dana felt sorry for the agent, but there was little she could do for him. He seemed grimly determined, and she heard the banked rage in his voice as he ordered the Bureau into action. An FBI SWAT team would move in as soon as possible. Colby ordered them to capture everyone in the compound, and to retrieve the body of Annie Ballard, the CIA remote viewer. Dana felt badly for the loss of the woman's life. It confirmed even more how dangerous Rogan Fast Horse was.

As the adrenaline left Dana's system, she began to feel exhausted. Chase must have sensed her fatigue, for he ran his hand gently across her shoulders.

"A little tense?" he teased her in a husky tone. Just kneading her shoulder fueled Chase's desire.

Her hair was drying in the welcome heat of the car, tendrils curling softly against her temples.

Her mouth twitched with a slight smile. "Just a little. I feel like I'm falling apart internally, one jigsaw piece at a time."

Nodding, he said, "That's how it is. The adrenaline is leaving and you begin to realize just how close to dying you really came." He squeezed her shoulder, then eased his hand away. "It makes you appreciate life with a new sense."

"That's the truth," Dana whispered. Traffic was light at this time of morning. The sun had crested the horizon. The moody sky and thunder beings were slowly dissipating. Dana had already sent many, many prayers of thanks to the sky spirits. Without them, she realized, Rogan would have found them for sure. The mighty sky beings had played offense to allow Chase and her to get the Storm Pipe.

She heard Colby get off the phone and snap it shut. Cutting a quick glance over her shoulder, she noted how exhausted he was, how battered.

"Don't you want us to get you to the hospital, Agent Colby? You look and sound awful."

"No, thanks. I'll give you directions on how to get to the FBI office. I want to be there to hear our team taking those people prisoner up at that compound." His mouth became grimmer. "And I want Annie's body retrieved. She didn't deserve any of this." He closed his eyes, as if the emotions overwhelmed him.

"I'm sorry, truly sorry," Dana told him. "Fast Horse is a dangerous, crazy man. It must have been an unending nightmare for the two of you."

Sighing raggedly, Colby whispered, "All we were doing was following up on her dream. And the man at the antique store, I'm sure, didn't realize how dangerous Fast Horse was."

Chase turned in his seat, resting his arm on the back of it. "Agent Colby, you're dealing with someone who hates white people. Fast Horse is a man with a mission. He's a homegrown terrorist as far as I'm concerned." Chase wasn't going to tell the agent about the Storm Pipe's involvement. Nor would he divulge that Rogan had killed the vice president with it. The FBI agent surely wouldn't understand or accept that explanation. Because Rogan had murdered the CIA psychic, he and his rabid band would be caught and put into prison, anyway. And that's all that mattered to Chase—an end to Rogan's hateful ways.

Right now, Chase wanted to drop the agent off at his office and hightail it out to the Navajo reservation to give Grandmother Agnes the Storm Pipe. And he wasn't interested in the FBI agent knowing why they'd been at the compound. Chase would stay out of this investigation as much as possible. That way, he and Dana could go to the winter hogan, rest up, heal and have quality time together. He had to play his cards right to avoid getting ensnared in the escalating investigation Colby was putting into play.

The agent looked out the window at the desert, which was green with vegetation here and there, the closer they got to town. There was some farming south of Carson City. "I'm going to need you to stick around," he told them. "You'll have to give me the name of a local hotel where you'll be staying."

Dana started to speak, but she felt the energy around Chase subtly change. Instead, he spoke for them. "Sure, no problem."

Dana frowned and kept quiet. Their agreement was to get the Storm Pipe back to Grandmother Agnes. The agent didn't know that, and she didn't want to divulge anything more about the pipe. If Colby found out it had been used to kill the vice president of the United States, he would take it away from them. And that couldn't happen. Colby was a white man, and he'd never understand the pipe's history, its use or why it had to be put in the hands of the right individual once more.

Drawing in a deep breath, Dana concentrated on driving. In another thirty minutes, they'd be in the capital of Nevada.

"Chase? Before we find a hotel, can we get you to an emergency room to check out your head wound? I don't think Agent Colby will mind if I take you to the nearest hospital?"

Colby said, "No, I don't mind at all. There's a hospital about ten blocks from the FBI office. I can give you directions. Once you're done there, just call me at this number and report where you're staying." He scribbled on a piece of paper and handed it to Chase.

"Of course," Dana said, playing along. Colby had Chase's name. He did not have hers. There'd been no time for introductions during the rescue. She worried that if they disappeared, they'd be breaking some kind of law. But which one?

Once Rogan and his women were captured, Dana wondered what they would admit to. Killing Annie Ballard? Rogan would probably get some smart lawyer who would tell him to keep his mouth shut and plead not guilty. Would the secret of the Storm Pipe remain just that? Her mind was spongy and whirling with different scenarios.

Tightening her hands on the wheel, Dana ached to be alone with Chase. To be in his arms, to be held. To let this entire nightmare slide away into oblivion… She knew it wouldn't happen, but she didn't have the stamina to even look at other possibilities right now.

When they arrived at the FBI office, the agent got out very slowly. Chase offered to help him, but he refused. He thanked both of them for their help.

There was a dark determination to Colby that Dana admired. He was met by two men in dark business suits, who helped him inside the three-story, redbrick building on the busy street.

Chase said, "Let's get the hell out of here. As far and as fast as possible. I want Colby to think you're taking me to the E.R., but that's not gonna happen."

Nodding, Dana put the van in gear and melted back into the burgeoning traffic. The sun was shining brightly, the last bits of fluffy cumulus clouds dotting the sky above them. "You got it."

"Colby is going to have his hands full," Chase told her. He reached out and slid his hand across Dana's right shoulder, giving it a brief squeeze. "How are you doing?"

"Okay," Dana lied. She concentrated on driving. What she wanted to do was concentrate on intimacy with Chase. Dana absorbed the contact like a dry sponge in water. It had been over two years since Hal's murder had hurled her into a dark abyss of pain and loss. Now, Chase was like dawn light to Dana. He filled her with hope that perhaps the worst of her own nightmare was finally coming to an end.

"You don't lie very well," Chase remarked, giving her a warm look. "You're a warrior at heart, woman of mine. You know that?"

"I don't feel very warriorlike," she answered wryly. "My insides still feel like Jell-O."

"Adrenaline letdown, is all," Chase assured her. He grinned. "And you're probably hungry."

"Starving to death."

"Yeah, that's how it happens." Chase looked around at the awakening city. It wasn't large compared to Reno or Las Vegas. In another ten minutes, they'd be south of the city limits and driving back into the Nevada desert toward the massive Navajo reservation. "If we see a motel on the way, let's stop. We'll get a room where we can wash up, put on clean clothes and find a place to chow down."

"Don't you want to get away from Colby?"

"He's occupied," Chase stated confidently. "It's time we took care of ourselves. He's got Fast Horse to deal with, and we both know that isn't going to be easy for his SWAT team. Rogan's probably already fled the compound with his women."

Grimacing, Dana kept her eyes on the road as they exited the city. She saw a sign for a motel about a mile farther. "If Rogan runs, the FBI may not find him."

"Oh, I think they will," Chase said, keeping his hand on her shoulder. "Colby is enraged over Annie Ballard's murder. I think he'll turn over every rock between here and hell to find that mean son of a bitch."

"I hope so," Dana whispered unsteadily. She braked and pulled up to the small white motel.

Next to it was a Denny's Restaurant, which was a perfect place for them to refuel. After shutting off the engine, Dana retrieved her identification and wallet locked in the glove box. "Stay here. I'll get us a room and be right back."

Chase nodded and eased his hand from her shoulder. Dana looked pale, her eyes dark with exhaustion. He wasn't doing so hot, either. His head throbbed where the bullet had creased his temple. But he knew if he could get some aspirin, the pain would go away. Right now, what he wanted most was a hot shower so he could wash his hair, clean his wound and climb into clean clothes.

Within five minutes, Dana was back with the motel key. She handed it to Chase and drove to the last unit at the end. Getting out, they quickly hustled all their gear into the room. It was barely 7:00 a.m., and Dana imagined people were still sleeping.

Inside, she gently placed the pack holding the Storm Pipe on a shelf in the closet. Her first and only duty was to protect it from ever being stolen again.

"You first," Chase told her as he closed the door and locked it behind them. "The shower is yours."

Dana started to protest, but was too weary to argue. He put the small suitcases they'd had waiting in the SUV on the two double beds. The room was simple but clean. It was decorated in a Western motif, the bedspreads a sky-blue with brightly colored cactus in flower. "What about you?"

"While you shower, I'll clean my wound," Chase stated. He unzipped his suitcase and took out a small first-aid kit. "Go ahead."

With a nod, Dana headed off to the immaculate bathroom. After closing the door, she quickly shimmied out of her spandex outfit, the dry mud dropping around her on the white tile floor. When she glanced in the mirror, Dana realized how awful she looked. There were smears of mud across her brow and cheek. Her hair desperately needed to be washed. When the elderly motel clerk had made a comment about her appearance, Dana had lied and said they'd been mountain climbing and got nailed by the line of thunderstorms. The woman had clucked sympathetically and given her the key. It wasn't a lie, Dana rationalized, just not the whole truth.

Heat and mist quickly rose in the glass-encased shower. She stepped eagerly into the warm, pummeling stream and closed the door. Unbraiding her hair, she turned around slowly, allowing the warm water to wash away all the terror, sweat and mud. She savored the hot spray massaging her tense body.

The bathroom door opened and closed, and Dana could see Chase's naked torso through the mist. He was at the sink, cleaning his head wound. Picking up the jasmine-scented soap, she didn't care if he saw her naked or not. Chase had seen her that way before. All she wanted was to get clean and wash away this nightmare.

Dana had no idea how long she stood relishing the hot streams of water on her body. Finally, she turned off the shower and exited. Chase was gone, but he'd thoughtfully left a fluffy white towel on the washbasin for her. He'd even left her a set of clean clothes.

Every movement was an effort as she dried her hair and body. A soft smile touched Dana's mouth as she pulled on the soft, stone-washed jeans, a loose-fitting, dark-green tank top and white cotton socks for her aching feet.

As she padded out of the bathroom, she saw that Chase had made them coffee. In fact, two trays sat on one of the beds. Chase had stripped out of his muddy clothes and wore a thin cotton robe that barely fit around his large, muscular form. He was grinning as he brought over a hot cup of coffee to her.

"Nice to have take out at Denny's, isn't it? I ordered breakfast for you. Here, sit down before you fall down, Dana. You're looking real tired."

She smiled and took the coffee. "I feel dead on my feet, Chase. Like I'm going to fall across that bed."

"You will soon enough. But first eat, Dana." He cupped her elbow and guided her to the bed.

"You've already eaten," she said, sitting down. Her flesh tingled delightfully beneath his fingertips.

"Yeah, you were in there quite a while. I was starving to death." He chuckled.

Looking up, she could see he had cleaned his wound. Now, it looked as if he'd just hit his head, not been creased with a bullet. An amazing transformation. "You look pretty good under the circumstances," she noted, pulling the tray over and settling it on her lap.

"Yeah, I feel better, for sure. I've had a couple cups of coffee and a big breakfast. I took some aspirin and my headache's gone, so I'm in pretty good shape, comparatively speaking."

"You know how to handle this kind of life-and-death stuff. I don't." Picking up her utensils, she eagerly began to eat.

Chase patted her shoulder. "Eat and rest, woman of mine. I'm going to take a long, hot shower and get cleaned up." Truth be told, Chase thought she looked fetching, with her hair curling slightly around her face and shoulders. But there were dark smudges beneath her eyes. "Fill your stomach and then stretch out and sleep," he urged her, turning at the door to the bathroom.

"I'm still worried about Colby and the FBI. Aren't we too close to Carson City?"

Shaking his head, Chase said, "Don't worry about it, Dana. We can rest for a while. By the time they get done with their SWAT operation, it will be evening. By then, we'll wake up and drive back to the res before they think about us."

That sounded good to Dana. She wanted to disappear off the radar of this FBI agent once and for all. "Thanks for the food, Chase. It's delicious."

He gave her a wolfish grin. "What I'm looking at is delicious."

CHAPTER TWENTY-FOUR

THE WORDS CHASE HAD so huskily spoken were the last ones she remembered. Shortly afterward, he had gone into the bathroom and shut the door. After setting her empty tray on the bureau, she pulled back the covers of her bed and crawled in, clothes and all. The moment her head sank into the pillow, she spiraled into a desperately needed sleep. With Chase's words, gritty and filled with promise, encircling Dana like the arms of a lover, she slept soundly.

Half an hour later, Chase emerged from the bathroom. He'd washed away the sweat, mud and fear that had caked him earlier. Wearing only a white, nubby terry-cloth towel low around his waist, he halted just outside the door as the steam escaped. There, on the nearest queen-size bed, lay Dana, asleep. His heart wrenched violently in his chest. Warmth drenched him, like the drizzle of hot honey being poured over his entire being.

Her hair was in soft disarray around her head,

an ebony halo that emphasized her golden skin. The tension was gone and her slightly parted lips beckoned to Chase. As he rubbed his clean-shaven jaw, he felt a scalding heat in his lower body. The desire to simply slide in next to Dana nearly unhinged him. He stood there, feet damp and creating dark water stains on the floor, wanting her desperately. Hadn't he called her his woman? A man didn't do that unless he'd laid claim to the one he loved. Scowling, Chase forced himself to move.

He quietly walked across the room, setting the second tray on the bureau beside Dana's. He knew he had to sleep in the other bed. It wouldn't be right to act on his instincts: to slide in beside her, gently ease his arm beneath Dana's slender neck, pull her back against him and curl his other arm around her waist, to hold her protected and loved within his embrace. No, he couldn't do that. Not yet...

The time would come, Chase promised himself. He glanced at his watch on the dresser. It was nearly 8:30. The sun was bright behind the dark-green, thick drapes, and blazed around the edges of the window. Enough light spilled into the room for him to see where he was going. Even though the threat of Rogan was past, and the Storm Pipe was safe in the knapsack in the closet, Chase trusted nothing. He took his pistol and placed it beneath his pillow as he sat down on the bed.

He released the knot and allowed the towel to

drop to the floor. As he gazed forlornly across the room at Dana, he felt his heart wrench again—with loneliness, with need. No, he had to wait until they got back to the reservation. The Storm Pipe had to be delivered to Grandmother Agnes first. Only then would he speak to Dana of what lay in his heart.

Chase lay down facing her. At least his last sight would be of her peacefully sleeping, those thick, black lashes fanned against her high cheekbones. He could hear her soft breathing and notice how she curled up beneath the cover. With these images, he fell into a dream-ladened world where he was making slow, passionate love with her.

DANA DROVE through the night, her hands gripping the wheel as they sped along the lonely roads from Nevada into Arizona. Chase fixed her coffee, which they'd bought after getting gas at the border. He poured in several packets of sugar and stirred it with a wooden stick.

Smiling softly, she absorbed the quiet and his nearby presence. "I'm so happy, Chase."

Looking up from his kitchen duties, he saw Dana's profile in the faint, greenish glow from the dashboard. His heart thudded with need of her. "You have a right to be."

"Are you feeling the same way?" She shot him a quick glance, then returned to her driving.

"Yeah. *Relieved* is probably the word I'd use."

"Relieved about…?" She reached for the coffee as he handed it to her. Their fingertips met; it was a delicious moment and Dana savored it. "Thanks."

Chase settled back with his own cup of black, steaming coffee. It was 2:00 a.m. The stars hung close and sparkled like gemstones in the sky. He liked traveling at night; there was little traffic, and the night sky felt safe and soothing. "Relieved that we got the Storm Pipe back." He sipped his coffee. "Consoled that we came out of this alive. And comforted by the fact that the FBI is going to find Fast Horse and his band of women and put them away for good."

Dana shook her head. "Things happened so fast, Chase. When I think back on our climb in that storm, well, there were times I didn't think we'd make it." She looked over at his rugged and handsome profile. "Did you?"

"That was the easy part, Dana—climbing the cliff. I was a lot more worried about getting into the compound."

"Maybe because you are so used to climbing."

He smiled briefly. "Maybe…"

"I can hardly wait to give the Storm Pipe to Grandmother Agnes. She's going to be so happy." Dana smiled widely, glancing again at Chase. His mouth was so strong and tempting. For many weeks, she'd fought liking Chase purely as a man. He had been her teacher and off-limits to her on a personal level. She hadn't even realized that she was drawn to Chase until he'd broken the news to her of how her mother and husband had died. Only then had Dana realized how much she liked Chase and needed him.

"Yes, I'm sure she already knows we have the pipe," Chase said. "She's so psychic."

"That's why she doesn't have a phone out there." Dana chuckled. Many people living in the Navajo reservation did not have a phone line or electricity available to them. The res was over a hundred thousand acres, the largest in the U.S.A., and it was like a third-world country in some respects. Yet many of the Navajo, particularly the older generations, had lived their whole life without a phone or electricity, and preferred it that way. Only the younger generations, wired with cell phones, iPods, computers and other modern-day inventions, wanted those accessories on the res.

"She knows we have it," Chase agreed quietly. He sipped the coffee, finding the hum of the tires on the asphalt lulling. They'd slept until 4:00 p.m., eaten a full meal at Denny's and by 5:30 were on the road.

"I feel like I'm coming out of a dream." Dana laughed. "Maybe a nightmare. I keep thinking about the five weeks at the res with you. My training. Wondering if I could do it…"

"Well," Chase murmured, "you did it, Dana. And you should be damn proud of what you pulled off. When I got hit by that bullet, everything fell on your shoulders. When I became conscious, cuffed to that pole in the lodge, I never expected you to show up and rescue me. That was…" Chase held her luminous gaze, "well, that was courageous. You didn't have to return. You had the pipe. You were out of the compound and safe."

Dana reached over and squeezed his arm. "I don't know why you wouldn't expect me to come back to free you. I waited outside the gate for you, and when I heard gunfire, I knew they'd found you. I didn't know whether you were dead or alive, Chase." Releasing his arm, Dana wrapped her hand around the steering wheel and stared out at the empty four-lane interstate. "I was so scared that they'd killed you. I thought the worst—a shot to the head."

"Well," Chase chuckled, "you were right on. I did take a shot to the head. Only I got lucky, and it was a graze and nothing more. Besides, holding the Storm Pipe bag, the pain and exhaustion are gone."

Relief continued to filter through Dana as she came off the adrenaline high of their mission. With relief came emotional awareness and the terror she had suppressed. "Chase, I was so scared for you, for me, as I went to hide the pipe and came back to get you."

"It must have been rough for you, Dana. I'm sorry."

"It wasn't your fault. Things just went crazy

inside that compound. We all did the best we could. If you hadn't been protecting me earlier, I might be dead and we might not have the pipe to give to Grandmother Agnes." Shaking her head, her voice filled with emotion, Dana whispered, "Chase, you're the bravest person in the world. You put yourself deliberately in the line of fire for me so I could escape with the pipe. I don't know how many sentries you took on, but you stood guard for me at that open gate." She choked back sudden tears. Her sight blurred momentarily and she blinked to clear her eyes. "You are my hero, in every way. I want you to know that."

Her words lit him up inside. His heart, long dormant, was awake and full of hope. Dana's confession was a healing unguent for him, for his brutal imprisonment in South America. In that moment, he finally forgave himself for that period of his life. When the time was right, he would share that sordid time in his life. Right now, they were too stressed to discuss such a topic.

Reaching over, he slid his hand tenderly across her shoulder. "And you're no less a heroine in my eyes and heart, Dana. Your courage was incredible. When I saw you appear in that room, for me and Colby, I couldn't believe my eyes. I was wrong about you in one way—I didn't think you had the backbone. You could have taken the easy route and left us. But you didn't. You risked your life for me." Squeezing her shoulder gently, Chase added, "I think we're a mutual admiration society, don't you?" He made himself lift his hand away and rest it on his thigh.

Warmed by his unexpected touch, Dana gave a broken laugh. "I guess we are." She sighed deeply. "Oh, Chase, I'll be so glad to get the pipe back to Grandmother Agnes. The Storm Pipe, when I held it, took away most of my exhaustion. I can see why the society wanted it back. Then I want to walk up to the winter hogan in the canyon—together. We have so much to talk about." She risked a quick glance at him.

His eyes glimmered and his mouth softened. "I want the same thing, Dana. You and me. We can stay up there for as long as we want and work on personal things between ourselves. That's what I'd like."

"Me, too." Dana's heart opened and joy spilled through her chest. By dawn, they would be at the hogan. For so long, ever since her world had been destroyed by Rogan Fast Horse, she hadn't had a home. And now a new world was taking shape, a joyous one filled with wonderful possibilities that all revolved around Chase.

GRANDMOTHER AGNES WEPT with joy as Dana knelt down and slid the Storm Pipe bag into her out-stretched, arthritic hands. "This is wonderful, children," she murmured as she cradled it in her left arm and pressed it gently to her thin chest. The warm, healing energy flowed into her aching hands and removed the pain. Dressed in her ceremonial garb of a deep-red velvet, long-sleeved blouse and skirt, a silver concha belt around her narrow waist, she beamed at them. "Thank you, both…so much. The Blue Heron Society owes you a debt we can never repay. In a special ceremony, at the next full moon, we will induct you into our society and give you the Storm Pipe, Dana."

Agnes gazed down at the pipe bag and stroked it reverently. "You two are truly courageous. We will pray for you at our next meeting and your names will be on our lips to the Great Spirit from now on. You have rescued one of the most powerful pipes known, and given it back to us." Patting it tenderly, Grandmother Agnes whispered, "You are one of us, my child. We welcome you."

As Dana knelt in front of the elder she could see the bluish-white light emanating strongly from around the beaded bag. Little waves of joy seemed to be surging outward, too, flowing through Dana and Chase and beyond the hogan. "I'm so happy for you, Grandma," Dana said, her voice tremulous. Reaching out, she gently touched Agnes's hand. "We are grateful it is back with you, with the society. I'll look forward to the coming ceremony at the next full moon."

Chase sat on a colorful woven rug near the

elder. This moment was historical, he realized. Few stolen ceremonial pipes were ever recovered. And ceremonial pipes were the backbone of a Native American nation. To lose one to theft, well, that was heinous and shocking. And a nation's spirit suffered because of it.

Once a ceremonial pipe was gone, it was usually gone forever. But this one time, they'd been lucky enough to find the pipe and get it back to its rightful place. Pride, warm and flowing, moved through him as he gazed at Dana's glowing face and watched her animated features. There was no doubt there was a bond between her and her adopted grandmother, one of pure love and respect.

Chase stared down at his folded hands. He wanted to share such a look with Dana. Would that happen? He wasn't sure. Until he heard her express that same wish, he was in the tortured position of a man wanting the world, but finding it out of his grasp.

Trying to remain tranquil while the two women celebrated the return of the Storm Pipe, Chase closeted his desires and wishes. The warmth in the hogan was building, even though the door was open, and he went and opened the windows to allow a breeze to come through. Sunlight from the east streamed in like a golden beacon, splashing its life energy throughout the home of the elder.

It was nearly 7:00 a.m. And Grandmother Agnes had been standing at the door, awaiting their arrival when they'd pulled up to her hogan. The old woman was clairvoyant, knew the pipe had been rescued and knew they were fine. She had hot fry bread, strawberry jam, eggs and bacon ready, and fresh coffee perking on the woodstove for them. Chase shouldn't have been amazed by such knowing, but he always was. Perhaps because so few people utilized their intuition, it looked magical. What a better world it would be if everyone did use their sixth sense daily, he thought.

His gaze moved back to Dana, who was laughing through her tears. Tears of relief. Tears of joy. Tears that had long been withheld due to her past trauma. How Chase wanted to hold her! Just hold her, keep her safe and let her know that the world wasn't always such a bad place, just chaotic from time to time. As he sat there, he yearned for a time of peace now. That would come, he was sure. And with it, the opportunity to share and talk with Dana, heart to heart. Mind to mind. Today, he hoped, he'd find out how she really felt about him, about them.

It was a sweet moment, and Chase clung to it. So much of his life had been harrowing, life-and-death, threatened or just plain lost to bigger events. Now, he wanted nothing more than the simple pleasure of having this woman in his arms, her mouth clinging hotly to his.

Would the Great Spirit give them this reprieve of time and space with one another? Chase prayed fervently that his request would be fulfilled.

Grandmother Agnes was beginning to look weary. Her face was alight with joy, but he saw the tiredness in her watery eyes. Dana seemed to sense and see it also, because she slowly got to her feet and turned to him.

"Chase? Want to walk up to the winter hogan? I think Grandma Agnes could use some time alone with the pipe."

Nodding, he unwound and stood up. "Sounds good to me. Grandmother? We'll drop in and see you for dinner tonight?" He knew Agnes would take care of the Storm Pipe until the transfer ceremony and that was as it should be. Agnes was the only one who could award a ceremonial pipe to a deserving woman.

"I'd like that, my children. We all need to rest. Our hearts and spirits have worked hard, and now we need to be quiet and be grateful." Gently patting the pipe bag, she added, "Rest, my children, for you are certainly blessed by the Great Spirit for what you have done. Tonight, at sundown, come and I will have fresh mutton, potatoes and gravy waiting for you. A celebration dinner. Also, we need to plan a sweat lodge at noon today for us to welcome the Storm Pipe back in the society."

Already, Chase's mouth watered. Mutton was one of his favorite dishes. He saw Dana smile, too. When she reached out and gripped his hand, his heart banged in his chest. Her fingers were warm and firm upon his. Dana's unexpected act was a sweet shock to Chase. He saw Grandmother Agnes's eyes sparkle with happiness—for them. Curling his fingers around Dana's, he said, "We'll be here, Grandmother."

"Come on," Dana urged Chase. "Let's go get groceries at the trading post."

CHAPTER TWENTY-FIVE

AT NOON THERE WOULD BE a sweat lodge ceremony to officially welcome the Storm Pipe to its rightful place with Grandmother Agnes. Chase knew in the past, the Storm Pipe had been with other nations, but always it belonged to the vaunted Blue Heron Society. Since their arrival, Dana and Chase had much to do. First, she dropped some of her belongings in the winter hogan. Outside, she heard Chase retrieving their groceries from the car parked down at Agnes's hogan. They'd driven to a nearby trading post and gotten provisions for their stay. It felt so good to be *home*. As Dana moved around the quiet hogan, its hard-packed dirt floors covered with beautiful old handwoven rugs, she savored the moment. Grandma Agnes had hung fresh sage in the four corners, a way of announcing their return.

Smiling to herself, Dana saw that the elder had also dusted and cleaned. As always, cobwebs were removed and spiders were taken into the wilds to live. A fresh bouquet of blue lupine sat on the small wooden table.

Chase walked in the door, arms loaded with sacks. Dana turned from the small kitchen counter and helped him set them on the table. The happiness burning in his eyes went straight to her heart.

"Any more stuff?" she asked.

"Yeah, mostly our clothes and climbing gear." Chase halted at the door. "We have to prepare for the sweat Grandmother will conduct for you, her and the pipe next."

"I know," Dana said, a little breathless as she put the canned goods away.

"I'll start gathering the wood for the sacred fire. I know a spot where there's a lot of kindling," he told her.

"And I'll help as soon as I get things squared away here in the hogan," she murmured.

He rested his hand on the rough timbers of the doorway. Dana looked incredibly beautiful. Her hair was in thick braids and she'd dressed simply in jeans, hiking boots and a pale-green T-shirt that showed off her womanly figure. "Sounds good. There's a bunch of dead juniper higher up in the canyon. I'll start there and bring it down for the fire."

"Right." Dana nodded. She was crouched before the shelves, placing cans into the cramped area, but turned and smiled up at him. "I don't know about you, but it feels so good to be home, Chase." She swallowed hard and added, "Home with you…"

Had she gone too far? Said too much? For a moment, Dana's breath hitched in fear. But when Chase's expression grew even more warm and open, her heart sped up. Deep in her body, she felt an ache to love him.

"You're my woman," he told her gruffly. "We have duties right now, to welcome the pipe back to the Blue Heron Society, but after that…" Chase gave her a hooded look. "When we're done with the sweat, we're coming home, together. We have a lot to talk about, Dana. Important things…*our* future."

Chase's emphasis and meaning were clear and deliberate, like a rainbow glittering against a stormy sky. Closing her eyes for a moment, Dana allowed his voice to caress her like a lover's hand. Then she opened them and held Chase's smoldering gaze. "Ours. Yes. For the first time in two years, Chase, I feel like living again. I have hope in my heart. Dreams."

How badly Chase wanted to pull Dana into his arms and love her—hotly, and for a long, long time. But the ceremony came first. Smiling rakishly, he said in a low growl, "I never thought I'd love, Dana. But you've changed that for me." He opened his hand. "There's so much I need to say to you, share with you."

"I know, the time isn't right." Dana smiled

crookedly. "After the sweat, our lives will slow down finally, and we'll have the time we deserve with one another."

Chase returned her warm look and watched as she finished shelving the canned goods. "Roger that, woman of mine. Well, I've got to start the fire for the sweat. I'll see you later, down at Grandmother's hogan, for the sweat."

"Right." Dana sighed as he disappeared out the door. Birds were singing, and she recognized a cardinal's beautiful melody from a juniper close to the hogan. Dana felt her tight shoulders relax. She was beginning to feel the aches, pains, cuts and scratches from her climb. Just the simple act of putting cans away soothed some of the shock and trauma. She'd nearly died out there on that cliff, and without Chase's strength and support, she surely would have. A fierce tide of love swept through her. She loved Chase. With all her heart and soul.

Finishing arranging the shelves, Dana straightened up. There was something satisfying about making the hogan their home. Oh, she knew they couldn't stay here forever, but for a week or two, it would be a wonderful place to hide away, a respite from the rigors of their mission.

An odd noise at the door interrupted her thoughts. Dana turned, and abruptly, her heart plunged in terror. Rogan Fast Horse stood in the doorway! His face was scratched and bloody, but his gaze burned angrily into her.

Was this a cruel trick? Dana stood there, frozen in place, as her worst nightmare suddenly materialized.

"You!" she finally gasped in a strangled tone. Instantly, adrenaline shot through her and she dropped into a crouched position near the sink.

"Yeah, bitch. *Me*. Where's the Storm Pipe?" Rogan blocked the entry with his frame. He'd parked away from Agnes's hogan, energetically cloaked himself so she nor a pipe of any kind could detect his presence. "And where's that bastard, Chase Iron Hand?"

Shaking inwardly, her breath choppy, Dana realized there was no escape. A hogan had only one door, in the east. And Chase was somewhere high in the canyon. He'd never know Rogan was here—until it was too late. Her mind spun with desperation. There was no place to run. And the pistols? Where had Chase put the pistols? Had he even unloaded them from the van yet? Dana didn't know. Suddenly, she felt overwhelmed. Her mind blanked out on her.

"I—Chase? He isn't here."

"Liar."

Rogan remained in the doorway, his hands anchored on either side of the frame. Dana's eyes narrowed. His clothes were torn and dirty. His hair, once combed, clean and in a ponytail, hung like filthy snakes around his narrow, long face. Rogan must have escaped from the compound, found a car and then found them.

"How did you track us?" Dana whispered, her voice squeaky with fear.

Giving her a lethal smile, Rogan said, "You stupid idiots didn't cover your energy trail. That's how. What's the matter? You think some white boy FBI agents are gonna find me? Trap me and take me prisoner?" Rogan looked over his shoulder. "Where's Iron Hand? I can feel him around."

Gulping, Dana saw that Rogan carried a gun in a holster, low on his right thigh. There was a knife in a sheath attached to his leather belt. Dangerous. Deadly. Rogan was going to kill her. Dana knew it with every short, anxious breath she managed to suck into her lungs. He would kill her and then he would kill Chase. Even worse, Rogan would eventually find the Storm Pipe down at Grandma Agnes's hogan.

They had thought they were safe. It was a stupid student's mistake not to cover their energy trail, Dana knew. They were just so exhausted, so happy to get the pipe back. But a good sorcerer could follow their trail like a blazing light in the Other Worlds.

Holding Rogan's dark-blue stare, Dana whispered, "Chase isn't here. He dropped me off. He's driving back to Carson City right now." It was a lie. She saw Rogan scowl.

"His energy path led here." Rogan's eyes were bloodshot, and while menacing, he seemed dead on his feet.

Dana knew that even a good sorcerer, if tired, hungry or stressed out, could not maintain the intense awareness of the Other Worlds. And Rogan looked as if he was laboring under all those conditions right now. That told Dana he couldn't continue to try and find Chase. But he'd had enough willpower and focus to trail them to the hogan.

Rogan's mouth was twisted, his face gaunt and pale. Sensing intuitively that he'd escaped, then honed in on them, stealing a car to follow them, Dana gulped hard. She and Chase had completely underestimated Rogan's ability not only to survive the FBI SWAT team, but to track Chase and her here, to the hogan.

"He was here," Dana admitted. She was going to lie, because she knew Rogan's psychic abilities were exhausted. If he was able, she was sure he'd have tracked Chase up into the canyon, but he hadn't. That told her he had to rely on her for information. "But he's gone now."

"Your van is here," Rogan said, his voice grating. Lucky for him one of his women found the keys to the handcuffs they'd put on him.

"Chase borrowed a friend's pickup. He's gone to the trading post for more supplies."

Snorting softly, Rogan looked around. "Where's the pipe, bitch? And don't stall. If you don't tell me, I'm comin' over there to beat the information out of you. So make it easy on both of us, will you?"

Dana gasped as Rogan stood to his full height, his hands falling to his sides. When astral traveling, she'd seen Annie Ballard's dead body. She knew he was good for his word. *Concentrate!* She had to make a call to Chase energetically. Closing her eyes, Dana pretended she was thinking about it. Instead, she sent her main spirit guide, a wolf, to tell Chase she was in danger and that Rogan was here. If Chase wasn't too tired, if he wasn't too focused on finding firewood, he'd hear the plea and come as swiftly as he could. After ordering her spirit guide to find Chase and deliver the message, she opened her eyes.

Rogan's glittering gaze cut into her like an obsidian knife. She trembled over the shock of having him here. And she was perfectly aware that he'd kill her. It was just a matter of time.

"The pipe is out in the van. I can go fetch it for you." Mind churning, Dana knew she had to get out of the hogan.

Rogan seemed to consider her words. "All right, go on." He pulled his knife out of its sheath and pointed it at her. "One wrong move, and you'll get cut."

Dana's knees weakened, and she gripped the counter for support. "I won't try anything." Her voice wavered, and Rogan seemed pleased. Fine, let him think she would be a victim to his threats.

Pulling away from the door, he snarled, "Get your ass out here and go get that pipe."

She forced herself to move, hoping she could walk at all. This wasn't the time to break down. Her hammering heart felt as if it would tear out of her chest as she approached Rogan. His face was a mass of cuts and bruises. Familiar with the brush on the mountain slopes, the cactus, she was sure he'd run blindly into the night to escape the SWAT team. His clothes were torn and ripped, stained with dried blood and mud. He looked like Death personified. And the knife he held was long and ugly.

As she moved out the door, Dana's skin prickled. Rogan was right behind her, and she tried to stop from panicking. She went to the rear door on the driver's side of the van. *Stay calm,* she ordered herself. Giving in to fear was never the answer. Rogan stood to her left as she halted at the door. The sunlight was hot on the metal handle of the vehicle, which she grasped. Chase had left most of their gear inside. She hesitated, stealing a quick glance up into the box canyon. No sign of him. Had he heard her plea and warning?

Right now, she was on her own, so she peered into the darkened glass. "See it in there?" she asked Rogan, pointing at the window.

He stepped forward.

In an instant, Dana jerked the heavy door open, and with all her strength, swung it into Rogan, who was leaning forward in its path.

The moment the door slammed into him, he was thrown backward, with a cry of surprise.

Dana took off running up the canyon. She heard him give a shout, then curse. *Escape!* The only place she knew to run was the canyon—which she knew like the back of her hand. No way would she lead him down to Grandma Agnes's hogan. No way!

Her boots dug into the sand as Dana plunged recklessly up the slope. She dodged the cactus and brush, and with each step, adrenaline added to her speed. Not far below, she heard Rogan cursing loudly. She only hoped he would stop and examine the van, to see if the pipe was really there. It would give her time. Time to hide among the trees up ahead.

"You *bitch!*" Rogan shrieked, pawing through the items on the backseat. All he found were two blankets, a pillow and two pairs of shoes. No pipe! Frustrated, he jerked his pistol out of the holster. He was hungry and exhausted. He aimed the weapon and fired off three shots at the fleeing woman. None of them hit her. Dammit!

He turned his focus back to finding the pipe in

the rear of the car. It could be hidden under the mess of ropes and tools there. Holstering the pistol, he climbed into the rear of the van. The pipe had to be in here!

She was halfway up the slope and winding through the trees when Dana saw Chase running toward her. His face was set. Hard. She gasped and waved her hand. Heart pounding, she stumbled over to him.

"Rogan's here!"

Chase gripped her by the shoulders and turned her so that his back was shielding her from below. "Are you all right?" Her eyes were dark with fear and shock.

"Y-yes, I'm okay. Chase, I lied and told Rogan the pipe was in the van. I—I think he's still there looking for it."

"Good," Chase exclaimed. "You make your way down to Grandmother's hogan the back way, through the trees. Get her and the pipe out of there in case something goes wrong."

"What?" Dana gasped, her knees shaking.

"I'm going after Fast Horse."

It was then that Dana saw Chase had out his Bowie knife. "He's got a gun."

"I heard him firing it. He followed our energy trail."

Dana threw her arms around Chase, her head resting momentarily against his massive chest.

"We screwed up, Chase. We got too confident and thought the FBI would find Fast Horse."

Chase caressed her shoulders in an effort to steady her. Dana was shaking like a flower in a thunderstorm. "We overrated them," he agreed grimly. "Listen, go get Grandmother. Put her and the pipe in her pickup, and drive as fast as you can to the trading post. When you get there, call the Navajo police on the phone outside. Get them out here, pronto." Holding her away from him, Chase drilled her with a steely look. "Can you do that for me? For us, Dana? There's not much time. Once Rogan figures out the pipe isn't in the van, he'll probably move into the winter hogan, thinking it's there."

Managing to straighten her spine, Dana whispered, "Y-yes. I'll do that right now." Gripping his arms, she begged, "Chase, be careful! He's a killer…." A sob tore from her.

Noting the abject terror in her eyes, Chase caressed her cheek. "Be brave, my woman. I'll finish this once and for all. Now, go on. Only one man is going to be alive when the Navajo police get here. I'll come and find you when it's all over."

Dana swallowed a cry of fear. Chase spun away from her and quickly disappeared down the slope among the cedar and piñons. She didn't have time to deal with her fear and grief. Every second counted. Turning, stumbling, she took off through the trees that would lead her directly down to Grandma Agnes's hogan. Time. They didn't have any.

ROGAN WAS FURIOUSLY tearing through the van in search of the Storm Pipe. Angry that he'd let Dana Thunder Eagle escape, he ripped through several stacks of clothing in a plastic green bag. They smelled. Obviously, their dirty clothes. "Shit!" he muttered, throwing them out the car door. And then he felt a warning....

Quickly exiting the vehicle, Rogan whirled around. Chase Iron Hand was standing twenty feet away. The warrior's face was hard and without mercy; his cougar-colored eyes were narrowed—on him.

Rogan dusted off his hands and said in a condescending voice, "Well, well, the prodigal son finally shows up. I hear they booted your ass out of Delta Force, Iron Hand." His pistol was on the front seat of the car. Was it in his adversary's line of sight? Because the door was wide open.

Nostrils flared with hatred, Chase hissed, "You slimy son of a bitch. I let you get away once when we had a fight and that competition. Now this is it, Fast Horse." Chase jabbed his index finger toward Rogan. "You murdered two people to steal the Storm Pipe. You set things in motion no one in their right mind would have done. You've abused the privilege of a ceremonial pipe, murdered for it, and misused it for your own insane plans."

Hearing the lethal note in Iron Hand's snarl, Rogan backed up to the front door, his hands raised in apparent surrender. He wasn't sure whether the ex-Delta Force officer had seen the pistol lying on the seat. Perhaps, from where he stood, the car door was slanted just enough to block his view. Rogan decided to play along and buy the time he needed to get to that gun. "That pipe is mine!"

"Like hell it is! It's a woman's ceremonial pipe, you dumb bastard."

Chest heaving, Rogan clasped his hands behind him and lifted his chin imperiously. And yet fear wove through him as Iron Hand advanced, an ugly, long Bowie knife in his right fist, close to his side, ready to use. "I remember our last knife fight," Rogan said in a conversational tone, smirking. "I cut you good. Twice."

"Yeah," Chase said in a guttural voice, watching Rogan back up to the passenger side of the car, "you did. But I cut you across the forehead. Look at your forehead, because the scar is still there to remind you of being a cheater, Fast Horse. Memories of me you can't erase." He grinned lethally at the medicine man.

Chase could feel Fast Horse was up to something. What? Dana said he had a pistol, but Chase didn't see it on him. Or was it in the car?

"Step away from the vehicle," Chase snarled. "Now." He raised the knife in a threatening gesture. There was six feet between him and Rogan now. Chase wanted to murder the bastard, not take him alive. But he knew Dana would call the Navajo police, and he had to do the right thing. Besides, he wasn't about to get strung up on murder charges over this worthless piece of garbage.

Rogan hesitated as he saw the fury darkening Iron Hand's eyes. The man's desire to kill was palpable. "You know, getting to use that pipe to kill the vice president gave me great pleasure. You should have been happy I made a strike against the white man, Iron Hand, for all Indians."

Spitting to the left, Chase tensed. "I don't share your hatred of whites, Fast Horse. And I sure as hell don't want to kill them now for what their forebears did to us over a hundred years ago. You're sick. You're stupid. And you're going to come away from that van and lie on the ground. I've got the Navajo police coming for your sorry ass. Move away from the car. *Now!*"

Cursing, Rogan took a risk. He turned and snatched the pistol off the passenger seat. As he whirled back around, he fumbled with the weapon. Rogan vaguely heard his enemy curse and then move like lightning toward him. Giving a startled cry, Rogan realized he wouldn't have time to grab the pistol correctly, aim and shoot the bastard.

With the kickboxing skills he'd learned in Delta Force, Chase lashed out with his foot, aiming at Rogan's hands. The instant his boot slammed into them, the medicine man was thrown into the side of the van. The pistol went flying over the hood and landed in the dirt with a puff of dust.

Rogan bounced off the paneling, but quickly recovered. He delivered a side kick, which struck the Bowie knife squarely. The tip barely scored the side of Fast Horse's Apache boot. But it was enough! With satisfaction, Rogan saw the pain transfer to Chase's face as the knife was knocked out of his hand.

Rogan grinned savagely and leaped away from the car. The knife landed a good ten feet behind Iron Hand. "Now we're even," he snarled. "And I'm going to take you apart, piece by piece, like I should have a long time ago." He held up his hands and took a stance that signaled he was prepared to do battle.

Snorting, Chase didn't even wait for the smirk on Rogan's face to get settled into place. He wasn't about to tell the overconfident medicine man he'd been kickboxing champion in intermilitary competition. Taking a quick hop, he shifted all his weight to his left leg, picked up and jerked his right knee back, then snapped his foot forward, aiming at Rogan's chest.

Unprepared for the assault, Rogan went wide-eyed with surprise when Chase's boot slammed hard into his sternum. With an oomph, he found himself sailing backward through the air, arms flailing like windmill paddles to keep from falling.

Chase didn't wait for Rogan to get his wits about him. As his enemy hit the dirt, he made a grab for his long, unbound hair. In that split second, Rogan rolled to his knees, gripped a dead juniper and swung.

The side of Chase's head exploded with light and pain. Grunting, he was thrown back, knocked semiconscious for a moment. He had to keep moving, so he twisted onto his belly. Through the dirt and dust rising around him, Chase saw the Bowie knife nearby. He breathed hard and ignored the pain to his hand. Fingers outstretched, he wrapped them around the leather handle of the nine-inch-long blade.

"No!" Rogan shrieked, leaping toward him, arms extended. He intended to knock Chase away from the knife. Instead, everything slowed down for the medicine man. The murderous look in Chase's gold eyes made him scream with terror. The Bowie in his grip, Iron Hand thrust it upward just as Rogan was coming down upon him.

The blade ripped through the sorcerer as he fell.

The pain in Chase's right hand forced him to release the blade; he couldn't take Rogan's full weight. He rolled to his side, dirt flying in the air. The medicine man gurgled as blood spewed out of him in geysers. Rogan's eyes went wide with surprise, and then horror. Blood stained his shirt as he frantically tried to pull out the blade.

Chase knew his opponent would die. No one sustained a wound like that and survived. A sense of finality flowed through him as he knelt there, panting. He wiped his sweaty brow with the back of his arm.

"You deserve this kind of painful death, Fast Horse," he snarled, leaning toward him. "As you lie here bleeding out, think about how you murdered Dana's mother and her husband. Think about how you made Dana's life hell on earth. You took the two people she loved most in this world away from her." Chase grinned with a hatred he could taste. "With every breath you take, you will pay one day for each of those fine people you murdered. I'm glad you're going to die, Fast Horse. And I'm going to stand here and watch it happen."

DANA SAT WITH Grandma Agnes on a wooden bench outside the Harley Trading Post. The elder had the pipe bag in her arms. Looking at her watch for the fiftieth time, Dana could barely sit still. An hour had passed. Was Chase dead or alive? Had Rogan killed the man she'd come to love? The man she'd never told of her love. Tears swam in Dana's eyes and she fought them back. Hanging her head, she whispered, "Oh, I wish we'd known this was going to happen, Grandma."

"Child, the Great Spirit never reveals our personal path to us. Many things are hidden." Agnes patted Dana's clenched hand. "Faith. We must have faith now."

Wiping her eyes with the back of her wrist, Dana said tremulously, "Grandma, I've already lost my mother and husband to Rogan. I—I don't know that I could lose Chase to him, too. It's just too much. I ache inside. My heart hurts. I'm so scared."

"I know you are, child. Just keep taking slow, deep breaths. Pray to the Great Spirit that Chase is not in harm's way."

Although Dana knew that the elder meant to soothe her, nothing could at this point. Her insides felt like Jell-O. The mere thought of losing Chase to that murderous Rogan Fast Horse caused a spasm of pain so sharp it left her breathless.

She'd just found Chase, just realized how much she loved him. And now he could be violently taken away from her. What kind of life did she have? Violence was repugnant to Dana, and yet it seemed to stalk her. She felt herself emotionally disintegrate beneath the weight of that realization. Would the Great Spirit never allow her to love again? To feel safe again? To have a life? A home? Oh, it was too much to think about.

Dana rubbed her face and tried to stop her tears. She didn't have Grandma Agnes's faith.

"Look…"

Dana's head snapped up when she heard the elder's voice. A white Navajo police cruiser was coming up the dirt road toward the trading post. Gulping back her tears, Dana stood. What had happened? It was impossible to see who was in the cruiser because it was a good mile away.

As the car pulled up and halted, Dana gasped. Her hand flew to her lips as she stood uncertainly on the wooden porch of the old trading post. There, in the front seat next to the deputy, was Chase. Relief was written across his bloody, bruised face.

"Chase!" Dana flew off the porch.

He exited the cruiser, his arms wide. "Dana!"

She leaped into his embrace, and instantly felt his strong arms wrap around her. "Oh, Chase! Chase! You're alive! I love you! I love you so much!" Dana buried her face against his neck and clung to him.

Groaning, Chase spun her around. Her body felt so warm, strong and supple against his. Whispering her name, he rasped, "I'm okay. Rogan's dead. It's over, woman of mine, it's finally over."

Tears flowed from her eyes as she clung to him. Finally, he set her down, so she could plant her feet on the red earth of the reservation. After pressing kisses against the thick column of his neck, his unshaved cheek, she framed his face with her hands and gazed up at him. Through her tears, she saw his eyes smoldering with feelings.

"I love *you*, Dana. And I always will."

CHAPTER TWENTY-SIX

"I NEED YOU, Chase." Dana spoke the words in a hushed tone as he reentered the winter hogan. Two hours had passed since Rogan's body had been removed by the medical examiner. Navajo law enforcement had come and gone. The FBI had been notified and they would be interviewed once they arrived, which would take hours. Grandma Agnes had been spared the gory details, and was safe in her hogan down below the canyon, the Storm Pipe in her possession.

Dana had remained with her grandmother to buffer her from the shock of Rogan showing up again unexpectedly. The sweat they'd planned for today would wait. Once assured that she was fine, Dana had trudged back up to the winter hogan, and was sitting at the table, her hand wrapped around her coffee mug.

Chase left the door open as he came in. The day was hot, the sun strong. He wiped his brow with the back of his hand and searched Dana's face.

"I need you, too, woman of mine." He managed a tight smile, then poured himself a cup of coffee and sat down opposite her. "How are you doing?" he asked.

"Not well. Shaky. The past coming back to haunt me." Dana bit her lower lip. "I'm in shock, Chase. The last thing I expected was for Rogan to show up here. I—I was so scared. I thought I'd end up like my mother, like Hal." She closed her eyes and gripped the mug tightly.

Lifting his hand, Chase touched her arm, then began to stroke it. "Shh, it's okay, Dana. Everything's going to be okay now. I talked to the chief of police. He said that the FBI caught everyone in the compound except for Rogan." Chase continued to soothe her and saw her mouth slowly relax. "Blue Wolf is dead. She chose to fight the FBI when the SWAT team entered the compound. The other women gave up and turned over their weapons. I guess Rogan left them earlier and headed up the mountain to hide. He stole a car and followed us." Chase grimaced. "We were in flight mode and forgot to cover our energy trail. And he was a good enough sorcerer to pick up on that."

Nodding, Dana relished the feel of Chase's rough fingers caressing her skin. With every gentle caress, a little more of her fear and shock dissolved. Did he know the powerful effect he had on her? So much was going on that Dana couldn't sort it all out. "We did do a stupid thing. We were sure the FBI would catch him. We shouldn't have assumed."

Chase agreed. He gently pried her hand off the mug. Sliding his fingers between hers, he asked, "What's going on inside your head?"

"I still feel so afraid. I know it's stupid, because you killed Rogan and he's finally gone. Knowing Blue Wolf is dead doesn't make me feel sad, but relieved. And here I am, believing in peace and goodwill between all beings. I'm sitting here happy that two humans are dead."

"Listen, if they weren't dead, we might be, instead. Including—" Chase lifted his head and looked to the south wall of the hogan "—Grandmother Agnes. I know this is hard on you, Dana. I know you believe in the goodness in everyone's heart. That's the way you're made in this lifetime. But not all people are like that. It's a slap in the face when you realize it. And a tough pill to swallow." Chase squeezed her hand gently. She looked lost. Broken. His heart swelled with fierce love for her.

"You're right," she admitted hoarsely. "I don't know how to make the two extremes come together in me."

"The tension of opposites," Chase agreed quietly, smiling. He sipped some of the strong, black coffee. Setting the mug down, he whispered,

"Dana, we're trained medicine people. Our entire life is about learning how to hold the tension of opposites within us. At some point, we'll be able to integrate this energy into us as one. This is why we came into this incarnation—to learn how to do this. Peace and war. They're two extremes, but we have to allow both possibilities to live within us."

Shrugging, Dana said, "I don't want to, but I know I have to try."

"Everyone lives and dies down here," Chase told her in a low tone. "The moment we're born, we're in a death spiral. It's only a question of when and how we'll die. Some people go in their sleep. Some have a violent end. Or some suffer a long, chronic illness and die an inch at a time. Maybe you have to reconcile that mystery within you, Dana. That doesn't mean you like the thought of a violent death, but it does mean you consider it a choice by the person who's picked that doorway out of this reality."

Again, Chase was right. "You sound so like my mother." Dana's lips twitched as she held his warm, caring gaze.

"Medicine people are taught all of this at a very young age. The hard part is reconciling it within yourself when you see some tragic or horrible things happen to people around you." Holding her hand firmly, Chase said, "So much is being asked of you right now, Dana. If you weren't in line to carry the Storm Pipe, you probably wouldn't have chosen such a rocky path in this lifetime. But you can't carry a ceremonial pipe and not hold the tension of opposites within you."

Chase grimaced. "There may come a time in the future when another person like Rogan will want to steal this pipe for his own means. To use it in a violent way again. You want to utilize it in a peaceful way—to bring rain to crops, to help and heal all our relations, so that they may not only survive, but thrive. Rogan wanted to use the pipe to kill. You see…" Chase shared a sad smile with Dana "…even a ceremonial pipe holds the possibility of peace or war within itself. It is the way the universe is made, duality and opposites, yin and yang. Only when a pipe carrier can hold these concepts within will the pipe and the individual be integrated as one."

Dana nodded. "I know this. My mother trained me well. I've just been a person of peace, that's all."

"Nothing wrong with that, because you hold a world vision of peace, Dana, for everyone. We need peacemakers now, more than ever." Chase released her hand and sipped his coffee. Warmth returned to Dana's eyes and her once wan flesh was now looking more natural in color. Chase understood that he needed to talk her out of her shock. He was more than willing to do it for her, because he loved her.

As she scrutinized Chase, Dana saw that his jaw was swollen and that the knuckles on his right hand were bruised and scraped. "Are you going to tell me how you found Rogan?"

Shrugging, Chase said, "I used the trees as cover, while he was tearing the van apart looking for the pipe, to get close enough to disarm him. It became a karate battle." Chase flexed his right fist, showing her his swollen knuckles. "Rogan was good and he took me down. But he made the mistake of going for the knife that he knocked out of my hand." Chase didn't want to get into too many details because he wanted to protect Dana from such violence. "He ended up with my knife in his heart."

With a shuddering sigh, Dana flinched. "I'm not sorry he's dead. I'm sure you're in shock over this, too." She studied Chase's hard, unreadable features.

"No one deserved dying more than he did, Dana. Remember? I'm the warrior to your peace-maker." Chase leaned forward and caressed her cheek. "Maybe by us being together, we will symbolize that tension of opposites."

Oh, how wonderful Chase's unexpected caress felt! Hot tears rushed to her eyes. Lifting her hand, she pressed his palm against her cheek. "Do you know what I want?"

"Tell me and it's yours," Chase promised, his voice gritty.

"I need to be away from here for a while. I know Grandma Agnes will be fine, because she's lived here all her life. Plus, she has neighbors who visit, and make sure she has enough food from the trading post. I know of a little cabin on Oak Creek, down below Sedona, that is isolated and beautiful. I'd like to drive down there for a month, Chase, and just be with you. Be there without any expectations, with no one knowing where we are, except, of course, for Grandma. I need time to heal, but I want that time with you, to see what we have. We'll have time to talk, to explore one another." Dana gazed into his widening eyes. "Will you go with me? Please?"

THE WHISTLE OF A wood duck plying the clear-green depths of Oak Creek announced to Dana that they were reaching their favorite picnic spot. Chase walked at her side, carrying a woven willow basket that contained their lunch. Dana brought a thin, blue wool blanket. The smooth white bark of some huge old Arizona sycamores hid this spot from the prying eyes of the world. Oak Creek flowed wide and shallow here, sparkling in the sun. The dappled gold highlights danced endlessly behind the brightly colored male wood duck. Somewhere, Dana was sure, mama wood duck had her babies in tow, looking for food along the creek banks, and daddy wood duck was playing the part of protector and guardian. Tall, waist-high grass lined the banks, a green border to an incredible view of the red, white and black rocks strewn along this stretch of the slow-moving creek.

"Here we go," Chase said. He stepped through the grass onto the smooth red sand beneath a sycamore. A perfect spot for their picnics, which they enjoyed nearly every day. The breeze was inconstant, the melodic call of a nearby male cardinal the perfect background music for their noontime meal.

Dana followed. She quickly unfolded the blanket and spread it across the sand. The creek was less than thirty feet away, with a perfect view of the wood duck following the grassy bank opposite them. She glanced over at Chase, who wore a pair of old, stone-washed jeans, his hiking boots and a dark-red cotton shirt with the sleeves rolled up to his elbows.

In two weeks, Dana's life had turned from terror-filled to peaceful. As she sat down on the blanket and settled the basket between them, she was amazed at how this time alone with Chase was healing her.

"What did you make today?" he asked. He'd just arrived back from Cottonwood, a town about ten miles south of the isolated cabin that had become their Eden and hideaway. While at the cabin with Dana, he saw his job to be getting the groceries and anything else she might need or desire. She wanted to be alone to do a lot of serious meditating, thinking and healing, and Chase hoped that he was giving her everything she needed, including space.

"Turkey and cheddar cheese sandwiches, some raspberry Jell-O with marshmallows on top, a thermos of coffee and for dessert—" she held up the plastic container "—your favorite."

Chase grinned. "Apple pie?"

"Yep. Homemade, the old-fashioned way. While you were gone to town this morning, I made the crust from scratch." Dana tested the bottom of the container. "I took the pie out just before you got home." How easy it was to say "home" to him. Dana smiled and set the dessert aside.

In the time they'd been together, Chase had been circumspect. The cabin had two bedrooms, and he went to his room every night. He seemed to sense that Dana wasn't ready to be intimate with him. But now she was. Chase had given her two weeks to get her own internal house in order. And now, today, Dana wanted to be assertive and let him know how much she wanted to share a bed with him tonight.

As she set the Doritos chips in front of Chase, Dana made herself go through all the positives of moving forward. For one, she knew that he loved her. And she loved him. It was a matter of timing, she realized, to seal their love with one another. When they sat on the porch swing together, watching dusk steal upon the cabin, Chase would wrap his arm around her shoulders and she'd willingly snuggle close to him. Many times, he would kiss her hair, her cheek or her hand, but never her mouth. He was waiting, Dana realized. And a fierce love for Chase, for his understanding, his care of her, welled up within her. That was enough for her. She would act today.

They started to remove the items from the willow basket and spread them out when Dana looked up into Chase's golden eyes. Grasping his hand, she whispered, "Come here." She gave him a slight tug.

Surprised, Chase saw a new glimmer in Dana's cinnamon eyes. Her voice was low, filled with promise of something he so badly wanted to share: his deep love for her. He cocked his head slightly and assessed her.

"Is this what I think it is?" Above all, Chase wanted no misunderstandings between them. Not now. Not on something this important.

Her lips curved softly, and the gleam in her eyes turned to a sparkle. "It is. I'm ready, Chase. We can eat later, if you want."

Ready. The word drummed through him and his heartbeat picked up and thudded heavily in response. Releasing her hand, he gave her a careless smile. "Okay, let's put all this food back in the basket, then. We need the blanket for ourselves, woman of mine."

Dana gave a breathy laugh and agreed. Within a minute, they'd replaced all the plastic containers and put the basket near the trunk of the sycamore. Her pulse accelerated as Chase walked back over to the blanket where she knelt. The look on his face sent a wild yearning through Dana. Eyes hooded and blazing with hunger, he settled on his knees before her. Lifting his hands, he framed her face.

"Let me love you, Dana."

"Yes," she whispered, closing her eyes as he leaned over to kiss her. She eased her chin up and waited a heartbeat in time. Then his mouth, strong and willful, met and melded with hers. As he eased her lips open, he took her warm breath deep into his lungs and then gently gave his back to her. The whistling of the wood duck, the trilling of the cardinal high in the sycamore above them, all melted away as she focused completely on Chase.

In all her life, Dana had never felt so loved. As his hands moved from her cheeks to hold her captive, she leaned against his hard, unyielding chest. Chase was at once dominating and sharing. Their breaths mingled and became one, coming more quickly as his mouth moved solidly and confidently against her lips. He was exploring her, appreciating her, and cajoling her to do the same with him.

It was so easy to open herself up to Chase. For as much a warrior as he was, he could also be excruciatingly tender. When his mouth left hers, Dana felt momentarily bereft. Opening her eyes, she was sure Chase saw a question in them.

He gave her a very male smile. "Turn around." He helped her settle with her back to him as he knelt on the blanket.

Dana felt him slowly unbraid her hair—first the left braid, then the right. Her mane reached nearly halfway down her back, and as he sifted his long fingers through the strands, her scalp tingled with pleasure over the simple, adoring act. She moaned softly as his fingers combed through her hair. Dana had never had a man treat her like this. She could feel Chase loving her with each stroke of his fingers. It was as if he was beginning to know her, to memorize each part of her in his heart and soul.

Her eyes closed when Chase turned her around and eased her down beside him. Dana understood the depth of his love for her as never before. It was a beautiful, shocking understanding, one that opened her wounded heart to new possibilities with him and him only. When he reached for her waist and tugged her pink top up, Dana relaxed and accepted the gift of his care and love. The warm breeze made her nipples harden as he pulled it over her head and dropped it on the sand behind her. When Chase gazed down at her naked torso, Dana felt her entire body respond to his burning, hungry look.

She began to pull the snap buttons on his shirt open slowly, one at a time. He gave her a wolflike smile as he sat up to get rid of the shirt. Pushing it aside, he took her hand, pressed the palm against his chest and whispered, "My heart is yours."

Those simple words made her want to cry for joy. Sitting up, Dana unsnapped her jeans and then leaned down to untie her boots and kick them off her feet.

"Here, let me help," Chase said thickly as he got to his knees and helped pull the jeans off her long, beautifully curved legs. Legs that were firm, in wonderful shape, and seemed to go on forever. He slid his fingers into the waistband of her white silk bikini briefs and pulled them downward. Dana's face glowed with the light of what Chase could only interpret as love—for him. That someone would love him with such fierce gentleness made him feel even more male and protective. The look in her shining eyes brought him to his knees, emotionally. There was such guileless beauty radiating from her.

She reached over to unsnap his jeans, and he helped her pull them down. Getting rid of the boots first, he was more than happy to remove his comfortable pair of jeans. And if Dana was shocked that he wore nothing under them, he didn't see it in her face, only appreciation. For him. For his obvious need of her.

Naked and wanting, Chase drew Dana into his arms, glad the sycamore was shielding them from the burning noontime sun. Her firm womanly form melted against him, and, as her arms went around his shoulders, she gave him a tremulous smile of wonder. Yes, loving her was more than a joy, it was a gift that he'd never thought would be bestowed upon him. And yet, as he drowned in Dana's luminous eyes, Chase understood the pure power of love as never before.

His hand touched her curving hip, her mouth molded with his own, and his maleness brushed between her welcoming thighs. As he slowly moved into her, Chase groaned and shuddered, his arms tightening around her yielding, soft form.

Dana moaned as she felt the surge of Chase coming into her open, greedy body. The union met with heat and friction. His body stiffened against hers, and she held him even more tightly. The sensation of moving together as one was the greatest pleasure she'd ever experienced. Their bodies were in sync, like a current of water ebbing and flowing in the creek. The restless wind cooled their damp, glowing skin. All the sounds and sensations melted into an orchestra of profound beauty and even deeper meaning for Dana.

As Chase's mouth sought and found hers, he arched deeply into her, until her entire body was thrumming. Moving sinuously against him, with him, she became the rhythmic pulse of water, of wind, of the breath of life itself. His mouth was strong and insistent, hers pliant and responsive. His tongue tangled gently with hers. Then Chase slid his hand beneath her curved, arching back and captured her hips against his.

The powerful, surging motion of his body into hers caused an avalanche of heat within her. As the shimmering eruption of light and warmth moved outward, a cry of surprise and happiness tore from her lips. Chase growled in response, a man claiming his woman in this most priceless and sacred of moments. Experiencing a pure, white-hot pleasure, Dana threw back her head, eyes closed, and dug her fingers spasmodically into his tense shoulders.

A rainbow of light filtered through her, one color at a time. First a white-gold tunneled down from the center of her head and deep into her singing body. It was followed by other vibrant hues, until finally violet flowed through her. The color was incredible, and reminded Dana of the ocean's flux and flow.

Chase groaned and found his release deep within her. The descending colors of energy melded with his pleasure. She could feel his joy over what they'd just shared. It enveloped them as they clung together hotly.

Dana had always understood the physicality of

sex, but now, for the first time, she'd experienced it on all levels simultaneously. As Chase buried himself within her, gave her the ultimate gift of himself, she opened herself up as never before to trust and love. Together they transcended time and space, and Dana floated in a blissful mix of color and light.

Their auras were glowing with energy and life, she realized, orbs filled with swirling rainbow colors. Dana watched as they overlapped, creating an eye, or middle oval, where they met. In that moment, Dana saw the many lifetimes she and Chase had shared. It was a swift-moving movie, so quick that she saw only parts and pieces of lives played out on alien landscapes, on planets she had no name for, as well as here on Mother Earth. There were times when she was a man and he was a woman, and vice versa. Sometimes they were married; often they were relatives or friends. She saw lives in China, the Middle East, in South America and on islands in the Pacific. There were so many Dana could not remember them all.

What came of this unexpected awareness was that she and Chase had been working together for hundreds of lifetimes. And in her heart, they were equals. Equals working to bring peace to this earth so ravaged with hate, war, prejudice and politics.

Drawing a deep, ragged breath, Dana pried her eyes open. Chase had pulled her onto her side, next to him. His arm was beneath her neck; her cheek lay against his damp shoulder. Slowly, the sense of time and place came back to Dana. She heard the joyous trilling of the cardinal somewhere in the branches above them. The soft breeze caressed her superheated flesh and cooled her. Her hair was damp and tangled around her shoulders, and partly covering her breasts. Chase was still within her, and Dana gloried in that oneness.

She lay a helpless prisoner to his caresses, his suckling, the slow, grinding thrusts of his hips, which gave her such raw pleasure. She had never experienced this level of oneness with another human being, not even Hal, whom she'd loved unequivocally. For whatever reasons—perhaps the ones that Dana had been shown earlier—Chase was her soul mate. Dana knew that when people who had shared many past lives met in this life, the old bonds would reactivate, drawing them to one another all over again, like a powerful magnet.

As she reached up and kissed Chase with all her womanly strength and love, she found herself smiling. Pulling away just enough to drown in the burning gold of his eyes, she whispered, "My love, my life, we're together. Again, as always." Dana dissolved beneath his male smile, that glimmer in his narrowed eyes. She knew he understood.

"Now you know the rest of our story, woman of mine." He eased his hand across her supple flesh, holding her firmly against his lower body. "We're one. We always have been. I couldn't tell you that, even though I knew. You had to discover this on your own."

Giving him a soft smile, Dana raised her hand and ran her fingers through his short, damp hair. "I didn't know," she whispered, "but I do now, beloved one."

Her words flowed through Chase like sunlight, releasing his heart, which had been imprisoned so long. Dana's fingers caused wild, hot tingles across his skin. And when she softly caressed his cheek with her palm, he opened his eyes and smiled down into her own. "We've earned this right to be with one another, Dana. And I don't ever want to leave you."

"You won't," she promised, moving her hips suggestively against his. Dana saw Chase tense, found his groan a sound of beauty. "From this day forward, we're together," she promised him.

"Forever…" Chase agreed.

* * * * *

Don't miss Lindsay McKenna's next story
A HEALING SPIRIT,
part of the Harlequin Anthology
SNOWBOUND.
Available January 2008!

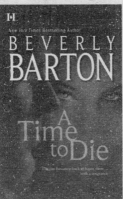

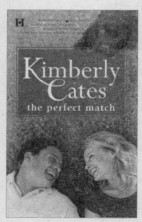

REQUEST YOUR
FREE BOOKS!

2 FREE NOVELS
FROM THE ROMANCE/SUSPENSE
COLLECTION PLUS 2 FREE GIFTS!

YES! Please send me 2 FREE novels from the Romance/Suspense Collection and my 2 FREE gifts. After receiving them, if I don't wish to receive any more books, I can return the shipping statement marked "cancel." If I don't cancel, I will receive 4 brand-new novels every month and be billed just $5.49 per book in the U.S., or $5.99 per book in Canada, plus 25¢ shipping and handling per book plus applicable taxes, if any*. That's a savings of at least 20% off the cover price! I understand that accepting the 2 free books and gifts places me under no obligation to buy anything. I can always return a shipment and cancel at any time. Even if I never buy another book from the Reader Service, the two free books and gifts are mine to keep forever.

185 MDN EF5Y   385 MDN EF6C

Name _____ (PLEASE PRINT) _____

Address _____ Apt. # _____

City _____ State/Prov. _____ Zip/Postal Code _____

Signature (if under 18, a parent or guardian must sign) _____

Mail to **The Reader Service:**
IN U.S.A.: P.O. Box 1867, Buffalo, NY 14240-1867
IN CANADA: P.O. Box 609, Fort Erie, Ontario L2A 5X3

Not valid to current subscribers to the Romance Collection,
the Suspense Collection or the Romance/Suspense Collection.

Want to try two free books from another line?
Call 1-800-873-8635 or visit www.morefreebooks.com.

* Terms and prices subject to change without notice. NY residents add applicable sales tax. Canadian residents will be charged applicable provincial taxes and GST. This offer is limited to one order per household. All orders subject to approval. Credit or debit balances in a customer's account(s) may be offset by any other outstanding balance owed by or to the customer. Please allow 4 to 6 weeks for delivery.

Your Privacy: Harlequin is committed to protecting your privacy. Our Privacy Policy is available online at www.eHarlequin.com or upon request from the Reader Service. From time to time we make our lists of customers available to reputable firms who may have a product or service of interest to you. If you would prefer we not share your name and address, please check here. ☐

BOB07

LINDSAY McKENNA

| 77142 | BEYOND THE LIMIT | ___ $5.99 U.S. ___ $6.99 CAN. |
| 77079 | ENEMY MINE | ___ $6.99 U.S. ___ $8.50 CAN. |

(limited quantities available)

TOTAL AMOUNT $ _____
POSTAGE & HANDLING $ _____
($1.00 FOR 1 BOOK, 50¢ for each additional)
APPLICABLE TAXES* $ _____
TOTAL PAYABLE $ _____

(check or money order—please do not send cash)

To order, complete this form and send it, along with a check or money order for the total above, payable to HQN Books, to: **In the U.S.:** 3010 Walden Avenue, P.O. Box 9077, Buffalo, NY 14269-9077; **In Canada:** P.O. Box 636, Fort Erie, Ontario, L2A 5X3.

Name: _____
Address: _____ City: _____
State/Prov.: _____ Zip/Postal Code: _____
Account Number (if applicable): _____
075 CSAS

*New York residents remit applicable sales taxes.
*Canadian residents remit applicable GST and provincial taxes.

HQN™

We *are* romance™

www.HQNBooks.com

PHLM1207BL